Praise for SIGNALS OF DISTRESS

'An authenticity of tone and time is one of the hallmarks
of Jim Crace's wonderful *Signals of Distress* . . . this is
unmistakably a Crace novel, fresh, vibrant and
unpredictable to the end'
HUGH MACDONALD, *Herald*

'Witty, descriptive, sharply observed, economic and,
above all, authentic . . . It is the characters who give this
novel such life . . . [a] marvellous demonstration
of traditional story-telling at its finest'
EILEEN BATTERSBY, *Irish Times*

'The novel, restless as a rip-tide, carries its shoal of
definitive characters in clear view; they are quite the most
memorable, momentous, and affecting Crace has created'
TOM ADAIR, *Scotland on Sunday*

'Crace is a writer of remarkable descriptive powers . . .
His characters spring to vivid life. The principal requisite
of a first-rate novelist is the ability to create an imaginary
microcosm as convincing in every particular as the
real world. This is what Crace triumphantly does'
FRANCIS KING, *Daily Telegraph*

'Crace weaves a progressive magic into this mythic plot
with masterful detail, luminous prose and
haunting characterization'
Boston Daily Globe

Signals of Distress

JIM CRACE is the author of *Continent*,
The Gift of Stones, *Arcadia*, *Signals of Distress*,
Quarantine (winner of the 1998 Whitbread Novel of the
Year and shortlisted for the Booker Prize), *Being Dead*
(winner of the 2001 National Book Critics' Circle Award),
The Devil's Larder, *Six*, and *The Pesthouse*. His novels
have been translated into twenty-six languages.
In 1999 Jim Crace was elected to the
Royal Society of Literature.

JIM CRACE

SIGNALS OF DISTRESS

PICADOR

First published 1994 by Viking

First published in paperback 1995 by Penguin Books

This edition first published 2008 by Picador
an imprint of Pan Macmillan Ltd
Pan Macmillan, 20 New Wharf Road, London N1 9RR
Basingstoke and Oxford
Associated companies throughout the world
www.panmacmillan.com

ISBN 978-0-330-45334-9

Many thanks to the Public Archive of Nova Scotia
for permission to reproduce the extract from *Oliver's Register* on page 296.

1 3 5 7 9 8 6 4 2

A CIP catalogue record for this book is available from
the British Library.

Typeset by SetSystems Ltd, Saffron Walden, Essex
Printed and bound in Great Britain by
Mackays of Chatham plc, Chatham, Kent

This stranger's footprints are engrav'd in frost,
But soon forgot.
The sun bedazzles. They are lost.
And he has not
Impress'd his passage on this spot
That rime's emboss'd,
Or left enduring signs
That he has cross'd
Our Parish lines.

ABRAHAM HOWPER,
Hoc Genus Omne, xvii

1. The *Belle* and the *Tar*

BOTH MEN were *en voyage* and sleeping in their berths. Hard winds swept in and put their ships ashore.

The coastal steampacket, *Ha'porth of Tar*, on which Aymer Smith had his cabin, had lifted before the wind that night as if it meant to leave the water and find a firmer passage in the clouds. It arrived at dawn off Wherrytown, hastened by the storm on its short journey along the Channel. Ten in the morning was its scheduled time of arrival. Dawn was too early for the harbour lightermen to be at work. No one with any sense was up and out in such a wind. The night was wild and cold. A few miles down the coast from Wherrytown, the Cradle Rock, which normally would take the efforts of two strong men before it began to seesaw on its pivot stone, teetered, fluctuated, rocked from just the muscle of the gale.

The *Tar* shipped heavy seas as it came into harbour. There was no choice but for the five-man crew to still its paddles and shut its fires. Its passage in the wind was more temperamental – and less pontificating – than its progress under steam. The *Tar* was thrown against the harbour boom, and then against the channel buoys which marked the vessel's road. The wind pushed north. The tide tugged south. The *Tar* was only fifty yards from shore. Two sailors had to land a line by rowboat and secure the ship to capstans on the quay. And then they had to coax the *Tar* to dock. Aymer lay awake. He wasn't any use on deck. His shoulder hurt from where he'd fallen from his bunk. The muscles in his throat and stomach ached from vomiting. His breath was foul. His temper, too. He should have travelled overland with the company carts, he decided. He should have stayed at home instead of meddling abroad. Yet now his ship had found a haven, he sought a haven, too, in sleep, roped to the granite of the quay. His dream was kelp and some young country wife, ensnared and going down, with Aymer drowning in the girl, the girl sucked under by the weed, the weed pitchforked like hay on tines of sea and wind.

OTTO, TOO, was not much use on deck. His berth, at orlop level on the *Belle of Wilmington*, was not secured. But Otto was. He was the ship's goat by night, its galley donkey during day. His ankle was held by a light chain, six feet in length and fastened to a timber rib. Shipmaster Comstock considered it a safety chain. Men far from home are boldened by the dark, he said. His African might settle scores at night, if he were left untethered. He might do damage to himself or to the *Belle* or to the crew or to the galley rations and the grog. He might cause mischief amongst the cargo of four hundred cattle which Shipmaster Comstock had taken aboard in Montreal and whose quarters he meant to fill on the return with emigrants to Canada, if he survived the storm. Wherrytown, the first port of call, could only be a few miles down the coast.

Without a porthole or any light, Otto experienced a partial storm. It wasn't wet for him. He couldn't see the waves slap up against the timber. Or feel the wind. His cabin was a tombola. What wasn't fixed – the stool, the water jug, the palliasse, the black man's boots, the bed – fell across the cabin. Otto fell as well. The chain cut into his ankle. But then he caught hold of the chain and pulled himself tight up against the timbers of the *Belle* so that, indeed, the chain did become a safety chain. He made a buffer from the palliasse so that the cabin's sliding furniture, the unsecured wooden pallet where he slept, would not cause too much bruising to his legs. The cattle – on the orlop level, too – were not so fortunate. They tumbled without benefit of chains. Some were concussed. Some broke their legs. They were too blind and winded to make much noise, except a tuneless carpentry as hoof and horn hit wood. Three cows at least had heart attacks. Another choked on its swallowed tongue. The bulkhead separating Otto from twenty of the cows could not withstand the buffeting of so much beef. It splintered. Then it fell apart. Two animals broke through the boards into Otto's berth and slid across the planking on their sides. They had no time to find their feet. The *Belle* made reckless angles in the gale. One cow fell against the palliasse and kicked to right itself. A hoof struck Otto on the ear. His head bounced off the wood. He fell six feet and swung like a carcass on a butcher's chain. The sea returned him to his berth, then dropped him on the chain with every ridge and trough of water. His swollen face and ear took splinters from the deck. The anklet etched new wounds. He was unconscious. He didn't feel the pain.

THE CAPTAIN did his best, according to the book. The foresail on the *Belle* was lowered, the mainsail double reefed. But still the wind at its stern hurried the boat bitingly forward towards the darkness of the shore. The fore and mizzen topmasts, with spars and rigging too, fell away into the sea. Part of the bulwarks went. And then the mainsail, taking off into the night like some great canvas albatross. Everything was swept off deck by long black hills of water, thirty, forty feet in height. The hands on board – at least those six of seventeen who weren't sick, and who had managed to hold on by their eyelids to the masts and rigging of the *Belle* – now waited for the lull following every set of seven waves and sent the anchors down. But the anchors slipped. The *Belle* heeled landwards. It went in two hundred yards, found some upright purchase on a sandy bar, and stuck. The crew, excepting Otto, took to what rigging had survived. They flew their signals of distress, though it would not take a flag when it was light to signify to those on land that the *Belle* was almost lost. Comstock fired the ship's double-barrelled cannon. He prayed the wind would take the sound into the bedrooms on the coast and that the people thereabouts had sympathy – and rescue boats.

Nobody came that night. But it wasn't long before the waves and wind abated, and a teasing, ruddy dawn thinned and thickened through the mist. The *Belle* was eighty yards offshore. The sea was still ill-tempered. Between the sandbar and a beach, however, the water was calmer. They checked the *Belle*'s four longboats. Two were lost and two were smashed. Would someone swim ashore? There were no volunteers. They were too tired, and fearful. The tide had turned and out-haul waves were rocking the *Belle* from the landward side. No human swimmer could achieve the shore in seas like that. But Captain Comstock put the ship's bitch, Whip, in the water with an ensign tied on to her collar, the red on white of I Need Help. They wouldn't let her climb back on board. At last, with the good sense and resignation of a dog, Whip headed for the beach. The cattle that had survived the night were not far behind. Comstock opened up the orlop hatches and drove them into the sea. He feared their frenzied restlessness would further destabilize the *Belle*. Many didn't make the shore. The ones with broken limbs or those too deeply shocked did not survive the swim. Others had no compass sense and headed off for Quebec. But three hundred cattle – maybe more – got to land that day and set to work on sampling the salty foliage of the backshore as if there'd never been a storm.

IT WAS SEVEN on a Saturday, November 1836, on that far angle of the English coast. Only strangers were awake. The Americans clung to rigging out at sea, impatient for a sign of life. Aymer Smith, ready to encounter Wherrytown, packed his careful travel stores by candlelight below decks on the *Tar*: his tarpaulin coat and leggings, his books and writing implements, some anchovy paste, a Bologna sausage, some chocolate, a great bar of black bread, three dozen cakes of soap, a jackknife and a leather flask. He wrapped them in a carriage rug which doubled as a bag. Otto bled into his palliasse. The cattle from Quebec moved on from backshore weeds and tested the corky grass of dunes which separated the hamlet of Dry Manston from the sea. The final strings and shreds of cloud stretched and disappeared. The water was as clear as gin. Whip ran along the shore, snapping at the waves and cows. And then she went in search of other dogs. She'd heard them barking, and soon had found the cottage where two large mongrels were secured by ropes to the porch. Whip found discarded bones which she could gnaw, and turnips. At first the mongrels went for her, but couldn't reach. They were too bored to persevere. Whip found a corner of a shed where she could sleep, her chin between her feet. The red on white of I Need Help had loosened at her collar. And help was not at hand.

It had gone nine before the mongrels were released. They ran at once towards the hut where Whip was sleeping. There were no men about. Whatever had been making her dogs uneasy, she'd have to handle it on her own. Rosie Bowe took a heavy piece of firewood as a cudgel and followed them. At best she'd find a hedgehog for the pot. At worst? Some thief who'd stolen lodging for the night would still be sleeping there.

She was perplexed when she found Whip, her back bowed and her tail between her legs, sheltering in the hut. Rosie knew the dogs for miles around, and this one wasn't familiar. She pulled the ensign from the collar and put it in her apron front. It was a tough and decent bit of cloth. She let her mongrels stay. Let dog police dog, she thought. It was too cold to kick the bitch herself. But the three dogs were in a playful mood, happy to chase tails. Rosie left them to it. She had work to do. There'd be storm kelp on the beach, easy to collect after such a tide and such a wind. Her cart would soon be full. With her daughter Margaret's help they'd have a dozen loads before the tide was in and (with the agent Howells paying thirty shillings a ton for prepared kelp ash) would earn a welcome three or four shillings for their efforts.

'Miggy! Miggy Bowe!' she shouted at the window of their cottage. 'Get yourself up and out of there. This in't the Sabbath yet.' She put her head round the door and spoke more gently. 'Come on, we'll get ourselves a good penny if we're keen.'

'No, Ma, it's hurtin' damp out there.'

'Warm yourself with work. Let's not be idle. I'll let the dogs inside to get you up. We've three dogs now. Our two have found a bitch to chase around.'

'Whose bitch is that?'

'She's ours, to keep or sell. She's sleeping in our hut, and that's the law. Or ought to be. Get out of there. Miggy! I'm warning you. It won't be dogs'll get you up, but me.'

Rosie stepped inside and showed her daughter the fire-wood cudgel. 'I can give a decent bruise to idle girls.'

'Oh, Ma! You gonna lay a fire, or what?'

'No fire on Saturdays. Not till it's dark at least. This in't

JIM CRACE

the inn. We'll have a fire down on the beach if you move fast. I'll bet there'll be the wood washed up. Did that wind wake you in the night? Does mutton dance quadrilles?'

'I'd like a bit of mutton though.'

'You'd better press your finery then and find yourself a farmer's son. There'll be no mutton till you do. Here, make yourself a gown from that!' She threw the red-and-white cloth on to her daughter's blanket. 'That should turn some farmboy's head. He'd turn away if he had sense.'

Miggy Bowe didn't mind. She knew enough to guess she was good-looking. 'It's off a ship,' she said. 'A signal flag.'

'The little dog was wearing it for a kerchief,' her mother said.

'What kind of dog is she?'

'A hairy little sharp-toothed bitch. Much like you. Only she's up and dressed for work and running in the yard, while you're still on your back. Come on now, Miggy girl. There's been enough of this. I'll get the cart and you can earn your supper.'

Miggy Bowe tied her hair back in a knot, put on men's working breeches and her thickest smock, and wrapped the *Belle*'s cloth call for help round her throat as a scarf. It gave a reckless dash of colour to a face that had no warmth. Her mother was the cheerful kind. Rosie Bowe would sing in rain and mud. But Miggy was young enough at seventeen to be a pessimist. Where would she be at thirty-four, her mother's age? Still carting kelp. At fifty-one? Cold as stone, with any luck, and nothing to her name except a wooden cross. She petted her two dogs and then inspected Whip,

8

her teeth, her paws, her collar, her little beard. With luck they'd get some puppies out of her in spring.

'Come on, you little lady,' she said. 'Let's have a look down on the shore.' Miggy and the dogs ran to catch up with Rosie, who was wheeling the handcart towards the dunes.

THEY SAW the cows from Quebec before they saw the sea. They'd never seen so many cows at once.

'You called for mutton, Miggy. The good Lord sends us beef.'

'Whose cows are they, Ma?'

'That little dog has come with them, that's all I'm certain of.'

'What's stopping us from salting one?'

Her mother didn't answer. She half guessed that there'd be some wreckage and some carnage on the shore – and, if there was, then who could stop them slaughtering one cow before the excise men got wind of it? There'd be better pickings than the kelp. Bullion, jewels and plate had been beached the other side of Wherrytown a dozen years before. Tobacco, tea and lace would suit them well. There would be sailcloth and timber for the house, at least. Winter beef. Wrecks were a godsend. Rosie almost ran.

Rosie Bowe was the first woman that the sailors had seen since they left Montreal. They watched her, strong and buoyant, pick her way between the cows and descend with her handcart down the backshore to the beach. They saw another figure, too – a smallish boy in breeches and a smock. He had three dogs. The Americans had spent six hours in the rigging but had been warmed and dried a little by the breeze and sun, so managed quite a spirited cheer when the seaman, Parkiss, who had the ship's glass, reported that the smallest dog was their own Whip. The dog, perhaps, had saved their lives.

They'd have to wait another hour. A kelper's handcart couldn't bring them ashore. Rosie sent her daughter running down the coast. The nearest fishermen were beached below the Cradle Rock, a mile away. They'd come out in their boats. She waved back at the sailors but didn't know how she could signify across so wide and watery a gap that help was on its way. She pushed her cart along the tideline and put the morning to good use. As she had expected, the storm had deposited a lot of kelp on the beach. She chose the knobweeds and the bladderwracks because their yields of soda were the best. She kicked aside the sugar wrack. A cartload of that would only give a quarter-bucketful of soda ash. She lifted the weed with her right hand and kept her left hand free to seize the crabs that often sheltered underneath the kelp or the lance eels which could be twitched out of the sand if she were quick enough. When she found timbers from the *Belle* and broken lengths of rigging she wrapped them up in kelp and hid them on the cart. She watched the water as she worked for bobbing bottles of brandy and liqueur, but all she spotted was the ready-salted carcass of a cow, floating on its side, and masts and planking from the ship tangled in the offshore weed. Quite soon her cart was full. She pulled it back into the dunes where she had built a stone pit for burning kelp. She buried what she'd salvaged from the *Belle* in a soft dune, and spread the load of kelp to dry over the disturbed sand. She'd gathered three more loads of weed before the seine boats of the fishermen appeared beyond the bar and breathless Miggy, her breeches caked in mud, her pulse quickened by the run and what was promised by the *Belle*, reappeared amongst the kelp, the wreckage and the cattle on the beach.

ONE MAN – Nathaniel Rankin, a seaman from Boston – was dead, concussed by falling timber in the night and drowned. But sixteen had survived. They had been fortunate to end up on the bar. The three seine boats that came to rescue them were secured to the *Belle*'s hull in water hardly deep enough for their keels. The dozen oarsmen helped the Americans to climb into the boats. They wrapped the men in blankets and gave them corn-brandy in water from their flasks. Comstock brought his charts and letters of command. He ought, perhaps, to leave a crew aboard or stay aboard himself. He ought to love his ship more than he loved his own life, but he didn't. The gear was clewed and stowed. The sails were off. The larboard bow was holed, but it wasn't shipping much water. Yet. What else was there to do? He dignified himself and called down from the damaged deck, 'I trust you gentlemen will help us salvage what we can when we are warm and dry.'

There were a dozen cries of 'Yes!' They all were keen to get back on the *Belle* again. Next time they'd charge a fee.

'There's one more man,' Comstock added. 'I ought to be the last to leave. We've got one injured party, on the orlop. Three men can shift him out.'

He took command and pointed at the nearest three – a

boatman called Henry Dolly, his wildly weathered, dark-haired son, Palmer, and one of their casual hands, an old and silent bachelor known locally as Skimmer. They followed Shipmaster Comstock below decks to Otto's berth. When the cattle had been driven into the sea, a crewman had released him from his chain and wrapped him in his palliasse to keep him warm. The cloth, to some extent, had stemmed the blood. The wound and swelling on his forehead were mauve. His ankle was stiff and raw with pus. He was conscious but inert. Only one eye opened. Only one eye could.

'Are you sleeping, Otto?' Comstock said. He was embarrassed by the silence and the stares of the three men. Perhaps they blamed him for the wounds. But they were speechless from surprise. They'd never seen an African before. The darkest they encountered was a youth like Palmer, a ripened russet face with sable hair. They weren't used to this topography. They couldn't tell his age or temperament or judge his character. His hair was like black chimney moss. He seemed to have a woman's lips. He hardly had a nose. They were reluctant to hold him by his arms and legs. They couldn't bring themselves to touch his skin. Instead they lifted Otto in his palliasse. He was a very heavy man, and it took twenty minutes negotiating the carcasses of cows, the timber debris and the companion ladders, before they reached the deck. They put him in the Dolly boat and pushed off for the beach. Already there were forty people and a dozen carts waiting with Rosie and Miggy Bowe. Two wagon-harnessed horses and one horse ridden by the agent, Walter Howells, and made frisky by the irritation of a loosening shoe, stood on the shingle with their backs against the sea. It was too cold to wade in to help the Americans ashore. They had to manage it themselves – except that when one older man, John Peacock, fell into the water, Walter Howells, to some derision mixed with cheers, rode his horse into the breakers and hauled the sailor out by the collar of his cork safety-jacket. 'Save a sailor from the sea,' someone recited, 'And he will prove your enemy. He'll have, once he is out of water, Your life, your money *and* your daughter!'

Otto was not touched. Comstock threw sea-water in his face to rouse him. Otto found the energy to swing his damaged legs across the bows of the rescue boat and try to find his footing in the shallows. He sank into the water. Its iciness shocked him. The salt was painful on the wounds, but cleansing, too, and healing. He was the last to make his way to shore. They found a bed for him, in seaweed on the half-loaded horse-drawn cart. They gathered round to point and shake their heads and giggle nervously. Miggy was the first to stretch her arm and touch him on the toe, where dry, dark blood had been made pasty by his short walk in the sea. Then everybody touched the toe, in turn. They ran their fingers across the nail and felt the skin, the pink below the toe, the brown above, the blood, and cold.

The beach was never busier, except at pilchard time. The sailors and the locals hugged and shook hands. Three dogs ran wild, experimenting with the sea and crowds. The cattle moved inland. Miggy looked for Palmer Dolly. Perhaps he'd shake her hand. Or they might hug. But he'd gone off in his father's boat. Instead she made do with the attentions of the younger Americans, who now could see, despite her breeches, that she was a girl, a pretty one. She wore their ensign round her throat.

'This miss is calling out for help,' they joked. 'All hands stand by.'

The sailor, Ralph Parkiss – blond, teasing and boyish – attempted first to take away her ensign scarf. And then, playing the innocent, touched her at her waist. The whole of Miggy flushed. She'd gladly press her lips on any young man there. A fire was lit – in her, and on the beach. They warmed and dried themselves as timbers from the *Belle* smoked grey. The three seine boats pulled beyond the bar and soon were out at sea. The *Belle of Wilmington* settled into the wet sand of the bar. It would not break up; the seas were sheltered there, and shallow. On Monday there would be a rising tide of sufficient depth, with luck and wind, to float it free again. Captain Comstock turned his back on his command. He'd have to wait and see what happened to the *Belle*, and he would rather wait and see in some dry place, on solid land. He was not the hero of the day.

The Americans, with Otto sleeping in the cart, and Whip in tow, embarked upon the six-mile walk to Wherrytown, where there was food and lodging and where, by now, Aymer Smith, that other dreaming voyager by sea, had found the inn. Walter Howells rode ahead on his laming horse to spread the news. The air – scrubbed and quietened by the storm – was now so still that Miggy and her mother could take a lighted piece of wood and carry it the half-mile to Dry Manston to start a celebration fire in their own home. And what was there to celebrate, besides the passage of a storm? Much. Much. Much.

2. The Journey West

AYMER SMITH was taken to the inn in Wherrytown by George, the parlourman-cum-porter, whose job it was to bully custom from any ship that docked. George didn't take to the *Tar*'s single passenger, the unpromising and unattractive Mr Smith. The man's breath was foul. And his bookish jollity, his height, his thinness, his insistence that they shake hands like old acquaintances and then take turns to 'bear the burden' of his carriage bag on the short walk between the quay and the inn, were misplaced, misjudged, unbecoming. If they had to share the burden, would they also share the tip?

The night gale, which had lifted tiles and flung back doors in Wherrytown, had left the quayside scrubbed and clean. Aymer Smith remarked it was 'a fresh and handsome town', but, steady though he was in conversation, he had climbed awkwardly from the cabin to the deck. His shoulder was bruised, or worse, from the tumble from his bunk. His throat was sore and hot. His legs were still at sea. He was shivering, from cold and apprehension and timidity. George could only guess what business such a man could have in Wherrytown at that time of year, but what he knew was this, that Aymer Smith would not be an inspiring presence at the inn. Here was a moper. Here was a book snuffler. Here was a man who couldn't sing.

Perhaps he couldn't sing, but God the man could talk!

'What kind of lodging are you taking me to?' he asked George, in a voice that attempted informality but managed to be both teasing and condescending. 'Tolerable, I hope.'

'Ours is the only inn,' George said. He could think of no better commendation. 'It's us or nowhere in this town.'

'What is the name of this grand inn?'

'It has no name – nor any need of one. It is the only inn.'

'Indeed, but then this is the only ship in dock, and I its only passenger, and yet we both have names. It would not do, I think, to call me simply "Passenger" or this vessel "Ship" because we are, for the moment, unique.' He allowed George a moment to keep pace with this Comedy of Wisdoms. 'Names, it is true, are mostly useful should one need to *distinguish* one man, one ship, one inn from another. But they are helpful, too, for *signifying* character. So, were your inn known as the Temperance, then I could well imagine its mood and its sobriety. The Commercial has a more convivial ring, I think. And the Siren or the Venus? Well, I should not wish to take a room in such a place, unless that room had thorough locks on every door. What do you say?'

'What should I say, except what I have said three times, and that is that there is no choice?'

'Say it three hundred times and still you fail to reassure me. What phrase is there to best describe your inn?'

'The only inn in town.'

'Ah, yes. You are right to stand firm against my questioning. Refuse to yield to me!'

'I don't know enough to yield or not – but I'm the only one in Wherrytown'll lead you to an empty bed. Except there's plenty barnyards in the neighbourhood, so long as you like rats.'

'The rat is much maligned...' But Aymer Smith's discourse on rats would have to wait another opportunity. The two men reached the lower entrance to the inn.

The inn was ideal for hide-and-seek. It was a warren, untouched by architects. The town rose steeply from the harbour front and the building had perplexing levels that placed the stable lofts scarcely higher than the scullery basement and meant that the attic box room looking south and the ground-floor parlour facing north were connected by a level corridor. An outside wooden staircase led from the seafront courtyard to a balcony and bedrooms, but there was no direct seafront entrance to the public rooms. There wasn't any logic to the place nor, even, any regimental regularity to the shapes and sizes of the building's bricks and stones.

'Accommodation for man and beast. Victuals, Viands and Potations,' said George. 'It's hay or cheese for supper.'

Aymer followed him up a narrow passageway of steep, pebbled steps that climbed through the heart of the inn. He didn't like the smell of fish and urine, nor the meanness of the alley, nor the pinched and sea-damp wind which rifted at his back. They came out in a lane, and for a moment Aymer was relieved to think their destination was some other, better place. But George directed him towards a

raised front door with a flat granite lintel, just to the right
of the alleyway. It opened directly into a low-ceilinged
parlour, empty except for a solid, black-haired woman on
her knees, removing ashes from the grate. She was, she
said, Mrs Yapp, the landlady, the innkeeper. She didn't rise
to greet her guest.

'Give the gentleman a bed,' she instructed George.

'Assure me that you have sheets,' demanded Aymer,
gripping his carriage bag and coat.

'There's sheets for those that ask,' said Mrs Yapp.

'And good, hot food that's fit for eating?'

'There's nowhere else,' she said. 'Unless you want to stop
with Mr Phipps, the preacher, who has a room for Christian
travellers. Sinners and repentants catered for. The bill will
be repented, that's for sure. It's good, hot food he dishes up,
and fit for eating, except it's Buttered Tracts and Bible Soup
and Psalm Tea.'

'. . . and Hebrewed Ale,' said George. He'd said the same
a hundred times before.

'. . . and the Word Made Flesh,' added Aymer, after a
short moment's silence.

Aymer had meant to make a good impression in Wherrytown. He knew that he would never have a reputation for
vivacity, and that he was more comfortable with documents
than company, but still he'd meant to be amusing and
relaxed, putting George at ease, demonstrating to Mrs Yapp
that he, though firm and businesslike, was happy to be
informal. But once he had been taken down two short
flights of steps and left alone inside one of the balconied

rooms above the courtyard he almost wept. He had, he felt, been treated with hostility. The woman hadn't even stood to greet him. That was not behaviour to admire. And George the parlourman had seemed to find his conversation comic, except when he attempted jokes. He hadn't even shown gratitude when Aymer had presented him with a bar of white soap by way of thanks.

His room was on two levels and had four curtained beds, none of which was welcoming, and none of which had sheets. There was no other furniture nor any draping on the windows. There was a chamber pot, a water jug and two small tin basins. The walls and floorboards smelled of fresh lime wash. At least the bedbugs had been treated. Aymer couldn't imagine spending a single night in any comfort there. Perhaps he could conclude his business in one day and take the Sunday return passage on the *Tar*, home again. He went out on to the balcony and looked across the courtyard and the harbourfront to where the *Tar* was docked amongst some smaller fishing boats that had been damaged by the gale. The cold, the breeze, the brightness of the sky, his shoulder pain, the dislocation that he felt from being far from home, brought water to his eyes. It didn't help that he had travelled all this way with nothing but bad news.

He chose a bed close to the windows, where there was light enough to read and write. He took a quill, some paper and a pinch of ink from his bag. He mixed sufficient ink with spittle and began to write, unsteadily, using his knees as a desk. He put the title of the family firm in capitals at the top of the page:

HECTOR SMITH & SONS
Manufacturers of Fine Soap

And then he added his address:

> The Only Inn
> Wherrytown
>
> Saturday, 19th November

Sir, he wrote, *I am this morning arrived on the coastal packet in Wherrytown and lodged at the inn. I would be obliged if we could meet at your soonest convenience. I have disclosures that concern our business interests and that I wish to communicate with some urgency.*

He added his own signature and then, on the reverse of the folded sheet, the name of the agent who at that very moment was riding in the shallows to haul a Yankee from the sea where the *Belle of Wilmington* had beached: *Walter Howells, Esq.*

Now he wrote a second letter, to his younger brother:

My dear Matthias, I am safely come to Wherrytown and have survived the worst of storms at sea. Already I have summoned Mr Howells and am awaiting his reply. I write this letter for the return of the coastal packet which will depart tomorrow, Sunday, in case my business does not allow a swift departure from this place. Despite my deprivations I am convinced of the propriety of my coming here, and hope that in my brief absence you will come to recognize that our responsibilities to these people could not

be satisfied by pen and ink and paper but only by the
presence of at least one son from Smith & Sons.

He read the last line several times aloud. He hoped his
brother would detect reproof but not the coldness that he
felt. Matthias was a businessman who had no moral code.
But Aymer? He was moral code and little else.

Aymer, at forty-two, was senior to Matthias by nineteen
months – yet he was the younger, lesser man in everything
but age. Matthias had a city and a country house, a wife,
two daughters and a son, a carriage and six servants.
Matthias was a Justice of the Peace. He was obese. He
sang, a decent baritone. And since his father died he'd been
the acknowledged master of Hector Smith & Sons. He had
transformed the business. The city works employed ninety
adult hands, as well as twenty children, and produced
forty thousand bars of soap a week. Smith's Finest Soaps
were used by royalty, but there were cheap, good-looking
soaps for working people too. Soon the company would be
renamed: MATTHIAS SMITH & SON.

Aymer had little interest in soap. He was a Sceptic, a
Radical and an active Amender. But, still, he was the junior
partner in Hector Smith & Sons. It provided him with
income, and notionally it was his task to help his brother
at the works. Matthias, though, had no faith in Aymer. He
thought he was a waster and a fool, best left alone to read
his riotous pamphlets and his volumes of verse than let loose
amongst the company's order books and ledgers. Yet Aymer
went to work each day. He had a sense of duty. There
was dignity in labour. The task he took upon himself was

not to help his brother but to check him. If Aymer could rename the company it would not be MATTHIAS SMITH & SON or SMITH BROTHERS, but SMITH BROTHER-HOOD or EMANCIPATION SOAPS. He didn't have an easy manner with the factory hands. He wasn't even liked. But he could fight on their behalf. To no avail he pressed his brother to provide gloves and leather aprons to protect the soapmakers from the boiling fat. He bullied for a shorter working day. He argued that the works should not employ children under twelve. He recommended profit-sharing schemes, and factory schools, and rights of Combination. He was, as Matthias said to Fidia, his wife, 'half-boiled, half-baked and half a man'.

'He's hell set on damaging his one true brother in the selfish interests of fraternity,' was Fidia's practised opinion.

At Aymer's instigation, three factory hands had formed a Works Committee and should be (Fidia again) 'sacked before they do some harm'. Matthias wished his brother were elsewhere, so that the sackings could take place without commotion. As in everything, his wishes would come true.

It was the plight of kelpers such as Rosie and Miggy Bowe in their rough cottages at Dry Manston that would provide Matthias with some respite from his brother's quarrelsome philanthropy, and bring Aymer on the journey west. For forty years Hector Smith & Sons had bought supplies of soda ash for soapmaking from the kelpers on the coast beyond Wherrytown. Walter Howells and Walter Howells's father before him had been Smith agents there, purchasing the kelp ash from the Dry Manston families and arranging wagons to deliver it to the manufactory, five days' journey overland to the east. Now thanks to Nicolas Leblanc, a French surgeon with a taste for chemistry, a simple process was established to extract sodium carbonate from common salt. It was pure; it was cheap; and when the railway was complete it could be delivered within a day. 'What is the point,' Matthias asked Aymer, 'in using Mr Howells when we have Leblanc?'

'The point,' said Aymer, 'is our Duty. The Smiths and Howells have been partners since we were young. Our fortunes have been interlocked. And Mr Howells has contracts – moral ones at least, if not legally established – with families who rely on stooping in the sea for kelp for their small incomes.'

'Well, let them give their backs a rest and let them dry their feet. We have no further need of kelp. I cannot argue further.'

'I will not let this rest.'

'Aymer. The choice is mine, not yours. You well know the stipulations in Father's will. Besides, my letter to Mr Howells is already written and ready for dispatch. I will not go back on my word.'

'You cannot break their trust by letter! What friends are we to hide behind the mail?'

'You would prefer, perhaps, to write a sonnet?'

'I would prefer that you and Mr Howells would sit down face to face . . .'

'You want me then to take an empty wagon back to

Wherrytown to tell a man whose face we do not know that we desire to purchase better, cheaper soda somewhere else? The man will take me for a fool, as, Aymer, I take you.'

'What of your duty, then? What of your conscience?'

'And what of yours?'

'My conscience remains clean.'

'Then you can take the wagon west. Why don't you? Or take the coastal boat, for all I care. Our father might have left the running of this works to me, but I do not think he stipulated how Duty and Conscience should be divided.'

'Well, then, if it cannot be you it must be me. I will travel to see Mr Howells with this bad news.'

'Then do so, sir. And do as little mischief as you can.' And may you break a leg en route.

Now Aymer was ensnared. He had no appetite for such a long and testing journey. He wasn't suited to the country-side. He'd never travelled far from home. But once arrangements had been made for his departure for Wherrytown he found himself aroused and impatient. Perhaps when he was away from the city and in a place where surely he might count on some respect, he could find for himself what more than Justice and Reform he had desired for all his adult life, a loving country wife.

So Aymer Smith had taken the *Ha'porth of Tar* on the journey west in a fearful and a hopeful mood. He was surprised how travel unleashed him, how he could talk to sailors on the boat with a freedom absent from his home and city life. He was encountering, also, that other libera-tion which is the gift of travel and unfamiliar places. He – the virgin and the masturbator – was poised, engorged and shallow-breathed with expectations and desires. So now, in Wherrytown, his tears short-lived, his letters written, he left his cold room at the inn ostensibly in search of George, but mostly to sniff round like a dog, to poke his nose in rooms, to seek a friendly face, to find the margins of his new emancipation. He went up two flights of steps to reach the ground-floor parlour. George was sitting with a pipe.

'Is there a boy to take these letters for me?' Aymer asked.

'There's only me.' George took the letters. 'What a place! No boys, no boots, no chambermaids! No tips!' he said, and walked out of the parlour without leave.

Aymer stood with his back to the grate which Mrs Yapp had cleaned and prepared, and waited for the lighting of the woods. He hadn't been waiting more than thirty seconds when a young couple entered from the lane, a thin-haired man with spectacles and a woman without a bonnet but kept warm by a tiered shoulder-cape which fastened at her chin. She would have been a fool to wear a bonnet. Her hair was held in one loose tress by black ribbons. It was so sandy in colour and so buoyant that Aymer could not prevent himself from staring.

'We were hoping for a bit of fire,' the young man said, rubbing his hands at the empty grate.

'Indeed, we all were hoping for some fire, but, it seems, our hosts do not subscribe to wasting warmth on guests,' said Aymer, blushing. He held his hand out for the man to shake. 'Aymer Smith. I'm rooming here. On business.'

He put his hand in Aymer's. 'And so are we, except it's not on business that we're here. We're taking passage on a boat to Canada. If it ever comes! It was due two days ago, but there's no sign of it. My wife and I have been walking on the quay and there are no sails on the sea except for fishermen.'

'Then you are emigrants?'

'We are. God Save Us. I'm Robert Norris. And this is Mrs Norris and has been for a fortnight now. Katie is her name.'

Aymer put his hand out once again and Katie put her hand in his. It was cold and smooth and dry, as flimsy and as modest as her hair was grand. 'I'm happy to meet you, sir.'

'A pity that our acquaintance will be so short.'

'Well, not so short,' said Robert Norris. 'I must suppose that we are trapped here for a few days now. I can't be sure if that is happy news or not.'

'Don't be so doubting, Robert.' His wife was the teasing not the bashful sort. 'They'll not want dismals like yourself in Canada.'

'It's not the colonies that bother me, but what we might endure on the passage there. I've not the constitution for the sea.'

'And nor have I,' said Aymer. 'But I have taken passage here by sea and I have ridden out the worst of storms.' He remembered now the bruising to his shoulder which, truth be told, had stopped hurting the moment Katie had come in. 'I tumbled from my berth and took a blow. But here you see me, well set up and only disembarked today. The observations to be made are these: on ship a passenger should have no fear of nausea if he stays off the deck and is not tempted by the portholes. Stay in your quarters. Let the wooden walls be the furthest horizons you allow. Let the deck above you be the sky. Take all your orientations from the space allotted you, and as the ship tips and rolls so you do too. Your body and your eye are in concord. But think to walk on deck to witness what a storm can do first-hand, and you will feel your body bucking like the ship. Your eye will sway between the still horizon or the stiller stars and battle with the masts and rigging of the boat so that your every step is like that of a drunken man. And thus seasickness will set in.' A pleasing and a helpful lecture, Aymer thought.

'It seems a pity to go so far and see so little,' commented Katie.

'The sickness is the price you pay for seeing,' said Aymer. 'I think there might be some general truth in that philosophy. To learn is to suffer. To suffer is to learn.' He chuckled at his observation. And Robert and Katie Norris beamed at him with such indulgence and such attention that he felt glad to be in Wherrytown. Normally he didn't welcome scrutiny. Not that he was the kind of man to command the stares of strangers. He liked to think of himself as a plain man, plainly spoken. He didn't care for adjectives, or anything that was too ornamented. He liked the force of facts and objects, and he endeavoured to make his conversation instructional. 'Still, such observations will not warm you from your walk,' he concluded. 'Our landlady is not at hand, it seems.' He stepped across to the parlour sideboard, lifted the inn handbell and shook it. 'That should bring our Mrs Yapp running.'

Mrs Yapp was not the sort to run. Anyway, she didn't

hear the bell. She wasn't in earshot. She and George were in her sitting room with Aymer's letters open on her table. Mrs Yapp had read them both out loud.

'So that explains the soap,' said George. 'Take care he doesn't pay for his lodgings here in bars of soap.'

'And you take care to pay the gentleman some respect, George. He's Smith & Sons. We'll have to treat him sweet. I'd better see if I can find some bed sheets.'

'What brings a man like that down here?'

'To talk with Walter Howells, that's what it said. Go on now, George. You'd better do as you've been bid and take these letters round.' She shook her skirt and pinafore. She checked her stays and laces in the glass. She primped the jug-loops in her hair. 'I'll go and see if there is anything he wants.'

'He'll have no need of soap.'

When Alice Yapp and George came into the parlour, Aymer Smith and the Norris couple were sitting round the cold grate in happy conversation, or at least the Soap Man was in conversation and the other two were listening politely to his remarks about the beneficial freedoms of the colonies. Katie had loosed her hair and let it hang in one long bunch across her chest. Her husband had removed his boots and had his stockinged feet on a fireside settle, as if they could be warmed and dried by the memory of fire.

'Mr Smith,' said Mrs Yapp, as if it were the most aristocratic of names, 'is it all pleasing to you?' She made a genteel sweep of her hand.

'We should like a fire.'

'George! Lay a fire for Mr Smith. And sheets. I promised sheets.'

'If that in't hospitality,' said George to no one in particular, 'then what the Devil is?'

Aymer was cheered by the change in Mrs Yapp. So were Robert and Katie Norris. They'd been at the inn for three nights and Mrs Yapp had not so far expressed any word of welcome or shown any sign of hospitality. They had not lodged in inns before and took the Yapp indifference to be normal. But now with Mr Smith she displayed an accommodation to his comforts that was almost worshipful.

George put tinder in the grate and set off by the lane and alley to collect dry kelp and logs from the courtyard for the fire. He'd scarcely reached the courtyard when – happy chance – Walter Howells rode in, his yellow leather breeches, worsted stockings and high-lows caked in mud, his horse a little lame from galloping with a lost shoe. George ran to take the reins and pass on Smith's letter.

'Not now, not now!' said Howells, brushing past George and stamping across the yard towards the alleyway of steps. 'There's been a wreck!'

'What wreck?'

But Walter Howells was out of sight and at the inn's front door. He didn't remove his leather hat which, low at the crown and turned up at its eaves, revealed red shock hair and a redder face. Mrs Yapp and three guests whom he had not seen before were in the parlour – a fine-looking young woman and two clerkish men. He didn't pause for pleasantries but broke into their conversation. 'Alice. Bake

some bread and pull some corks. You've got a full house for
a night or two. That Yankee ship we were expecting has
beached at Dry Manston and all the sailors on it are coming
here and seeking beds.'

'Dear Lord, how many beds?'

'Oh, sixteen, seventeen. And a little dog! And they've
got a Negro in a cart.'

'You're joking with me, Walter Howells.'

'I am not.'

'A Negro in a cart, you say? Well, we'll see.'

'You will indeed. You can expect them in the hour and,
in that hour, I'll have to find myself the smith. My horse
has dropped a shoe.'

Aymer Smith – somewhat startled that this muddy,
florid man should be Howells the kelp agent – stepped
forward and offered his hand: 'Please allow me to introduce
myself. You say you need a smith. And I'm a Smith, but
not much use with horses . . .'

'Then, sir,' said Walter Howells, 'you're not much use to
me.'

3. Shared Beds

FOR THAT ONE HOUR between Walter Howells's 'You're not much use to me' and the arrival of the sailors from the *Belle*, Aymer viewed his task in Wherrytown with less timidity. The obligations of Duty and Conscience were unchanged, of course. He could not take pleasure in the lecture-with-regrets that he would have to deliver on 'The Local Implications of Monsieur Leblanc's Liberties with Salt'. But Walter Howells's ill-manners in the parlour with Katie Norris there to witness had made the prospect of the lecture sweeter.

Aymer stood at the window of his room. In the courtyard Mr Howells was leading his unshoed horse to the smith that, for the moment, he might imagine more consequential than a Smith. Aymer could be patient. He would let Mr Howells absorb the wincing implications of the letter to him and its signature. How could Aymer know that George still had the letter – both letters – in his pocket and in the fever of 'There's been a wreck!' had forgotten it? The letter was at that moment (he imagined) waiting on the agent's parlour table. It would not be long, a couple of hours at the most, before Aymer could expect the verbose opportunity to accept the man's apologies.

'Matters of propriety and dignity do not engage me,' he would say. 'I have not weathered storms at sea in my passage here to Wherrytown to benefit from local courtesies and etiquettes or to test your manners, good or ill. We are plain men, I think, and plainly spoken. Indeed, I already have experience that you can speak your mind. So, sir, you will not take amiss the unhappy news that I must give to you. You may not know of it, but the industry of a Monsieur Nicolas Leblanc, a Frenchman, has made a mark on yours. And you, for all my efforts in your name, must be the poorer for it.' Aymer could imagine the hunted, baffled, deferential look on Howells's face as the bad news encircled him and taunted him but would not give its name until the Lecture nearly was complete. 'I think your already spoken view,' Aymer could conclude, 'that I am little use to you assumes a sharper meaning now.' Mr Howells would have no repartee for that. Aymer's Duty would be done. Then there would be time to eat a country meal (with the Norris couple as his guests, perhaps; he really was determined to scrape acquaintance with them), to sleep well at the nameless inn and to take the return Sunday passage on the *Tar*. What further obligations could he have in Wherrytown?

He would, he thought, find Mr Norris and his wife, to enquire if they would like to share his dinner table. He had information on the topography of Canada that they would benefit from hearing, and some advice, too, on Self-Reliance. He took some soap for Katie Norris. Five bars. He imagined they'd serve her well on her long sea voyage. Perhaps she'd save one as a keepsake of her mother country, stored beneath the crapes and linens of her clothes drawer, in the timber bedroom of her cabin, on the virgin land, deep in Canada. Perhaps she'd wash her hair in Smith's Fine Soap.

The thought of Katie Norris with her hair in suds hastened Aymer, but his bedroom door was opened before he could reach it. Mrs Yapp came in with sheets and bolster cloths.

'You shouldn't give no thought to Walter Howells,' she said. 'He didn't know that you were Smith & Sons, the soap. He'll be back and limping like his horse when he finds out.'

'I would not waste a second thinking of it, Mrs Yapp.'

'There, then, there's no harm done.' She set about making up Aymer's bed. 'We'll get you comfortable,' she said, 'and then I'll have to shift them other beds. You heard what Walter said. We've boatloads coming here and it'll be a squeeze to find the rooms for them. Those Norrises will have to share, or sleep out in the corridor. I can't be bothered with a fuss. You should've seen his wife when I explained. The blushes on that girl! You'd think I'd asked her to share a bale of hay with horses. I said, "You don't get private rooms for what you're paying me, not when there's other guests to satisfy." Still, it'll be a taste of Canadee for her.'

'You mean she'll have to share a room with sailing men?'

'There's nothing wrong with sailing men except they're rough.'

'For how long will this be?'

'Well, here's the pattern to it, Mr Smith. The Norrises have passages aboard a ship that's called the *Belle of* . . .

some place I forget, and that's the one that's beached along the coast at Dry Manston. If they can get her off the bar and seaworthy and she's not broken up for firewood, then the Norrises can leave and be in Canadee within the two months.'

'If not?'

'If not, the Norrises will have to share a room until they find another ship, or turn around and go back home, wherever that might be.'

'It is not thinkable that they should share, even for one night.'

'They've not the choice. I'll not have shipwrecked men sleep in the street or in the stables. This isn't Bethlehem. It's damp and cold out there. I never heard that blushes did more harm than damp and cold. Besides, she'll only have to blush a while and then they'll all be shipmates, just you see. There's plenty women in this town'd be glad to share a room with three or four Americans. Young Mrs Norris can take her pick!' Her laugh was uninhibited and unoffending. She was a woman in her forties, playful, forthright, savoury, with some remains of beauty in her face if not her figure. Hers was a case for stays, although she was the sort whose stoutness was a charm. 'There, that's your bed dressed for the night,' she said. 'You'll sleep like royalty. Don't be surprised if I creep in between the sheets, it looks so clean and welcoming . . .' Aymer reddened. He put his hand across his mouth. 'Now, that's me being comical,' she said, noting Aymer's discomposure. 'I'll not go uninvited anywhere. So there's your sheets and there's your bed, and anything you need from me is there for asking. You'll not want soap, I see.' She nodded at the stack of soap in Aymer's hands. 'They must be Smith's.'

'Please take some, if you want.'

'I like a luxury,' she said, and took three bars, and curtsied, plumply.

Aymer was alarmed. He couldn't be sure if she'd been flirting. What was the 'anything' she'd offered him? Food? Hearthside hospitality? Or sin? Would she try to slip between his sheets – and legs – at night? And if she did, would Aymer take her in his long, thin arms, or would he flee, in his nightshirt, onto the balcony and down the wooden staircase to the cold and salty courtyard? Were blushes really so much healthier than cold and damp? He didn't have the courage to find out.

'There is no need to move the other beds,' he said. 'I'll share a room with the Americans. I think we must allow the Norrises to keep their privacy.'

'No, Mr Smith. I cannot let you sleep with sailors of that kind. Same as I said, they're rough. Their language will offend you, and their nighttime habits . . .'

'Well, then, perhaps it would be better if Mr Norris and his wife were to share with me. Shift out two beds for sailors, and let the other two remain. Our beds are curtained, so we can count on privacy. My language and my nighttime habits can give no offence. Besides, I am already acquainted with Mr Norris and he has introduced his wife. Perhaps, if my business can be completed rapidly, I will depart on the coastal packet tomorrow, and then this room can offer total privacy again.'

'That is a rare suggestion and a kindly one.'

'Surely I can make this sacrifice for just one night.' Aymer put the remaining two bars of soap on the widest of the beds.

OTTO WOULD NOT get a bed. There were no volunteers to share with him, though there were many townspeople in the inn's courtyard keen to stand around and stare, to examine his face, to try a smile, to test a word or two, to comprehend this first encounter with an African. What did they know except what they'd learned at fairs or from sailors or in the farthing pamphlets they'd bought from pedlars? That Africans were ruled by dogs or dined on dogs or smelled like dogs? That Africans didn't wear clothes and had no tongues, no names, no navels? That black men didn't dream? The Wherrytowners did their best to catch sight of a navel or a tongue, to find his oddities. 'Well, Blackie,' one man whispered in Otto's ear, 'what news from the Devil?' But he didn't wait for a reply.

Otto was conscious and in less pain. His ankle wounds had crusted. The bruises on his forehead were already blue. His eyesight was restored. He sat on the seaweed in the cart, eyes closed, and did his best to think of other things. But the oddness of the leafless trees he'd seen, the hardness of the sky, the stony torpor of the land, the mud, unsettled him so much that he was close both to tears and to fury. He had to concentrate, amid the din, to steel himself against the courtyard ghosts. He'd learn to dream himself elsewhere, but first he wanted things for which there were no words. He wanted warmth and food and sleep, and could not summon them. Shipmaster Comstock and his crew could be excused their neglect of him. They all were bruised. They all were cold. Their tempers were worn thin by the six-mile walk along the coast and by the prospect of some weeks ashore. They had no energy for anyone except themselves.

They put Otto in the tackle room beneath the wooden balcony. They covered him in horse blankets woven from rough perpetuanna wool, and made him comfortable on straw. They shut the bolts. 'It's best to let him rest,' Shipmaster Comstock said. The captain had more pressing problems than the African. He had his ship wedged on the bar. He had fifteen sailors and a dog to feed and pacify. There were hard letters to be written: to the owners of the *Belle*; to the various agents further down the coast who had arranged passages from several ports for emigrants to Montreal; to the Bostonian family of the seaman, Nathaniel Rankin, who had drowned; to the livestock merchants who had shipped the cattle that now were grazing freely at Dry Manston, still a half-day's voyage short of the *Belle*'s second destination, and their owners at the port of Fowey. He had to find the means to dislodge his vessel before it broke up on the Monday tides, and dock it in Wherrytown. He had to find the wrights and riggers to carry out repairs. He had to justify himself. Thank God that there were men like Walter Howells. In their brief conversation on the beach, the man had introduced himself as someone who could alleviate the captain's burden, for some decent recompense. Already he had undertaken to herd the cattle at Dry Manston and find secure grazing for them. And he had promised more.

Comstock and his men were tired. They ate the bread

and soup which Mrs Yapp prepared. They longed for sleep.
It was midday. Aymer had stood on the bedroom balcony
and watched the caravan of men arrive. The Norrises were
there below, their passage tickets in their hands, anxious to
discover what their travel prospects were. A small, untidy
dog with a bearded throat and white hair on its chin and
eyebrows ran wildly in the yard, barking at the townspeople
as if they were the newcomers and the dog belonged. The
horse-drawn cart was stabled with its horses. George began
to unload the bed of seaweed and stack it in the inn's fuel
store. Aymer couldn't see the African. The sailors who
carried him into the tackle room obscured the view. At last
the sailors followed Mrs Yapp into the inn. The Norrises
walked once more down to the quay, and the townspeople
returned to their nets and pots and laundry. Now the
courtyard was empty except for the dog which was turning
horse manure with its nose and eating some.

Aymer came down from the balcony by the wooden
stairs. He tried to see inside the tackle room, but the single
window had been boarded. There was no sound. Aymer
knocked on the door and then drew the bolts. The black
man had his back against a saddle and a saddle-cloth. It was
too dark to see his face, although the draughty winter light
that slanted through the open door displayed the healing
rawness of his ankle where the chain had been.

'Are you sleeping?' Aymer said. Evidently not. The
man's reply was a fusillade of words. Aymer couldn't recognize the language but he knew the tone. Here was a man
who, had he got the strength, would have taken Aymer by

the throat. The shouting brought the dog to Aymer's heels. She spread her legs and growled into the vociferous darkness of the room.

Aymer put the bolts back in place. He went into the warm breath of the stables where he could hear George at work. 'Is there a good physician in Wherrytown?' he asked.

'There's not,' said George. 'Are you unwell? That shoulder's giving trouble, is it, sir?'

'It is, indeed. But I was thinking of that poor man who is locked up.'

'The African?'

'He has a wounded leg and should be seen.'

'There's no one here to see him, except the horse doctor, but I suppose the fellow won't want shoeing or getting his tail docked. I hear, though, that those Negro men have tails . . .'

'You are a provocation, George. No doubt, in time, I will learn to treat your banter as comedy. But for the moment I would be glad to hear you talking plainly. Tell me, to whom do you resort if you are ill?'

'I resort to bed and hope that Mrs Yapp will tend to me.'

'Is Mrs Yapp a healer, then?'

'No, she in't.'

'What must I do to get an answer out of you?'

'It seems to me you're getting answers by the score.'

'But not the one answer that I seek.'

'What answer do you seek? You say, and I'll repeat it for you, word for word, so long as it is short.'

'I do not know the answer that I seek and that is why
... Dear Lord, I need someone to treat a wounded man.
Is that not plain enough?'

'It's plain you want a healer, then. There's only one, and
that is Mr Phipps, the preacher. He pulls the Christian
teeth round here, and sets the bones for those that are
contrite.'

'Then kindly fetch him.'

'I've my work to do.'

'I'll see to it that you are recompensed.'

'With something shinier than soap, I hope.'

'A shilling, George. Produce the healer here at once. Be
my man while I am lodging at your Inn-that-has-no-name,
and the shilling will be yours. Can I count on you?'

'You can count on a shilling's worth.'

Aymer went back to his room to find some gift to pacify
the African. He took a cake of soap, but wondered if the
man might take offence. And so he added his dry rations,
the food he'd brought from home in case the catering in
Wherrytown was bad: the great bar of black bread, the
Bologna sausage, the chocolate, the anchovy paste. He took,
too, the jug of sweetened drinking water from his bedside.
He could have called on Mrs Yapp for provisions, but
Aymer felt that in some way the African was placed in his
safekeeping. Once more he drew the bolts on the tackle
room and opened the door. The little dog accompanied him
and didn't bark. There was no fusillade.

'What is your name?' asked Aymer. No reply except a
sigh. 'I've brought you food to eat.' He mimed the cram-
ming of his mouth, then put his gifts in the shaft of light

on the bricked floor between the man's good ankle and his bad. There was no hesitation. Otto drank the water from the jug. He ate the sausage and most of the bread. He smelled the soap and anchovy and put them to one side. He smelled the chocolate and rubbed it on his lips before dispatching it. He didn't mind the dog sniffing at his ankle and then licking the dried blood. He stroked her neck and chin. It seemed they were old friends, the least regarded creatures on the *Belle*.

'I've sent for a physician. A Man to Make You Well,' Aymer explained, thinking that emphatic language would be understood. The African stayed in the shadows. He made no sign of gratitude. He turned the dog's ears in his hand, the double-sided velvet skin. He tugged and stroked the long, dung-crusted hair beneath her chin. At last he seemed to speak. But if this was speech then it was meant for the dog and not for Aymer: 'Uwip. Uwip. Uwip.'

Aymer didn't like his philanthropy to be less heeded than a dog. He wanted Otto to himself. So he repeated what he heard, 'Uwip'. The dog's ears straightened and her head turned. 'Uwip, Uwip,' said Aymer, with more force. The dog came to him and pushed her nose into the crotch of his trousers – expecting what? Some treat perhaps. Again, Otto called to the dog. He didn't like to lose the animal. 'Uwip, Uwip.' The dog returned and for her trouble was rewarded with the anchovy paste.

'Her name is Whip!' Aymer said, delighted at his deduction. 'So now we have a word in common. And I will teach you more. My own name . . .' He pointed at his chest. 'Aymer Smith of Hector Smith & Sons. Can you say Smith?

Smith. Sm.Ith. Smi.Th.' He wasn't listened to. He had no audience. A cold and wounded man abducted from his home has no appetite for lessons.

It wasn't long before George returned with Mr Phipps. The preacher first examined Aymer's shoulder in the court-yard, asking him to hold his arm above his head and then to exercise his fingers.

'The bone is bruised,' he said. 'I cannot find a fracture, but your shoulder is inflamed. You should rest the arm. It would be wise to strap it to your chest. Sleep on your side. Are you in pain? Then purchase laudanum, and ask Mrs Yapp to prepare a poultice of witch hazel and cicely. That will thin the bruise, with God's good offices.'

'Is there an apothecary where I can purchase laudanum?'

'No, there is not. You see the kind of town we are. But Walter Howells who is a trader here has some supplies. Our Mr Howells has some of everything, excepting virtue. Now let me see this other injured man.'

They brought a lantern from the stable and hung it from a rafter in the tackle room. The preacher didn't speak. Nor did he touch the patient. He peered into his face and examined the damage to his forehead and eye. He looked for several seconds at the weeping ankle.

'My knowledge does not stretch to Africans,' he said. 'I do not know their constitutions. I would not wish to interfere. More harm will come of that than good. Our remedies are not for him. A medicine that makes us well might make him feverish.'

'You cannot tend his wounds?'

'I cannot stand between this man and God.'

'You will not save him, then?' Aymer was perplexed.

'I can and will if there is water left inside that jug. For water is the Almighty's medicine. The greatest service I can render this man or any man is baptism, the wet cross on the forehead. If he devoutly wishes it.'

'He cannot understand a word you say.'

'Then he is an Innocent and we should pray for him. That is the balm and poultice I prescribe. His wounds will heal in God's good time.'

'Or he will die.'

'We all will die in God's good time, but not, I think, of bruises. The man will be mending by tomorrow. It will be the Sabbath. Come to my chapel for evensong and we can offer prayers for him. You are baptized yourself, I trust?'

'I am a Sceptic, Mr Phipps.'

'Then we shall pray for you as well.'

Aymer would make do without the laudanum. He didn't want to trade with Walter Howells. The pain didn't merit it. But he persuaded Mrs Yapp to make a warm compress and find the linen for a sling. He walked down to the quay in search of the Norrises and to deliver a newly written letter for his brother, Matthias. If he encountered Walter Howells then it could do no harm to have his arm strapped up. It made him unassailable, he felt, and just a little dignified. The *Tar* was being loaded with its homeward cargo: fresh and salted fish. Its decks were being scrubbed in preparation for the passengers. Aymer would not be aboard. He had decided he would stay in Wherrytown.

My dear Matthias, he had written,

*I am arrived in Wherrytown and have sustained an injury
at sea during the worst of storms. I am not well enough to
travel yet and so I must remain amongst the kelpers here.
Already I have seen our agent, Mr Howells, face to face,
and we are making progress with the bad news that I bear,
though he is not a man of feeling or of judgement. My
lodging is tolerable though I must share with sailors. They
are Americans, wrecked in the same storm that injured me.
Amongst their cargo was an African, a slave. I know you
think it is my duty to be at your, my brother's, side at
Smith & Sons, but I would claim a greater duty to a
greater Brotherhood. I think it is my task and obligation
to serve the sacred cause of Negro emancipation by visiting
upon this man the benefits that Mr Wilberforce has brought
about in our own land but which, alas, do not yet flourish
in America. Despite my deprivations I am convinced of the
propriety and fortuity of my coming here. It may be that
Smith & Sons are obliged to break the kelping contract
with their friends, but I can make amends on both of our
behalves by offering the Freedom of this land to a man
whose prospects have been nothing more than Slavery and
Chains. Do not concern yourself for my well-being.*

Aymer gave this second letter to the *Tar*'s mate. He
waited on the quay for the return of his first, but the mate
could find no trace of it. What would it matter if both
were delivered to Matthias? Aymer had, after all, relished
the final line of the original letter and didn't wish his
brother to be spared. He was invigorated, flushed with his

philanthropy and a touch in love. His cheeks were pink with wind and optimism. He would be admirable. He would excel.

At last, he saw the Norrises returning from their walk, arm in arm, along the front. He waved with his free arm and almost ran to meet them with the news that they could share his room and were invited to share his table, too. Katie's sandy hair was a flapping flag of colour on the sea.

4. Aymer's Duty

Mrs Yapp had baked squab pies, with horse bread and potatoes. Winter cooking.

'What's squab?' asked Captain Comstock. He'd come to collect food for Whip and Otto, but had stayed for warm brandy and kitchen comforts. 'Fish, fowl or fur?'

'That depends,' said George, 'on what the cook's got spare.'

'And what is spare today?'

George prodded the meat off-cuts and bones on the kitchen block, the hardened autopsist. 'It might be cormorant,' he said. 'It could be cat.' He put his nose into the meat. 'It in't fish. And that's a blessing and a rare thing in this town, to eat a pie that has no fish.'

'At least we know what it's not,' said Comstock.

Mrs Yapp took a handful of grey feathers from the waste, and showed them to the captain. 'This squab is pigeon,' she said. 'There's apple, bacon, onions, mutton, pigeon. Makes it nice.' She made a well in the crusts of three pies and broke a raw egg into each. Then she poured in beer. The gravy of the pies steamed like chimneys on a pastry thatch.

'That's to still the squabs,' George said. 'They'll be too drunk to fly.'

Comstock sniffed the steam. He couldn't wait to eat. He'd lived too long on pickles, salted meat and biscuit on the *Belle*. 'My dog'd love a bowl of that,' he said.

'Your dog? I'll not bake pies for dogs.' She gave the captain two chipped bowls. 'There's scraps and gravy for the little dog. And bread and pilchards for the black fellow. Will he drink beer?'

'Best not. His temper's unpredictable.'

Comstock found his way by lantern light into the upper lane and down the open and bladdery alleyway into the courtyard. He called for Whip and took her and Otto's food into the tackle room. He felt embarrassed, waiting on the man who had been the *Belle*'s galley boy. The two men didn't speak. Comstock satisfied himself that Otto had recovered from the storm and from the tumbles he had taken. The ankle was mending. He seemed both calm and comfortable. That was a blessing. The last thing that the captain needed, on top of all his other woes, was a riotous and ailing slave. The tackle room would be a decent billet – and a kennel – for a night. Tomorrow was the Sabbath. Captain Comstock would see if there were warmer quarters for Otto, inside the inn perhaps – but he suspected that the Wherrytowners would not welcome an African beneath their eaves. They'd stared and pointed at the man as if he were a creature at a fair. A slave was worthy of more respect than that, so long as he was biddable, and free of vices and diseases. Perhaps it would be for the best if Otto were kept out of sight in the tackle room, away from local eyes and fingers. Matters would improve, he hoped, and Otto could enjoy more latitude once Wherrytown was used to him. So long as he was supervised, his muscle would be useful in the restoration of the *Belle*. Comstock watched his man and dog eat for a while and then he shut the bolts on them, though Whip could get out if she wanted to. There was a cat hole in the door, and Whip was hardly larger than a cat. He hurried back to squabs and Alice Yapp. He had an appetite for both.

THE INN PARLOUR and the adjacent commercial room were rarely busier. Eighteen men and Katie Norris were waiting for their dinners. Aymer's invitation to the Norrises to share 'his' table had been too optimistic. There were two tables only, the large oak formal table in the parlour – waited on by Mrs Yapp herself – and a softwood trestle in the commercial, reserved for the more raucous of the Americans and served by George. Everybody shared, though Katie had been spared the pressing thighs and invasive elbows of her fellow diners. She sat at the head of the parlour table on a seat with a straight, spindled back, and a laced cushion, much like a governess with eight slow learners. She was the closest to the fire. She felt both vulnerable and powerful, with such a retinue. All the men had narrow places on backless benches. Aymer Smith, with one arm strapped to his chest in its sling, could hardly find room to place his elbow on the table, but he was in no mood for complaining. His life had never been as purposeful as this. Even the unruliness of the Americans, even the wooden plates and earthenware cups (despite the evidence of glass and china in Mrs Yapp's buffette), could not disturb his feelings of well-being.

Here were two universes, the solemn and the jubilant, the reverential and the scurrilous, connected by an open door. The ten young 'castaways' (as they had named themselves) in the commercial were intemperate with beach-fever. They hadn't spent a night ashore since leaving Wilmington, Carolina, with cotton for Montreal in mid-September. Now that their cargo east – the four hundred cows – had been prematurely landed, they would not sleep at home again until the westward cargo of emigrants from Wherrytown, Fowey and Cork had been shipped to quarantine at Grosse Isle in the St Lawrence and – the fourth side of the merchant square – a consignment of Canadian logwood taken south to Wilmington. They'd be hammocked for ten more weeks at least, curled in sleep like prawns – if, that is, the *Belle* was saved. If not, who knew when or how they'd see their families again? They were becalmed and idle and, almost, bored. Boredom, with such unpolished turbulents as these, would turn to mischief given half a chance – with women, money, fists. Their heartiness would sour unless the *Belle* was soon back at sea.

Already there were one or two who'd seen a chin they'd like to punch, a silver timepiece or a pair of boots they'd like to lift, a mouth they'd like to kiss. But for the moment, over squabs, they were content to be at ease. At least there were no midnight watches to be kept. They'd not be called away from their food to pull in canvas. The sea would not upset their plates nor put a reckless angle on their drinks. They – almost – could forget the sea, and make the most of being safe and far from home, except they all had boat cough and their throats were never clear. They raised their

drinks to the *Belle* ('Long may we sail in her!') and to
America and to baffling 'George, the parlourman!' who kept
their cups topped with rough beer and wine. They smoked
their rations of Virginia. Soon they were singing in praise
of squabs and calling out what fine pigeons Mrs Yapp and
Katie were. 'Would the ladies care to dance or sing a verse?'
If only Katie were a flirt! If only Mrs Yapp had Katie's hair
and throat! What then?

The mate had chanced his arm with Mrs Yapp. He'd
put a hand across her back when she'd reached over for the
empty pie dishes. She hadn't seemed to mind. He'd try
again – and somewhere fleshier. 'Don't organize a search
if my bed's empty for the night,' he said. 'I'll be in safe
hands.' The sailors laughed in unison at that. The mate was
always claiming conquests, though he wasn't equipped to be
Lothario. His nickname on the *Belle* was 'Captain Keg',
perfect for his size, his shape, his hollow self-importance
and what mostly he contained, gas and beer. The only
reason Mrs Yapp hadn't pushed his hand away was because
the mate was too much a gargoyle to be threatening,
particularly in that low, unsteady light of oil lamps.

If any man there was equipped to win the admiration of
women it was the straw-haired deckhand, Ralph Parkiss.
He was nineteen, tall and beautiful. This was his first trip
on the *Belle* – and at least some of his adolescent softness
had – so far – survived the rough life of the decks. He
was not the hardened sailor yet. He had the kind of easy,
guileless smile that could turn ice to steam.

'That Mrs Yapp hasn't even noticed you,' one man told

the mate. 'She's only eyes for baby Ralph. She hoped it was his hand across her butt, not yours.'

'You keep off, Ralph,' the mate said. 'The lady's mine!'

'There's younger and there's finer down the coast!' Ralph Parkiss defended his embarrassment by deepening it. 'I've found myself a sweetheart already.'

'Who is she, Ralph? A she-goat or a ewe?'

'I know her name is Miggy, and she's a fine sight. That girl down on the beach when we were rowed ashore, the one that had our ensign round her throat . . .'

'The one dressed like a fellow, Ralph? You'd best find out what's hidden in her breeches before you buy the ring.'

'I will find out. If I've the chance.'

'You better had. A cork's no good without the bottle.'

They drank another toast, 'To Ralph and Miggy. Long may he sail in her!' They banged the trestle with their pots. They shouted to be heard. They coughed, and laughed, and thanked the heavens that the *Belle*, with them aboard, had not gone down at sea.

Next door the parlour company was less jubilant. The five oldest sailors talked quietly at one end of the table, uneasy in the company of the sandy-haired woman and the two dull-looking men, and wary of the captain. He introduced himself to Aymer, and tried to reassure the Norrises that the *Belle* would soon be fixed and heading off, with them aboard, for Canada. 'There's not a ship afloat that could have ridden out that storm last night and not had damage done,' he explained.

'You have no need to give the details of the storm,' said

Aymer. 'I was at sea last night myself. I cracked a shoulder bone.' He didn't want to say to the captain that he had tumbled from his bed. 'I fell across the deck when we were struck and scarcely kept aboard.'

'You've been baptized then, Mr Smith . . .'

'No, Captain, I'm a Sceptic.'

'. . . and need not fear the sea again. You've sea salt in your blood.'

'We have no need to fear the sea at all, I think. And as for sea salt in my blood, then that is true of all of us, whether we be sailing men or Hottentots.' He gave the captain time to contradict, and set a thoughtful profile for Katie Norris. 'I speak, of course, about the chemistry of blood. It is not much known, but the elements of calcium, potassium and sodium are found in equal rations in our blood as in the oceans.' He sought a metaphor that was grand enough, and memorable: 'Our veins are tides. Our blood is brine. The organisms of our blood . . .' (are fish, he'd meant to say. But this would strike a comic note) '. . . are common to us all. The grandest captain of a ship, the meanest Negro slave, are both ancestors of the seas. What is your view?' He hoped the captain had the brains to take the hidden meaning.

'My view is, Mr Smith, that I leave chemistry to chemists. And they, I hope, will leave me well alone and let me go about my business. That's all that any man can ask.'

'That is exactly what we seek in Canada,' said Robert Norris, seeking something else as well, to keep the evening civil.

'You'll find it, sir, so long as you're not frightened of

hard work, plain food ... and ice! They've winters there that make the weather here seem tropical.' The captain called along the table to a stringy, grey-haired sailor, the one whom Walter Howells had hauled out of the sea that day. 'John Peacock, tell these good people that tale we had the other night, about the frozen boat.' Anything to keep Smith quiet!

John Peacock put his pipe down on his plate and, winking at his comrades, commenced with 'It was last October and ...' He told – in fixed and tested sentences which seemed as mannered as a psalm – how two brothers from below Quebec agreed to row a gentleman from Boston across the St Lawrence to the southern bank: 'They should've known better. At that time of year! But they couldn't refuse the fare he'd promised them. They'd end up rich, and wouldn't have to row a boat again, except to get back home. And why go home when you are rich? They got midstream. And then they felt the tugging on the oars and something banging up against the boat. They thought it must be beavers, snapping at the wood. A beaver's got more tooth than brain. But it was ice. And ice with teeth that's worse than beavers' teeth. It lay hold of the keel. And all their rowing, all their prayers, all their cursing language, couldn't get them to the bank.'

The Norrises were grimacing, not sure how seriously to take the sailor's tale. The talk of storms and ice was not encouraging.

'Perhaps we'd better take a passage to Australia,' said Katie. 'They've no ice there.'

'There's ice-mountains floating in the Tasman Sea,' said

Aymer. 'You should read the journals of Captain James Cook or Sir Joseph Banks. They had their share of bergs off Botany Bay . . .'

Comstock hushed Aymer with the flat of his hand (the selfsame hushing gesture that Matthias, his brother, used) and said, impatiently, 'Listen, sir, if you will. He's not done yet. Come on now, John. Let's hear the end of it.'

'The end of it is that the brothers' boat was frosted into solid water, so suddenly they hadn't any chance of being saved,' continued John Peacock, looking Katie Norris in the face.

'Why did they not simply walk ashore on solid ice?' asked Aymer. He would not be an uninquiring listener.

'Like penguins, sir?'

'Why not, indeed?'

'Because their hands were frozen to the oars and – excusing me my language, Captain, and the lady – their backsides had iced on to the boat . . .'

'Then why not shout for help?'

'Ah, when they opened up their mouths, to cry for help, as you advise them, Mr Smith, their tongues and lips were welded by the cold.' He pointed at the Norrises. 'You'll need to watch for that when we set sail for Canada. Best not to talk on deck.' For once the laughter from the parlour matched the drunken din in the Commercial. 'Their families drove a cart and horses out on the ice to rescue them. They lit a fire – midstream – to thaw them out. But that hard river ice did not give way. Nor did the boatmen or their passenger begin to melt. It wasn't till mid-March that the ice released the boat. And then it went downstream towards the sea before it could be saved.' He held a finger to his lips. 'It isn't over yet.' He picked his pipe up, drew on it to keep the tobacco burning. He made the silence at the table last. He took his time. He much preferred to smoke than talk.

Now – his voice macadamized by nicotine – he told the diners at the inn how the brothers and their passenger floated down the St Lawrence 'sitting as straight as three proud men in church', with backbones of ice and oars frozen to their hands. 'You'd think they were alive,' he said. 'Or ghosts.'

'They were picked up within a day by a sailing ship. She was the *Lizzie Wilce*, and she was heading out off Anticosti Island in the Gulf for Liverpool. The boatmen and the Bostonian had been dead five months. But they looked as fresh as eels. The captain tried to bring them round with slaps across their backs. And brandy. He thawed them out in front of the little grate in his cabin. Two of them had to be buried at sea. They stank like mackerel. The third, though, looked more like salmon. He had a touch of pink around the gills. So they put him in a hip-bath and covered him in steaming towels and let him soak. By the time the *Lizzie Wilce* had crossed the mid-Atlantic ridge the man was calling out for grog. And by the time they'd reached the Irish Sea he was full enough of life to win ten dollars off the captain in a game of five'n'one. You'd never know he'd been iced up all winter. Except the ship's surgeon had to cut away two toes. And half his nose. He could neither walk nor talk without a limp. He drank and gambled his way to Liverpool. He liked it there; the mildness of the

winters, the thinness of the ice. He stayed. Now he's got a
chandler's business, on the dock. He vows he'll never step
aboard a boat again, nor risk another nostril in the ice.
I've seen the man myself. I bought this pipe off him. We
shared a drink together. He told me how he'd lost his nose.
I didn't see his feet, or count his toes. Nor can I tell you
who he was. One of the brothers? Or the Bostonian? He
wouldn't say, for fear of it getting back to his family. And
every word is true. What say you, Mr Smith?'

'I say, you'd think the way he spoke would give the
man away,' said Aymer, meaning to demonstrate his good
humour. 'What kind of accent did he have? I suppose a
gentleman from Boston can be distinguished from a Canadian boatman.' John Peacock pinched his own nose
between his fingers. 'I gould nod dell,' he said. 'I gould nod
unterdand a wort he sait. He hagn'd gok no dose!'

'Then, if you did not understand a word, how, how did
this story . . . ?' said Aymer, but his question was drowned
in the applause which Aymer took to be at his expense.
Even Katie Norris had clapped her hands.

The captain slapped him on the back: 'What would your
chemists say to that?'

Aymer did his best to join the laughter. He clapped his
hands too – a little late – and swung round on his seat to
deflect their attention. He saw that Mrs Yapp, who'd been
listening at the parlour door, had a pair of arms around her
waist and was holding a man's finger in her hand. It was
Walter Howells, less muddy than he'd been but still with
traces of the coast on the lappets of his jacket. He laughed
longer than the rest, and then stepped forward to the table.

'Captain Comstock. Good evening, sir.' They shook hands. And then the agent offered his hand to Aymer, without the least trace of discomfort or apology. 'Mr Smith. I'm pleased to see you so established in Wherrytown. You should have sent me word of your arrival.' There was no choice for Aymer but to be civil.

'Perhaps we should go to a quieter place so we can talk. I've bad news . . .'

'There's no news that's so bad it won't wait till tomorrow,' Howells said. 'Enjoy your supper and your beer. I've business with the captain for tonight. And they are pressing matters.' He gave a short and portly bow to Mrs Norris, nodded at her husband, banged John Peacock on the back with a 'Bravo, sir!' and went out of the parlour with Captain Comstock at his heels.

Aymer did his best to recompose himself. He entertained the company with his opinions on Reform, Phrenology and Agriculture. He disclosed for them his whole budget of alerting anecdotes. When the treacle pudding was dished he refused his portion, and was admired for it, he thought, especially by Mrs Norris, who was unable to clear her plate entirely.

'I take no sugar,' he explained. 'I eat my supper bitterly, but with good conscience, sugar being the consequence of slavery. Slave dust, that's my name for it. There is no place for sweetness on my plate.'

'This is the man that begs for sheets,' said George, placing Aymer's pudding in front of John Peacock. 'Now there's an oddity.'

'I do not see it, George. What oddity?'

'They's cotton sheets. And cotton is the consequence of what? I'll have your bed stripped back to the bolster, so you can sleep in peace. Just say the word.'

'A nice distinction, George,' said Aymer, and stopped the laughter with a yawn.

AYMER SLEPT WELL for the best part of the night, despite the concert of coughing sailors and, occasionally, a barking dog. He was asleep when Katie and Robert Norris came to the room, a little before midnight, after their habitual walk down to the quay. He didn't hear their whispering. Nor the rustle of their clothes. He'd drunk more beer than he was used to. So, though his sleep was fast and deep, his dreams were urinous. He dreamed he'd wet himself, and then that he was passing water in the office at Hector Smith & Sons and that Matthias caught him doing it. He dreamed that Mrs Yapp had slipped between his sheets. She took his penis in her hands and she relieved him – but of what? The urine and the semen were confused.

He woke to whispering and low light, which lay in a broad band across his blankets where the curtains round his bed had parted. He'd slept till dawn. He'd have to rise and go down to the alleyway to urinate. He couldn't use the chamber pot, not with the Norrises so close. Their whispering began again. He didn't move, but tried to catch the words. It was Katie hushing Robert, giggling, saying what? Was it, 'I can't, I can't'? Aymer turned onto his side. What was more natural for a man with one bruised shoulder than to seek to ease the pain by lying on his uninjured side? He held the bed curtain back an inch or two so that he could

see into the room, but not be seen himself. He couldn't
see the Norrises nor where they slept. They'd taken care
to seal themselves.

Aymer must have slept again. When he next held the
curtain back the morning light had filled the room. He
heard the other bed give way, and then two bare legs
appeared below the screening curtain. It was Katie. When
she stood and stepped into the light her nightdress fell to
hide her legs down to the ankles. Her calves were stocky
and lightly freckled. She was the colour of a thrush. Robert's
hand came out and pinched the loosest flesh on her backside. She put a finger to her mouth and pouted 'Ssshhh!'
She tiptoed to the bed end and half obscured from Aymer
by the curtains she stooped to find the chamber pot, to
rid herself of last night's beer. She had her back against
the light. Her sandy hair was thick and carroty against the
cheap plantation cotton of her white nightdress. Aymer
didn't dare to breathe. He watched her shorten as she
squatted on the pot. He couldn't see her urinate. But there
was sound and smell. She stood and put the pot away and
then, pulling the curtain aside, returned to bed. Her husband pushed her nightdress up, above her knees, beyond
her thighs. He showed her buttocks to the room. Aymer
couldn't see their heads, but he could watch their bodies in
that early light embracing, wrapping, bending like a pair of
fish: a stringy eel, a plump and mottled salmon.

Aymer hadn't seen a naked woman before. Katie was his
first. He was surprised how broad she was, and how thickly
– and darkly – the hair grew between her legs. Robert had
his spectacles on and a hand on each cheek of her buttocks.

He pulled on her as if her flesh was dough, except this dough was pink and glinting at its heart.

Aymer had held his breath so long he coughed. He couldn't stop himself. He coughed repeatedly. He might only have breathed in loose lint from the sheets, but it felt as if he'd swallowed his tongue. He heard the Norris curtains draw shut, and whispers, giggles once again. What should he do? He didn't know the protocol. Should he pretend to sleep? He'd coughed too much to sleep. Besides the coughing had made his bladder ache. He didn't want to wet himself. He got out on the sea side of his bed, found his coat and boots and went out to the balcony above the courtyard. He pulled his coat over his sling so that only his good arm was sleeved. He secured his boots. He crept downstairs, bare legs beneath his coat, no shirt. He looked like an adulterer. An unsatisfied adulterer, because his penis was enlarged and pushed against his coat.

He found a dark part of the alleyway and urinated carelessly. A minor, unaccommodating stream hit his lower leg and ran into his boot. He tried to put a picture in his mind of Katie Norris, her face, her buttocks and her hair. But he was now too breathless and too exercised to concentrate. His forehead almost rested on the brickwork of the alleyway. He didn't feel the cold. He didn't feel any pain in the busy arm which he had freed from the sling. He ejaculated on the bricks. He swayed, for a few seconds at the most, and then the outside world blew in. Peace had been restored. He felt entirely tranquil now. Katie Norris was a thousand miles away. She was in Montreal. He cleared his throat and spat on to the wall. The little ship's dog, Whip, joined him. She smelled his urine, licked it from his leg. She went up on her hind legs and pushed her nose inside his coat. Her tail was like a metronome.

Aymer didn't want to go back to his room. He wasn't welcome there. He didn't want to sit inside the parlour, with flirting Mrs Yapp. His flirt had disappeared. It hung like giblets in the alleyway. He walked down to the quay with Whip. The *Tar* was ready to depart. Its steam was up. The sailors waved at him. Their steam was up as well. They didn't seem to mind he had no trousers on. They wanted to set sail before the black clouds to the west came in and dropped their tons of snow.

The streets of Wherrytown were quiet. It was the Sabbath and the townspeople could indulge their sins until Evensong and then poultice them with hymns. Aymer knew what he would do. He'd not bother with Mr Howells. The man had missed his opportunity. Two opportunities! 'I have done my best to try and make acquaintance with him,' Aymer told himself. 'I met his roughness with civility, to no avail.' So now, he'd make a pedestrian tour along the coast that day – at once, at least as soon as he had put some trousers on. He'd tell the kelpers face to face what Smith & Sons had decided. What Matthias had decided. The kelpers were the victims, not Walter Howells. Aymer could ease their suffering with bars of soap and, perhaps, a shilling for each family. He'd make his mark.

He walked back to the inn's courtyard. He pressed his nose against the window of the tackle room and tapped on the boarding. Better than a writ of habeas corpus, Aymer thought. The world would change at once. The bolt was

stiff and cold. Otto wasn't sleeping. He was hoping for
some food. Aymer didn't smell of food. He smelled of
animals. He smelled of damp. Otto let him take his hand
and shake it. He let the man sit down beside him on his
blankets. He listened to the sentences, the grinning storm
of words. The man was pointing at the open door saying,
'Go! Go! Go!' Whip was barking, running in and out the
tackle room. Otto couldn't bear this loss of privacy, nor
the commotion that the bare-legged man had caused. He
stood and tested how his ankle would support his weight.
He wrapped a blanket round his shoulders, put on his boots,
said, 'Uwip, Uwip,' and walked out into Wherrytown.

5. Dry Manston

SABBATH SNOW was coming in from Canada, preceded by a morning of tepid and deceitful air. There was no frost and just an ounce of wind, but anyone could tell that cold was on its way. The sea was pearly with pilchard shoals; seals and porpoises were seeking shelter close to shore; cormorants meditated on the rocks and did not fish; and there were hardly any penitents in Wherrytown who'd left their beds for morning prayers with Mr Phipps.

At Dry Manston the cattle from Quebec stood in squads or lay under the few low thorns between the high ground and the beach, their backs against the wrecking sea. Miggy and her mother hoped it would be easy to trap one of these mournful, docile cows. They'd have fresh meat, and what they couldn't eat within the week, they'd salt. They were up and out soon after dawn and planned to have one killed, butchered and concealed in an hour. They each had rigging ropes, flotsam from the *Belle*: one rope round the neck would hold the cow, one round its hind shins would bring it down. It should only take a single blow with a rock between the eyes to make the beast insensible. Then perforate the spinal column with a knife and cow was beef. That was the principle at least. They'd never had to kill a cow before. They hadn't had the chance. The most they'd done was club a seal to death and skin it on the beach.

The cows were wary and unpredictable. They wouldn't let the Bowes get close. They put their haunches in the air, hauled their bodies from the ground, and stood, face on, whenever Rosie or Miggy approached. They lowed in protest at the cold. They weren't fooled by gifts of grass. They backed away. They ran.

It was amusing for a while. Rosie tried all kinds of tricks to trap a cow, and entertain herself. She crept up on the cattle from behind, but got no closer than before. She tried to hypnotize a cow with weaving hands. She'd seen a donkey hypnotized that way at the farthing fair in Wherrytown. She made a sudden dash – with no success – and then fell down into the spongy bracken, laughing unselfconsciously. Miggy was embarrassed by her ma. She wanted beef. She was too old to be amused.

'We'll never get one if you fool around,' she said.

'Don't be so frownin', Miggy. We'll never get one anyway. Those cows in't wanting to be caught. I'm getting back indoors. My feet and back are soaking through. You coming with me, or will you stop and sulk?' Rosie was annoyed. Her daughter wasn't much of a companion. She was as clawed and joyless as a cat.

Miggy let her mother go. She liked to be out on the coast alone, the windswept heroine. Besides, she'd seen a distant figure on the path. It wasn't usual to see strangers – or officials – walking on the Sabbath. That's why Miggy and her mother had chosen Sunday to help themselves to beef. There was a chance, then, that it was Palmer Dolly.

Might he come by? And let his black hair mix with hers? Miggy wanted to be kissed. What must it be like to be kissed by someone other than your ma? More nourishing than beef! Sometimes at night she practised kissing her own mouth. She wet the insides of her lips and let them slide. She teased her palate with her tongue. She skimmed her chin and cheeks with her fingers. She licked the tissue on her palms. She found that, by touching the folds between her legs, she could reproduce the breathless tremble that she felt when she encountered men of her own age. A better place than home was just a touch away.

She'd not been alone for long when she discovered one of the shipwrecked heifers, grazing in an impasse of rocks and furze above the coastal track. She only had to stand resolutely at the open end and make a noise to trap the cow. It backed in more deeply. It dropped its head, either in resignation or to butt its captor. Miggy looped a rope round its neck and kept it back by slapping its nostrils. What should she do, with Rosie gone? Slaughter it alone? There wasn't any way that she could drag it home herself, or whistle it. The cow was not a dog. She'd have to brain it with a rock and butcher it before the crows and gulls found out. Would she have the strength and resolution? Could she relieve her boredom on the cow? Would Palmer Dolly come in time to help? The walking figure she had spotted earlier was getting closer.

There was a sharp, pointed stone almost within reach that would do for butchering. Miggy turned to pick it up, and stole a glance along the coast. It wasn't Palmer Dolly on the path. This man was blond. It was the sailor from the

Belle, the one who'd held her waist. Ralph Parkiss was honouring his sailor's boast, to see what she'd got hidden in her breeches. He'd volunteered to walk the six miles to the ship to discover how it had fared since it had beached, but he was looking for the girl. He couldn't fail to see her. She made a din – in case he passed her by.

'Is that you, Miggy?' He climbed up from the path across the winter bracken. 'Well now, that's fortunate. I never thought I'd see a friendly face.' Miggy's face was hardly friendly, though. She judged a smile to be unladylike, particularly as she had lost a bottom tooth and her lips were cracked and dry. She knew she had good eyes. Her mother told her so. She did her best to widen them, and not to blink. Ralph spoke the line that he had practised for six miles: 'I came to see the *Belle of Wilmington* and found myself the belle of Wherrytown instead . . .'

'It hasn't shifted much last night,' Miggy said. She wished she'd put a ribbon in her hair. They both looked down across the beach towards the *Belle*. It wasn't showing any sail. Its masts and rigging looked as bare and clean-picked as finished fish-bones. The carcasses of three drowned cows were floating in the shallows.

'I see you've roped yourself a cow. Is this one off the *Belle*?' Miggy let the rigging drop. She'd not be caught red-handed, poaching cattle. She was ambitious, but not for travel in a prison ship and not for Botany Bay.

'I wasn't stealin' it,' she said. 'Don't say I was.'

'I'll not say anything. Steal ten, and still I'll not say anything.' He picked the rigging up and handed it to Miggy. 'Go on. The captain won't miss one. He doesn't even know how many got ashore. Don't sell the steaks in Wherrytown, that's all.' He was unnerved by her round eyes. 'Is that our ensign round your throat?' he said. 'It suits you better than the *Belle*.' And when she didn't reply, 'I thought you were a boy. Those breeches aren't for girls. You're not a boy, I hope. How can a sailor tell?'

'I got a dress at home.'

'What colour, then?'

'White. Blue ribbons. I got long hair, 'cept it's up.'

'You can let it down so I can see.'

'I can't.'

'What will you do?'

'I'll not do anything. Why should I, anyway?'

'I walked six miles for nothing, then? Must I go back without a kiss? Miggy? Miggy? It's *twelve* miles, not six, by the time I'm back in Wherrytown. I tell you what. You kiss me once and then I'll dream of you.'

'I've got no time for kissin'. Kiss the cow if you're so keen on it.'

'I will, if you say no. And then I'll dream of cows, and you won't be my sweetheart any more.'

'Am I your sweetheart, then?'

'You are if you will kiss.'

What was Ralph Parkiss hoping for? The only girls he'd kissed before had been his sisters or, most recently, the cheap lorettes and dollar doxies in harbour inns in Montreal and Charleston. With prostitutes he'd put his lips and hands exactly where he'd wanted to, exactly when he'd wanted to. The women didn't care if they were in his dreams or not, so long as he could pay and finish what he'd come to do in less than half an hour. There wasn't any need for strategy or sweetness. They hadn't touched or kissed him in return. He'd had to serve himself. There was no happiness in that. Yet Miggy – who, so far, refused to kiss – made Ralph Parkiss feel as fragile as a blown egg. And happy too. He didn't mind her boyish clothes, her chilled, unsmiling face, her lack of decoration, her stillness and her secrecy. Such rapt, unconscious gravity was irresistible. Thank God the *Belle* had beached him here. Thank God for storms.

'What will we do then?'

'You can help me if you want.'

He helped her pull the cow out from the rocks and coax it down the incline to the path. He used a strip of gorse to beat the cow forward. He even risked a playful gorsing of Miggy's thighs. Try as she might she couldn't stop her smiles. Miggy had two creatures captive on her rope, the heifer and the man. She felt as mossy as the ground. She'd give Ralph a kiss of thanks when she got home for helping with the cow. Where was the harm in that? Thank God the *Belle* had beached him here. Thank God for storms.

They were halfway to the safety of the cottage and thinking only of themselves when Aymer Smith, touting his Duty along the coast, caught sight of them. He was in a cheerful mood. What a relief it was for him to be free of the bells, the guests, the corridors of the inn, to walk, and contemplate the fascinations of the coast. He had noticed, as he progressed away from Wherrytown, how one mile differed from the next, how landscape could transform in minutes from welcoming to inhospitable, how vegetation changed from rich to meagre, how time appeared to wind back on itself so that the 1836 of Wherrytown, its modest comforts and its steadiness, seemed a hundred years away as he approached Dry Manston. There weren't many trees for shelter now. And what trees there were, compared to those around the town, were angular. They shrank and thickened; they turned their trunks against the wind, and wore more bark. The people did the same. Aymer could regard himself as lean and willowy compared to them.

He called to Ralph and Miggy to wait for him, with a directness and informality that in a town would be considered improper. A morning out of Wherrytown had taught him that the diffidence and the reverence that marked the Spirit of the Age when strangers of two classes or two sexes met on city streets had not yet migrated here. The kelping families he'd encountered hadn't been paralysed by such a visitor. They didn't gape or turn away. They spoke to him openly, shook his hand and asked unsolicited questions. Boys and girls – children in nothing else but size – investigated him, pulling his clothes, pressing the leather of his boots, and treated Whip, Aymer's new companion, to strips of fish, yet didn't offer Aymer anything to drink.

He rehearsed with their parents the innovations in the soap industry, and what it meant for kelpers. 'We'll manage without kelp, God willing,' they said. 'The fishing's good enough these last few years. There's pilchards up tonight and we'll do well.' Aymer wondered why he'd come so far, with such a conscience, if the damage to their lives when the patronage of Hector Smith & Sons was withdrawn would be so inconsequential. Perhaps, if they had offered some brief signs of dismay, he would have felt less slighted.

'You'll miss the money, surely?'

'Hah! Mr Howells has most of it!'

The kelpers took Aymer's shilling and some bars of soap, and called their daughters for inspection, the ugly and the lean, the comely and the plump, the sour and the sweet, and all of them smiling wildly. This Kitty, fourteen years of age, was healthy and hard-working. She'd make a decent maid. This Mary, only ten, was useful round the house and would be glad of any work in Hector Smith & Sons. This Janie, seventeen, could work as hard as any man, 'Look at her muscles, Mr Smith!' and she could wet-nurse, cook or scrub. Did Aymer know of anyone who could offer employment to any of these girls? Aymer wrote their names down in his notebook and made promises he knew he couldn't keep. They'd let him take their daughters there and then, he felt, and not expect to see them any more, so long as they had 'prospects and positions'.

Aymer's appetite for kelpers and their daughters was diminishing when he saw Miggy Bowe and Ralph Parkiss with their stolen cow.

'Good morning, sirs,' he called, a long man in a black tarpaulin coat, hurrying to catch up with them on the path. 'Please stand and wait for me.' They turned to answer him. He waved. They stood stock-still, uncertain what to do. Miggy knew the type of man he was, though he was out of season, a winter cuckoo. From time to time, usually in the spring and summer, she'd come across such pale-looking fellows walking on the coast, with knapsacks on their backs, and walking sticks. These were the only people that she'd ever met that were more than a day's walk from their homes

– apart from Ralph. They might be alone, in pairs, in groups of four or five. Often they were lost. They asked directions to the Cradle Rock which, it seemed, they'd travelled all this way to see. Their purpose was to touch and sway the Rock. They'd missed it by a half a mile or more. There'd always be a penny in it if Miggy would lead them to the Rock and show them where they had to put their backs to set it in motion. Sometimes these men took their easels to the beach, or sat on dunes with sketch pads on their knees. Sometimes they came with hammers and broke up rocks, fossil-bibbing, or spent inexplicable hours attending on the sea birds. Miggy would then earn pennies by showing where the razorbills were nesting, or clambering down loose cliffs to collect gulls' eggs for them. Occasionally there were ladies, too, with umbrellas and clothes that were, for Miggy, colourless and disappointing. One of Walter Howells's men from Wherrytown or George from the inn was often in attendance as a guide and porter. Then there'd be a picnic on the sand and Miggy, if she smiled and was polite, could importune some bread and mutton for herself. She dreamed some man – some gentleman – would buy her for a penny and take her far from home.

Aymer didn't have a bag or easel. She presumed he was a man who'd missed the Cradle Rock. Except he didn't seem lost, but purposeful. Perhaps he'd come about the *Belle*. An excise man? No, he was far too tall and clerky, and excise men didn't work on the Sabbath. A shipping agent, then? Someone with proper title to the cows? Now Miggy was alarmed. He waved at them again, and whistled. A dog – the same small bitch that had gone off with the

American sailors the day before – ran out of the furze,
circled the stranger, and then ran barking towards Miggy,
Ralph Parkiss and the heifer. The young cow broke away
and ran. Miggy didn't attempt to hold her. She let the rope
fall. She waved back at the man, and when she lowered her
arm tucked her neckchief, the red-and-white ensign from
the *Belle*, under her smock. Perhaps he was a ship's officer.
He had the ship's dog, after all. And one sleeve of his coat
was armless. Perhaps he'd hurt it in the storm. Perhaps he'd
lost it in a brawl with pirates, or a whale, or in the war with
Bonaparte. Perhaps he'd seen they'd roped the cow. Ralph
would be in trouble. Miggy Bowe rocked from foot to foot.
She was set in motion by two men like the Cradle Rock,
swaying, heavy, inconsolable. Her heart was beating fast.

'Is he your captain, Ralph?' she said.

'I don't know who the fellow is. I saw him at the inn last
night.'

The dog did not respond to Aymer's 'Down, Whip.
Down.' She'd found two friends, one who smelled of other
dogs, and one who was a shipmate. She nuzzled Ralph. She
jumped at Miggy's legs and licked the stains of breakfast
from her fingers.

'Good morning, gentlemen.' Aymer reached them on
the path. He put his hand out, first to Ralph. 'I know you,
sir, I think. We dined together at the inn. Yes, yes. I know
a face.'

He turned to Miggy.

'My little lady,' Miggy said, using Whip to shield her
from the handshake that Aymer was offering, 'come to see
us, have you, sweet? Is she yours, this little 'un?' Aymer

blushed. Not his first blush of the day. He hadn't known she was a girl, a pert-faced, handsome girl at that. She was dressed like a farmboy.

'I'm Aymer Smith of Hector Smith & Sons,' he said. His face had quickly cooled and paled. 'And you? What are your family; kelpers?' Any hopes that Miggy had that this man had lost an arm to whales were shattered. His voice was not heroic, but clipped and fussy. You might imagine him to be distinguished, dashing at a distance, but now his face was close she saw he was quite old, older than her mother anyhow, and gaunt. He had a second arm, as well. It moved below his coat.

'We kelp a bit,' she said.

'And do you supply Mr Howells with soda ash?'

'Walter Howells? He has our kelp.'

'So then, what is your name?'

'I'm Miggy Bowe.'

Again he offered her his hand. She hid her hands, and backed away. 'I'm only seventeen,' she said.

'What does that mean? That you're too young to shake my hand?'

'I never had to shake a hand before.'

'My dear Miss Bowe,' he said, 'it is not important that you shake my hand. I merely offered it to mark our meeting and to introduce myself. A dog that rushes to you with its tail in motion is a dog you need not fear. And so it is with strangers, except of course we shake our hands and not our tails. A footpad or a common thief does not hold out his hand to shake, but only to relieve you of your watch or silver. But still, I will not trouble you to shake my hand.

You should not do what does not suit you, or else you will be unhappy all your life.' He put his hand into his coat. 'Here, take some soap,' he said. 'It is more useful, I agree, than handshaking.' Miggy Bowe, who had no watch or silver and *was* unhappy all her life, could not see the relevance of soap. She turned her back and ran. She didn't think that she'd be caught by Aymer Smith. He was too flimsy to give chase. But Ralph and Whip were fit. They soon were at her side.

ROSIE BOWE released her mongrels and went out, stick in hand, to meet the man that Miggy and the sailor had described.

'We'd roped a likely little cow, Ma, and got it halfway home and then he tries to fetch hold of my hand. I don't know what he might've done if Ralph didn't come by. I never seen a man so long and thin and strange. He's talkin' like you never heard before. He had his arm hid in his coat. He might've had a pistol there. He said I was to tell if we sell kelp to Walter Howells. And then he gave me soap.'

'Let's see the soap.'

'I wouldn't take no soap.'

'Miggy Bowe, if this is lies . . .'

'It in't no lie. I wouldn't tell no lie on Sabbathday.'

'She's right,' Ralph said. 'The fellow's got a pocketful of soap. And when he talks it's like a sermon.'

The man, when he arrived, it's true, was tall – but Rosie felt no fear of him. He was a spindleshanks. He wouldn't have the strength or pluck to trouble them. She calmed the dogs and put her stick away. She even shook his hand. She didn't want him in her home – where Miggy and the sailor stood behind the door – and so she made him state his business in the cold and open air. She listened as he gave his name and that of Walter Howells. She'd heard of Smith & Sons, of course. She knew her soda ash was sold to finish up in soap. She guessed as soon as Aymer mentioned Duty and Conscience that there would be bad news.

'Alas,' he said, after what seemed an endless doorstep homily on everything from soap to sin, 'my brother has no further need of kelp. His business with Dry Manston and with you and Walter Howells cannot survive the summonses of science or of progress. I come to thank you for your efforts in the past and to present you with a shilling for your troubles, and some soap.' He put five bars of soap down on the yard bench. Whip sniffed at them, but wasn't interested. Rosie felt the same. Already, she was angry with the man. How would they live without their thirty shillings for a ton? And then he held the shilling up. 'For you,' he said. 'By way of thanks. And may it bring you better fortune.'

Rosie couldn't stop herself: 'That in't no use. You think we're going to bake our bread from soap? How will we live? A shillin' is a fine price to be paupered by. It's a bad-luck shilling and we'll have none of it.'

'I intended it to be . . .'

'Intended in't enough!'

Miggy put her head around the door. She thought she'd turn a shilling to a crown: 'I had a cow roped, Ma. He chased it off. And now we're gonna starve.'

Aymer blushed again. He'd already spotted Miggy with the young American, peeking from behind the door, and though she was no Katie Norris, she was alluring in a colourless and undramatic way. He liked her peevish, boyish inhibition, and didn't want to seem a fool in front of her. He didn't know what he had done to cause such anger, except be honest and considerate. 'You should not blame me, Mrs Bowe,' he said. That would have been enough, but he was ill at ease – as ever – and couldn't stop the puffing elongation of this simple self-defence. 'I have been the kelper's friend.' A pause to find another reason to demand their sympathy and thwart their anger. 'I have braved a storm at sea in order to be here. Indeed, I've sustained an injury. My arm and shoulder bone are cracked.' (Now his sentences were under canvas. Their sails were full of wind.) 'But pain has not deterred me from my duty. I have walked a fair few miles from Wherrytown, and it is cold, and there are many kelpers to be spoken to. Your neighbours took my shilling and my soap. I've been this morning to the homes of Mr Fowler, Mr Dolly, Mr Hicks . . . All kelping families, but they were civil.'

'They've got the reason to be civil, in't they? Kelping's not their meat and drink. They've sons, and boats. Fish is their livin'. Kelping's for their daughters and their wives to earn a bit of extra for the pot. But we've no men or boats.'

'I beg you, Mrs Bowe. Do not upset yourself.'

'I've got a right to speak my mind. You're standing on my step, and I *will* speak my mind. What'll we do without our kelp? Who'll take my Miggy off my hands, if we've no work to keep us proud?' Aymer waited for Rosie Bowe to sing her daughter's praises, how she could cook and sew and be a lady's maid if only Mr Smith would write her name down in his book and find employment for her. But she said nothing more. She simply shook her head and looked at Aymer's boots.

'I'm sure your daughter has more worth than what you earn from kelping . . .'

'There in't no worth to being poor, not when it comes to marrying.'

'Oh, Ma!'

'"Oh, Ma," she says! She's no idea, that girl. She's living in her dreams. No man will take a pauper for his bride.' Behind the door, Ralph Parkiss had his hand on her daughter's back. She let his fingers tell a rosary of vertebrae down to her waist. She stopped his hand with hers and held his fingers tight. A thought occurred to Miggy Bowe that she would never let his fingers go. She'd hold them here, and on the sea, and in America. She rubbed the rope burns on Ralph's palm. She faced the stranger in the doorway and she smiled.

A thought occurred to Aymer Smith as well, an extravagant, rushing inspiration which, had he been at home, amongst the comforts of his sitting room, or in the prudent offices of Hector Smith & Sons, might not have found the thinnest purchase on his imagination. But here, emancipated by the open air, by the distance he had come, and by the dislocating alchemy of sea and loneliness and strangers, and by the smiles that he had got from Katie Norris, his head was free for reckless possibilities. There was no one to rein him back. No one to stop him thinking that, perhaps, he'd found a wife at last. What better man than he to take a pauper for his bride? The thought was not preposterous.

He'd dress her well. He'd mould her into shape. She'd learn to read and write and cypher. She'd pick up the proprieties of city life and adopt a more womanly demeanour, not gaping or being quite so busy with her legs. She could be taught to breathe through her nostrils and not her mouth. He'd turn her into Katie Norris. She was too gauche and innocent herself to mind that he was inexperienced and old and would not make a pattern husband. He'd offer her the wealth, the education, the status, the emancipation that otherwise could only flourish in her dreams and prayers. She'd bear him children: Aymer Smith & Sons. What would Matthias make of it? He'd be appalled. And jealous, too. Fidia Smith, Matthias's wife, was thirty-six and pinched in everything but shape. But Mrs Miggy Smith was like a chrysalis. Her best days were ahead. And so were his. So long as he could mend the damage done and earn the sanction of the Bowes.

'I did not mean ... to ...' Aymer said. 'I take the shilling back.'

'You'd better grab it, Ma!'

Rosie did what Miggy said. She wasn't angry any more. Her passions were short-lived, and hardly worth a shilling. She put the coin in a jar.

'You can come indoors,' she said. Aymer was relieved and startled by her change of voice and countenance. 'I'll get you something warm to drink before you set off back.'

The Bowes had lit a Sabbath fire of kelp, cow dung and timbers from the *Belle*. It burned in colours that Aymer thought he'd never seen before, colours that an artist could not mix. Miggy and her mother sat together on a bench, their faces halved and reddened by the floating firelight. Ralph Parkiss, petting Whip, squatted on the floor, which was simply earth, flattened once a week with a shovel. He didn't speak. Aymer had the only chair. They'd made both men hot mahogany, with water, country gin and treacle. (Aymer did not require them to remove the sugar from his drink.) It smelled of fish. The whole place smelled of fish. Smoked herrings hung across the fire. Tubs of salted pilchards were stored beneath the bench and chair. A leather bucket held fish oil, for cooking and for light. Great white wings of fish stiffened on ropes around the cob-and-wattle walls like lines of underwear.

The single room was divided by a sacking curtain, with a box-bed in the almost hidden part. It stood on bare earth which rain had softened to a paste. The only touch of colour to the room was a red petticoat, thrown over rising dough to keep it warm. There weren't any curtains, cushions, rugs or tablecloths. There was no ceiling, but a raft of timbers made from wrecks. A little light and some dust from the thatch of turfs came through and peppered Aymer's hair. There were no ornaments, except an embroidered passage from the Bible on the chimney breast:

> Weep sore for him that goeth away:
> for he shall return no more,
> nor see his native country.
>
> Jeremiah

Aymer found the room a little disconcerting: the fish, the petticoat, the privacy, the lack of daintiness, the quiet. But soon the dancing semi-darkness shut out the universe and made their silence comfortable. The two men concentrated on their drinks. Miggy Bowe untied her hair. Rosie had her first chance now to wonder how they'd cope without the benefit of kelp. Some farmers to the east of Wherrytown used untreated seaweed to fertilize their fields, but they would only pay a shilling for a wagon-load. There would be work in summer on the farms across the moor – but what a walk for fourpence a day! Who could live on that? What could they do, then? Find some work in Wherrytown. Cut peat where they had rights of turbary. Joust fish for the boatmen on the coast. Scrump nuts and apples. Poach rabbits, heathcocks, lapwings' eggs. Glean oats and nettles for bread and soup. Cadge clothes. Steal turnips. Emigrate? They'd find a way. Rosie Bowe was not a melancholic. She had no time for lasting sorrows. Like many people living by the sea she had the bedding of a beggar but the spirit of a bull. There was no denying that the man who sat in her one chair had beached the family just as firmly as the gale had beached the *Belle*. Their masts were down. Their sides were holed. And they were stuck. But not for long.

'Well, then . . . So that's the way the bad luck settles in. It's muck and nettles from now on,' she said, and looked at Aymer in the bending flattery of light, defying him to say another word.

Aymer kept the silence easily. He didn't know what he could say. He knew, though, what to do. He'd take the Bowes beneath his wing. A shilling was a paltry sum, a blushing sum. It was what he'd paid to George for merely fetching Mr Phipps. Aymer would give the Bowes more than a shilling's worth if he could find the means . . . to what? To be straightforward and suggest the benefits for everyone if Miggy ... Margaret. He'd have to call her Margaret ... would come back on the next *Tar* with him to be his wife. He wouldn't mention love. He couldn't love the girl, not like the love that danced till dawn in fairytales or books. He was too old for dances and for dawn. But he could *liberate* the girl. What better dowry could there be? He'd break her chains of poverty, just like he'd snapped the chains of slavery for Otto. He looked across the room at Miggy's silhouette. Her face was fine enough. Her skin was pale and clear. Mrs Margaret Smith, a healthy country catch, a woman less than half his age. He wouldn't want a wife too well experienced. He didn't need to win her heart. But he could court and win her head. Her body, too. She'd use the bedside chamber pot. He'd run his hands across her thrushy thighs. Her hair would hang in one loose tress. It would be best, he thought, to talk first to her mother. She'd understand the common sense of his proposal. She wouldn't have much choice.

Aymer felt light-headed. Excitement? Fish fumes? Or the gin?

'I'll go,' he said. 'I cannot trust myself to find the way when it is dark.' And then to Ralph, 'Will you be walking with me, sir? A companion shrinks the miles.'

'Gladly, Mr Smith,' he said. He couldn't tell the truth, that he would rather stay and spend the night exactly where he was. Both men stood up, pulled on their coats and jostled at the door. Whip ran through their legs into the open air.

Aymer made a parting speech: 'I promise you I will return within a day or two. I will consider some proposals that might ease your condition. You have accepted my shilling with reluctance, but you will, I hope, accept my friendship and my help with . . .' He could not find the proper words. *With greater deference*, perhaps? Or *with docility*? He left the farewell uncompleted. For the third time that day he offered his hand to Miggy Bowe. She stretched her arm and touched him on his finger ends, much in the way that she had touched the African's toes on the beach the day before, much in the way a child would dare to touch a jellyfish. His hand was damp and hot.

'I would've had that cow if you in't come,' she said.

Aymer Smith was not a Revolutionist. He could not abet the theft and slaughter of a cow, and square it with his conscience, or with the excise men, or – more to the point – with Walter Howells, who'd taken on the task of rounding up the cattle from the *Belle*. But what if the cow was not alive? 'I saw three dead cows, ready salted, in the shallows of the wreck,' he said. 'That's flotsam, isn't it? I do not know the finer points of law. But isn't wreckage floating in the sea the property of those who find it? And what is a lifeless cow but wreckage of a sort – just leather, horn and flesh? Who will oppose you taking meat out of the sea? It is fishing by another name. Besides, the flesh will putrefy unless you rescue it. It is almost a duty to oppose such waste.'

And so they took a handcart, a wood axe and some heavy knives and went down to the sea. The Bowes and Ralph waded in, despite the cold. Whip ran barking at the waves. But Aymer didn't want to chance his boots. He used his strapped arm as an excuse for staying idle. One cow was almost beached. Between them and the free help of the waves, the Bowes and Ralph managed to drag it into the shallows. Its orifices drained of water and lance eels squirted through a thousand punctures in the hide. Its eyes had gone, and crabs were feeding on the titbits of the skull. Its tongue was white and bloodless. There was some evidence already of putrefaction in the head. The women would not take the tongue or brains. But the clammy, musty, tainted meat from the neck and clod would still be edible if washed in ashy water and then roasted. They went to work without emotion, beginning at the leg and cutting meat from off the bone up through the topside, silverside and flank into the aitch bone. The salty water caused the fibres of the open flesh to contract and drew the juices from the cow so that the sea became a rosy brine. The women stood in water that was tumbling with tiny, feeding fish. By the time they'd reached the rump and sirloin the water and the sand were red. Gulls were circling so close that the mayhem of their wings was louder than the sea.

Aymer found the fish more shocking than the cow. He was used to seeing fish on plates, cooked, gormless, dressed, not tumbling like molten lead, not smelling so. He retreated up the sand. He couldn't help. He had only one arm. They posted him to stand with Whip next to their handcart, to keep birds off. No tumbril in Robespierre's Paris could have been as bloody or macabre, or smelled as bad. He turned his back to it and looked along the shore, where turnstones and oyster catchers were picking through the beached and draining kelp. Aymer had seen these seaweeds many times before, and knew their names in Latin: *Ascophyllum nodosum*,

Fucus vesicolosus, Laminaria cloustini. There was a folio in
the offices of Smith & Sons, with over fifty specimens
pressed, labelled and isolated on smooth sheets of white
paper like doilies or like fans. When they were boys,
Aymer and Matthias had learned to recognize each species.
'I suppose that now,' thought Aymer, 'there'll have to be a
folio with specimens of Monsieur Leblanc's common salt.'
He knew the *shapes* of the weeds, perhaps. But the *colours*
were a shock. The folio seaweeds for all their dry and
flattened delicacy were only brown and black. But on the
beach the living kelp was as polished and as leathery as a
prince's boot, in mustards, crimsons, purples, tans. In the
shallows, where the tide was frowning white round rocks
and bars, the deeper kelps and wracks spread darkly on the
surface, or danced arabesques in undulating groves of weed,
like spirit-women at a ball in heavy satin frocks. Aymer
looked beyond the kelp, beyond the figures in the sea,
beyond the *Belle* abandoned in the suds, into the feeble,
sombre sky. There was so little daylight left, that winter
afternoon.

'We'll have to go now, Ralph,' he called.

They left the Bowes to push their meaty handcart home
alone, and set off with the dog, at a pace too fast for Aymer,
towards Wherrytown. Miggy – her hands as red as two
anemones – called out to them, 'You've got to come again!'
Both men replied, 'I will!'

At first, Ralph's shoes made rodent noises as he walked.
But soon the sea drained out of them. His legs and feet
were wet and cold.

'We've done a decent job today,' said Aymer. 'They'll not want for meat.'

'We have,' said Ralph, smiling to himself.

'Good women, too. That is, when one considers all the deprivations in their life. The daughter, don't you think, might make a tolerable wife for a man? She has the country virtues.' Ralph did not reply.

The path was level as it skirted round the bay, and soft underfoot. First there were dunes which shielded them from the cold and bloody solitudes of the seashore. Then there were salty flats with skew trees and flood-tide debris, and tracts of open, windblown heath where grasses mocked the sea with mimic waves and clapping stalks matched the distant, wet applause of tumbling pebbles in the tide. But soon they had to scramble over rocks, and Aymer, with one arm in a sling, made clumsy progress. Ralph waited on the headland for his companion to catch up. Someone had set a wooden bench across two rocks and Aymer, when he arrived, sat breathlessly on it, while Whip went rabbiting and Ralph displayed the patience of a sailor by carving 'R.P.' in the bench with his clasp knife. Other names were carved in it with dates: Thos. Pearson 1829; C. Stuart, Edinbgh. May '33; Bartolli, Claudio, ROMA 1831. There were initials, too, with hearts and arrows. Aymer, motionless, was feeling cold and hungry and wearied by the ceaseless noise and wind. The inn was still two hours' walk away. He'd allow himself a minute more of rest. He tried to make his weariness seem purposeful by identifying, for Ralph, the hornblende and the feldspar which added the white and flesh-red garnish to the granite thereabouts. He grubbed out coloured stones which enamelled the turf at his feet and rubbed them clean between his fingers. He broke free crusts of salt and mustard lichens. He murmured his familiarity with them, by naming them in Latin and in English. Ralph shook his head at his companion's learning. 'I don't know names for those,' he said. And then, 'I do know other things . . .' Ralph's was a stranger's ignorance. Aymer's was a stranger's knowledge.

A narrow side path led down from Aymer's bench, through boulders, to a grassy bowl, and then rose steeply to a tonsured promontory where the granite was too exposed for ferns or lichen or algae. It was a perfect paradise of rocks, much loved, in summer, by watercolourists and lizards. But in the winter, with so much grey about and so little light, the dull pinks of the exposed stone were warm and beckoning. No child could pass it by without first attempting to climb the tumbled pyramid to reach the square mass at its summit. If it was natural masonry, then it had been weathered by a geometric wind and shaped by architectural frosts. This topmost block – the shape and size of a small stone cottage – rested with solid poise on the nipple of a flat but slightly rounded rock. If anyone sat, like Aymer, on the bench and stared for long enough it could seem the block was hovering an inch above the world. It had a tarred cross on its side.

'So that's the Cradle Rock,' Aymer said, pointing.

'What is the Cradle Rock?'

'A rock that moves when it is pushed. Let's go and see.

I think we can afford the time.' Even Aymer couldn't pass it by.

They found a way between granite slabs marked by tarred arrows and climbed to the rounded platform where the Cradle Rock rested on its pivot. Reaching it wasn't as easy as it looked. Aymer couldn't find footholds. He had to accept the sailor's hand around his wrist, and then his palm against his bottom. The Rock, they saw, was not a square on every side. Its hidden part was thinner and irregular. Ralph clambered up twelve feet or so and soon was standing on its summit, testing where the balance was. But Cradle Rock was so exactly poised that Ralph's weight only deadened it. He couldn't make it move. Both men searched the two sides where they could find safe footholds. At one point, on the southern face, the stone was worn away. The feet and shoulders of a thousand visitors had rubbed it bare.

'Try here,' Ralph said.

'I'll need both arms.' Aymer shook off his sling and threw it to the ground. His shoulder didn't hurt at all although his arm was a little stiff from its confinement in his coat. The wind picked up the sling and turned it once or twice, then took it on a seagull flight inland.

They put their backs against the naked stone, wedged their feet and pushed. At first their task seemed hopeless. But on their third and fourth attempts they sensed the softness of the mass. They moved across a foot or two and tried once more. Again the Rock seemed to give a quarter-inch against their backs. They found a rhythm to their exertions, with Ralph, experienced at team-work on the

Belle, calling out, 'And push! Let-her-go. And push! Let-her-go.' The quarter-inch expanded on each push, and soon the Cradle Rock made grinding sounds as it ascended and declined at its own pace. Ralph and Aymer were redundant now. They stepped back to a safer spot and watched as eighty tons dipped and rose like a child's cradle, with a displacement at its outer edges of nine or ten inches. Ralph was laughing at the joy of it. And Aymer, too, had seldom felt such unselfish pleasure. With just their backs, and half a dozen curses from the American, and some barks from Whip, they had rocked the grandest boulder on the coast. And left it rocking.

They were too pleased, at first, to feel the snow. But soon the Cradle Rock, its motion halting imperceptibly, was capped in white. They wanted to stay where they were until the Cradle was at peace. But the snow came driving in too thickly; soft snow, not wet. It fell inertly for a few minutes and then was taken up by a gusty wind. Both men were badly provided against such weather. They had no hats or gloves. Only Aymer's tarpaulin coat was waterproof.

They climbed down to the path and left the Cradle Rock to tremble in the snow, unwitnessed. Ralph was too cold to talk. Aymer was too nervous and elated to stay quiet. He asked about the seaman's family, but couldn't tell if Ralph had heard. He gave his solo verdict on the Bowes, on 'rocks that rock', on emigration, the American 'language', slavery, the beneficial properties of sea air, everything except the aching wetness of his knees and calves and boots. He pointed at and named the trees, the rocks, the fleeing birds, until there was nothing left to see or name excepting snow.

Their path had disappeared. Their legs and faces nagged with cold. Their clothes and hair turned white. They couldn't see the sea. It boiled with pilchards which would, at least, be safe until the Sabbath ended. On this God-flinching coast it was bad luck to catch or eat a Sunday fish. But then – at midnight – all the boats would put to sea for this godsend of oily flesh. It wouldn't matter that it snowed. Snow can't settle on the sea. They'd shoot their nets into the lanes of pilchards and pack their stomachs, lamps and purses with the catch. 'Meat, money and light, All in one night.' And what a night, for fishermen! Snow. Pilchards. Floating cows. The flotsam of the *Belle*. And twenty yards below the Cradle Rock the sea-logged, bloated body of a man. Not the African. He has his first experience of snow. But Nathaniel Rankin, the Bostonian, drowned for almost two days now, and ready for the nets.

6. Evensong

THE SAILORS from the *Belle* were bored. The Sabbath was a torment. What could they do all day, except sit round an idling fire and regret their ship had not been grounded off some other town, where there were breweries and brothels, or, at least, the liberty to work on Sundays? After breakfast they'd watched the *Tar* dimming out at sea. With the backing of a westerly it chased its own steam trail and then it was evaporated by the light. That was the entertainment for the day. They should have volunteered to walk with Ralph Parkiss to check the fortunes of the *Belle* at Dry Manston. At least there would've been flirting on the coast, and some amusement to be had with rocks and cattle. At least there'd have been some noise, if only gulls and wind.

The captain wouldn't tolerate their singing or any horseplay in the inn. His mood was murderous. George, the parlourman, whose conversation at its best was cryptic, had brought the news, 'Your blackie's gone back home to Africa.' Someone, he said, had released the bolt on the tackle-room door. All that remained of Otto now was dry blood on the straw. Who should they blame but Aymer Smith, the meddler with the soap, the sugar abolitionist? George said he'd seen the man a little after dawn, down on the quay. He

had Whip at his side and was talking to the sailors on the
Tar. He hadn't any trousers on. What should the captain
make of that? He whistled through a window for his dog.
She didn't come.

The captain went down to Aymer's upstairs room with
Mrs Yapp and George. The carriage bag, some clothes
and books were on his bed. The man himself had disappeared in the middle of the night, Robert Norris said,
embarrassed, evidently, to have slept through breakfast and
to be discovered in his barely curtained bed with half a pot
of urine at its foot. He and his wife – who looked a touch
too flushed and ample for a Sunday – hadn't seen or heard
of Aymer Smith since then.

'What does that mean, do you suppose?' the captain
asked George. 'Not wearing any trousers? Is this a jest or
your invention?'

'It in't any jest. I'd not invent such indecorum. As
barelegged as a seagull, he was.'

'He didn't even settle his account,' said Mrs Yapp. 'Or
pack his bags. Too rushed to put his trousers on! Well
now . . .' She laughed. She couldn't help it. She put her arm
around the captain's waist. The poor man needed cheering
up. But when she saw the temper on his face, she let him
go and busied herself with the empty bed. 'He had clean
sheets and hardly dirtied them. Now, there's a wicked waste
. . . Who wants some soap?' She took the few remaining
bars from Aymer Smith's belongings and offered them first
to Katie Norris ('We have some, thank you, Mrs Yapp')
and, then, to George ('Enough! Enough!'). Alice Yapp
removed the sheet from the bed, bundled Aymer Smith's

possessions – the soap included, and his books – in his bag and took them to the door. 'We'll see if we can fetch a shilling with these to pay his bill,' she said, and then, by way of explanation for the profit she could make, 'The man has gone. So's the dog. So's the African. And so's the *Tar*. We've seen the last of them!' She prodded the Norrises' piss-pot with her toe. 'Take care of that,' she said to George. 'Before there's kick and spill.'

The captain spent the morning at a table in the snug, placated every half an hour or so by a shot of 'Mrs Yapp's Fortified Tea'. (It would make her rich when she was in her sixties.) He needed fortifying, Mrs Yapp insisted. He'd been 'stormed-up about the blackie and the *Belle*'. A little 'lively tea' would settle him and let the anger out and only cost two pennies for a pint. 'You're sitting stiff,' she said. 'Don't be so starchy down your back. Better bend than break. There, now.' She squeezed the tendons in his neck and shoulders until his back relaxed. 'Anything you need from me, just ring the handbell in the parlour. Or else you'll find me in my room.' Was that an invitation to her room? The captain couldn't tell. She was so brisk and democratic. But her fingers and her tea had done their job. He felt more lively now, though, thanks to Mrs Yapp's plump gen-erosities, he was stiff and starchy in places other than his neck. He was stormed-up in ways that no man, even agent Howells, could relieve.

The captain had arranged for Walter Howells to visit him that afternoon. That's why – he needed no excuse – he hadn't gone with seaman Parkiss to Dry Manston to check on the *Belle* himself. For the first time in seven years of captaincy he would have to pass a full day without seeing the ship under his command. 'No choice, no choice,' he said aloud to himself, and tried to concentrate on his letters and his log. He did his best to calculate the dollar-damage that the storm had done. How would he pay for the repairs? What would they cost? He made a list of urgent tasks: the rounding up of cattle, the purchase of timber and rigging, the disciplining of his men who, given time and liberty, would turn feral. He wrote the names of Whip and Otto at the bottom of his list. And then the name of Aymer Smith. The three of them would be, by now, miles down coast and nothing he could do would get them back. Otto would cost a hundred dollars to replace at A. K. Ellis, the Negro Broker and Auctioneer in Wilmington. More trouble and expense! What kind of man would steal an African in such a blatant way? What kind of man would steal a little bitch like Whip?

'A bloody fool, that's who!' was Walter Howells's opinion when he arrived for their meeting in the late afternoon. 'I have the man's address. You send a bill for the slave and the dog to Hector Smith & Sons. And if he doesn't pay, then send him something to remember you by.'

'Like what, Mr Howells?'

'Like someone to torch the factory. Why not?' Why not, indeed? Now that the Smiths had no need of Walter Howells's kelp, their place could burn for all the difference it would make to him. 'I'd gladly torch the place myself, and him inside of it. It's little more than common theft, to take a man, no matter all this Wilberforcey bosh.'

'To steal a *dog* is worse,' said Comstock, 'because a dog

cannot express itself. I'd like to get my hands around the fellow's throat.'

'Don't take no risks yourself that you can pay for and forget about.' Walter Howells leaned forward in his seat, and topped the captain's drink. He pointed at the list on the table. 'I'll take care of all of that, if we can settle on a price and you can provide a promissory note,' he said. 'Let's get the Sabbath on its way, and then tomorrow morning I'll have them cattle rounded up. The tide is on the up. We'll see if we can tug your ship free of the bar and put her into Wherrytown. I'll fix up all the timber that you need, and I've the carpenters.' He worked down the list with a stubby finger, until he reached the last name at the bottom. 'And as for him. Well, now, you keep your own hands clean. I'll see he gets a beating. There's fellows that I know will gladly break a bone or two and only charge a sovereign. I'll write a letter to a man I have up east. He's in my debt and has a decent fist. He'll sort out Aymer Smith. He'll finish him! We'll leave the fellow black and blue. He'll wish he'd never come to Wherrytown. I'll write that letter straight away, and pay the sovereign out of my own pocket to show my good intentions. What do you say? Shall we play duets?' He put his hand in Captain Comstock's. 'We're partners, then?'

'Yes, sir, I think we are.'

'And if there's any, what should we call 'em . . . ? candle-ends . . . ? left over when the job is done, then share and share alike is what I say, and mum's the word.'

Captain Comstock was too far from home to understand the half of what he heard. But this he knew for certain. No trouble and expense would be too much to get the *Belle* afloat again and sailing home, away from snow and joyless Wherrytown where bad luck seemed to be as common and as unrelenting as the gulls. It didn't strike him as anything but fitting, as he now looked out beyond his saviour Howells into the lane, that dusk and snow were coming down in a chilling, felting duet of their own, while a horn warned shipping of the fog.

'There's snow *and* fog in these parts, Mr Howells?'

'Not fog. That's Preacher Phipps's chapel horn. It's evensong, and time for me to get along.'

'You're going to evensong, then?'

'No, Captain Comstock, I am not. I have no business with the chapel. I'm not the prayerful kind.'

'My men might benefit from getting out of doors, and singing hymns. We'll let the Wherrytowners see our faces.' The captain hoped a hymn or two would calm him down before his rage at Aymer Smith transferred to someone innocent. And, then, perhaps a Sabbath night with Mrs Yapp – plump and attentive in her bed – would draw the venom out of him if evensong did not.

The sailors from the *Belle* weren't the prayerful kind, either. They weren't used to worship, except at sea. Their God was weather. But, once the order had arrived from their captain that they must all attend chapel, the younger ones were glad to be at liberty in Wherrytown, sliding and snowballing on the way to evensong.

The town, just like the inn, was made for ambushes and hide and seek. It was a warren, with perplexing levels in which steps up led only to steps down, and parlour windows, at ankle height from outside, were head high from indoors.

There weren't streets or civic places, just a lattice of steep intersecting alleyways and lanes, some no wider than a horse and none with any compass sense or geometric logic. The uneven coastal ridge where it was built determined Wherrytown, and determined, too, that when the sailors' God – the sun, the snow, the wind – came in from the sea it beat on every door. There were a thousand places for the men to hide and throw their snowballs: behind the sheds and peat stacks in the public lanes, or amongst the hanging nets and timber piles that occupied every spare corner of the town.

Is *town* the word for Wherrytown? Or *village*, even? To these Americans, most used to spacious, open, ordered cities, it seemed entirely indiscriminate, a reckless labyrinth of farm outbuildings but without the redeeming focus of a farmhouse. The only building of any imposition was the chapel and the only imposition that the chapel had was its situation on the highest ground. It had views across the sea, and sight of every bedroom in the town. It didn't have a tower or a bell. That's why, when it was time to come and pray, Preacher Phipps blew the brass foghorn which had been salvaged, God knows when, from a Dutch wreck. He blew it hard that Sunday night. He feared the snow would keep his congregation home. But overcoats cannot resist the snow, and even as the preacher blew his horn the whitening lanes of Wherrytown were busy with parishioners. Mr Phipps would seldom have again so large and boisterous a congregation. The pilcharders were there, with lengths of net for Preacher Phipps to bless before they put to sea at midnight. And all the Wherrytowners, too, except for

Walter Howells. They were sufficiently alerted by the snow, the promised pilchards in the sea, the presence of Americans on land, the rumours of an African at large, to submit themselves to hymns, hard seats and draughts.

The sailors – minus Ralph Parkiss, who hadn't returned so far from his twin errands at Dry Manston – were undiscriminating with the snow. They pelted cats and confidants and strangers. Their play was cruel and jealous. The Norrises who were walking to evensong beneath a tempting umbrella were struck a dozen times until someone succeeded in separating Robert from his hat. They didn't snowball Captain Comstock, though. Led by George, with a lantern on a pole, he walked a dozen yards behind the slowest of the crew, with Alice Yapp on his arm. The captain was too self-absorbed to pay attention to his men or make snowballs of his own. If he threw snowballs now, then someone's head would break. He was unsettled by the mocking logic of the ship's horn on the land and all the fish nets dragged through snow, uphill. He half expected to find the *Belle* perched on the summit of the ridge in a saltless sea of snow, with its flags invisible on such a starless night and its rigging trimmed in white and not a chance that they would reach America again unless their ship would fly.

The preacher took his text from the Very Reverend Alfred Sleigh-Russell's *Ornithologia*:

All birds migrate, if it be only half a mile or so. For though the friendly sparrow does not range the oceans as does an albatross, he has good cause when it is cold or there is competition for one meal or there are cats, to move away from home, which is the wood or field where he was hatched. But when the cat has gone, or else the warmer weather manifests, he must go back to whence he came, just as the albatross, though he may fly ten thousand miles, must navigate each spring to his cold islands in Antarctica. For birds, like men, are allocated places on this earth to which they must return or perish, by the Almighty to Whom they will return for All Eternity or else will perish in the Fires of Hell.

The book was closed. The Bible was not touched. The preacher prided himself on his earnest eccentricity and the directness of his homilies. 'We have amongst us strangers, far from the woods and fields where they were hatched; exotics amongst indigenes,' he said. Mr Phipps did not approve of pulpits. He walked through his congregation with his hands behind his back, like a factory overseer. 'My brothers and my sisters, look around at unfamiliar faces.' He waited while Americans and Wherrytowners inspected each other, while sailors tried to catch the eyes of fishermen's daughters, while Captain Comstock and Alice Yapp touched hands beneath her shawl. 'You might recall that there were egrets on the beach in June, brought in from Spain by hot winds. And now we have with us sailing brethren from America brought in by colder winds. And also two young people here . . .' (he placed his hand on the bonnet of cream terry velvet that covered Katie Norris's hair) '. . . who are embarked upon their own migration westwards to the shores of Canada. The seas tonight are full of fish whose journey takes them to the east. And there are nets to bless for our own fishermen who, when the Sabbath horn is blown, will take to boats. God's creatures all are journeying, alone, in shoals, by sea, by foot, by air, and with God's blessing. May all His children travel safely in the world, and may they all come home again to die in Christ where they were born in Christ. Amen.'

He spoke a little of the Soul, and of the body too. But what he did not mention was the heart. And here in his congregation were a hundred hearts, in love, or grieving, or resentful, or simply fearful of the midnight fish, or palpitating with the guilt of failing to be saints. There were no paragons. Were Mr Phipps to go round as his congregation sang its final hymn ('Our Home in Thee, Our Lord') and place his hand upon the hair and hats of thieves and adulterers and bullies and those who failed to love their neighbours as themselves, then there wouldn't be a head untouched. But what about those absentees, Aymer Smith and Otto? If they had been amongst the congregation, perhaps the preacher's hand would hover at their heads and hesitate to touch. Otto was untouchable, as Preacher Phipps had found out in the tackle room the day before. Was he a bully? An adulterer? A thief? Was he a paragon? How could anybody tell? And Aymer Smith? It could not be said he was a thief. He didn't covet anything enough. Nor an adulterer; he was a celibate. Nor much of a bully; he was too tall and flimsy both in manner and in build. He even loved his neighbours as himself, because he didn't love himself at all. Nor was he loved by anyone. And he was hated by a few. The preacher wouldn't touch *that* head.

By now, in the last hundred yards through Wherrytown, Aymer Smith and Ralph Parkiss were far too cold to speak.

Their six-mile walk had been ten miles. They'd faltered in the snow and dark, misled by the preacher's foghorn into believing that the sea had moved inland and they were lost. They'd had to trust Whip to set the path. At last they'd seen the harbour light and found the inn courtyard where the tackle room, its door left open all day, was piled with drifting snow. The covered alleyway offered their first shelter from the night. All they wanted now was a fire, some dry clothes and Mrs Yapp to fortify them with her tea against the influenza which Aymer promised would justly follow on from such 'a foolish expedition'. The inn was empty, though. And cold. Just like a ghost ship. They rang the handbell in the parlour a dozen times, but no one came. They searched the rooms. Aymer would have changed into warmer clothes, except his bags and books and clothes were gone and his bed was stripped. He felt a little stripped himself, and liberated too, of home, possessions and proprieties. He even put his arm round Ralph's big shoulders and called him 'Friend'. They had been friends – if *silent* friends – as soon as they had swayed the Cradle Rock.

Ralph managed to coax the parlour fire alight. He knelt in front of it and toasted herrings from the kitchen for their supper. Whip fell asleep at once across the hearth. Aymer did his best to dry himself in the low heat. He smelled of smoke and herrings, and the smell spread through the empty levels of the inn. It was Ralph who guessed that everyone had gone to chapel. The pair of them chuckled like boys; to have escaped the hymns was almost worth the journey. They would be comrade-masters of the inn, until the captain and his men came back to find the meddler Smith and the dog returned and not fled on the *Tar*. But not a trace of Otto. Where is he now? Why did you let him go? would be the only questions to be asked. But there were deeper mysteries in Otto's first night out. What comforts would he find in snow? What would he have for supper? How would he reach his allocated place on earth and die where he was born, Amen? How joyous was he to be free?

7. Sitting on Blisters

AYMER SMITH had fled the smoke and herrings of the parlour. ('My chest and throat are raw, Ralph. My nose already is a tap. I shouldn't be surprised if I were feverish by breakfast time.') He was sleeping, fully clothed, on his sheetless bed. Whip, exhausted by the snow and cold, curled at his side, her nose tucked in between her legs. She didn't know or care that Aymer was (brother Matthias's judgement, endorsed by faithful Fidia) a blunderer, a bore, a hypochondriac, a meddling and self-serving man. She had adopted him.

Robert and Katie Norris hadn't waited at the chapel door to shake the preacher's hand. They had returned from evensong ahead of Mrs Yapp and all her other guests. They hurried through the parlour, nodding briefly at Ralph Parkiss by the fire, took a lighted candle from the mantel, and almost ran along the corridor and down the flights of steps to what they thought would be an empty room. They hadn't come out of the chapel edified by hymns or by Mr Phipps's passages from *Ornithologia*, but impassioned rather by the holy, warming congruence of worshippers at church, their thighs in contact on the pew, their two thumbs touching on the shared hymnal, their voices mating when they sang.

Katie Norris had forgotten how beautiful her husband's voice could be. His voice, her hair. She didn't mind that he was not a handsome man, that he was thin-haired, short-sighted, bony, clerkish in his manner and his speech. What mattered was his kindness to her, his steadfastness. Who'd emigrate to Canada for the sake of curls, blue eyes, a lordly nose, fine skin? *Good looks do not the lover make.* No, what a woman needs is not a beau but someone – Katie Norris loved the word – *resolute*.

Katie had a resolution of her own, that she would be with child before she put to sea. A pregnant woman, she'd been told, would get a bunk on board a migrant ship, a decent place at table, and generally would be coddled by the sailors. But, more than that, she wanted to take away a child from home, a child not made in Canada, a blessed, honeymooning child. She'd only hoped that Robert would indulge this wish without inflicting too much hurt on her. In those days before the wedding to Mr Norris, the local notary-cum-ledgerworm, and their departure from the village forty miles inland from Wherrytown, her elder married sister and her ma, not pleased to lose their Katie to the colonies, had warned of 'duty' and 'indignities' and 'getting used to manly ardours'. They had not mentioned that manly ardours might be shared by wives. Perhaps they didn't know. So no one had prepared Katie for how satisfying baby-making would prove to be. Their wedding night, just a fortnight and one day ago, had been a shock, a revelation. To think that mellow-singing, thin-haired Robert could be so *resolute* in bed! Where had he learned such sorcery?

Her husband had, on that first night of 'duty and

indignities', proved to be a virtuoso. The man could sing *and* touch! He'd caressed her beneath her wedding shift until her breathing had seemed so frail and heavenly, her mouth so dry, her thighs so open and invaded by his hand that she had cried out in the night too loudly. And Ma, a wattled wall away, had cursed 'that Robert Norris' for his cruelty and called to the newly weds, 'Enough's enough!' For Katie Norris, babymaking was no indignity. So when – in Wherrytown chapel – her husband sang, 'Our Home in Thee, Our Lord, Thy Life and Light Afford, A Pathway to Thy Side, and Let Our Love Abide', and every syllable of his stood out so that the other women turned around to see whose voice it was, Katie let her thumb cross over his. She stroked his fingernail. She couldn't wait to get him home in bed, alone. They wouldn't have to suffer Mr Smith's foul coughing nor the fear that he might hear them making love, or see her passing water in the pot. Thank heavens that the tiresome man was gone! They'd have the bedroom to themselves. She'd wrap her hair around his head. She'd count his ribs and nipples with her tongue. She'd sit on him by candlelight while he sang hymns to her.

Robert had his hand on her bottom as they ran along the corridor. Already she had got her bonnet off and pulled the ribbon from her hair. He lifted up her skirts when they arrived outside the bedroom. She yelped and snapped his hand between her thighs. His fingers were icicles. His face was icy too.

'Let's get warm in bed,' she said.

They'd hardly entered the room and dropped the door latch when Whip was barking at their knees and jumping up at Katie's skirts. She tried to force the dog outside. The candle toppled from its holder, fell onto the bedroom boards and lost its light. She put her boot against Whip and pushed her into the corridor. 'Where are you, Robert, my sweet love?' she said. 'Come here.' And then again, more softly and more richly, 'Come here. Come. Here.'

'Hello. Is that you?' said Aymer Smith. He sat up now in bed and could be seen in silhouette against the windows of the room. 'Mr Norris, Mrs Norris? How very pleasant. And so you are returned?'

'We are,' said Katie, 'yes.' Her bones had liquefied. Her chest and throat were quivering like some trapped thrush. She found her husband's hand, still icy cold.

'Then, pray, will you address yourselves to this small mystery, which causes me, perhaps, some distress but which might afford a little entertainment for yourselves.' He sniffed and coughed and chuckled. Good humour in adversity. He judged it struck the proper note with Katie Norris and her hair. He wished there was light enough to see her hair. 'I have returned from my expedition along the coast to find my bedclothes taken off and my belongings stowed somewhere – perhaps *else*where is better said – and no one in the inn to put the matter right. Do you suppose there are sheet-thieves about? Hot beef, stop thief. Is that our cry? Or should we look to that odd fellow George, or even Countess Yapp, to shed some candlelight upon their whereabouts?' When there was no immediate answer from his fellow guests, he cut short their silence: 'And you, dear friends? You passed a tolerable day, I trust? Myself, I have been lost in snow, and taken on the meanest touch of influenza, but not before I shook the Cradle Rock. That is an excursion you are advised to take before you leave these shores . . .' Again he coughed and sniffed and chuckled. He couldn't stop himself. He was so happy.

Katie Norris whispered something. And then she spoke a bit too audibly, 'You tell him, Robert!'

'Your clothes and bag, your cakes of soap, your books,' said her husband, 'are taken by our landlady . . .'

'Indeed?'

'Indeed, they are. I do believe she thought you were not here. That is to say, she feared you might have left. And that your few possessions might be payment for your bill . . .'

'The Inn-that-has-no-name, has no rhyme nor reason to it, either. Excuse me while I solve this mystery . . .' He blundered to the door. The Norrises were forced to stand apart and let him through. He smelt of fish and damp. 'I will return with light,' he said. He and the dog had gone before the Norrises could say another word. Perhaps the less they said the least harm done.

Robert put his arm round Katie's waist.

'Not now,' she said. 'He'll be back too soon . . . I wonder if he's got his trousers on?'

Aymer found the parlour occupied by an advance party of some of the younger fishermen. Their nets had been blessed by Mr Phipps. Now they were hoping to have their spirits fortified by Mrs Yapp's hot wine and beer before the Sabbath ended and the moment came to set off for the pilchards. Aymer rang the parlour handbell, but no one came.

'They's steppin' down from chapel,' one man said. 'There in't no point in shaking that, not till they's back inside.'

Aymer took his damp tarpaulin coat off its hook and went out of the inn's front door. He put his coat on, underneath the granite lintel, and went down into the lane. He was impatient to be back amongst the Norrises in candlelight, with Katie Norris in her nightshift just three yards away. And Miggy Bowe to dream about. How fortunate, for him at least, that Duty had brought him west, the bearer of bad news. His life had blossomed since the *Tar* had docked in Wherrytown and he had come ashore! He'd moved the Cradle Rock. He'd freed an African. He'd bested Mr Walter Howells. He had new friends, the Norrises, Ralph Parkiss, some of the kelpers at Dry Manston. Even George the parlourman. The dog! The hairy little dog was his friend, too! And, best of all, he had the prospect of a wife – though, when he tried to summon Miggy Bowe in his mind's eye, he couldn't picture her. What colour were her eyes? How had she worn her hair? Instead, his mind was full of Katie Norris, her freckled calves upon the pot, her sandy hair a flapping flag of colour on the sea.

An older fisherman approached the inn, a length of newly blessed net on his shoulder. 'Good evening, sir.'

'Indeed it is.'

'A bitter night, though.'

'But a well-shaped Universe,' Aymer said.

'Amen to that. That's worth a cup of anybody's time.'

Aymer waited while Whip relieved herself against the stone and then went chasing smells. The snow had almost stopped, but what had already fallen was hard and biscuity underfoot. Aymer put his hands into his coat, whistled for the dog and set off up the lane.

The next men that he met were two sailors from the *Belle*: 'Captain Keg', the portly mate, and a taller, younger deckhand. 'Good evening, gentlemen. Or should I say the contrary, that it is a dreadful evening and fearful cold?'

The Americans stared at Aymer with theatrical delight. 'Well now!' the mate said to his companion. 'And lookee lookee here, see what the dog's brought home!' They stopped and grinned at him. Aymer was impatient with their 'sauciness'. He walked on. They followed him until – to loud American guffaws – he collided with George the parlourman.

'Ah, just the fellow. George? Let's see if you are worth the shilling that you've had.'

George seemed at a loss for words for a moment, and then he said, 'It'll take more than a shilling to save your tail . . .' and added, '. . . sir!'

Again the two Americans were laughing, inexplicably. Aymer felt excluded from some joke. It was a feeling he was accustomed to. He joined the laughter with a lifeless 'Ah-ha', and then took George by the elbow and spoke softly: 'We must not fence, George. It is too cold and late to fence. Can you throw any light on this? My bed is stripped. My bag and my possessions are no longer in my room and Mrs Norris says that Mrs Yapp has taken them in lieu of payment . . .'

George was smiling now from ear to ear. 'We thought you had eloped with the captain's dog,' he said, 'and taken that Otto Africanus as your valet. But now you're back, so that's all right, so long as Otto's nice and snug on this cold night inside the tackle room. I hope he is.'

'Well, he is not . . .' Aymer hadn't given much thought to Otto. He'd provided food. He'd sent for a physician. He'd set the fellow free. And that was that. The man would be, well, sleeping somewhere else by now and on his way to . . . Aymer didn't know the names of any towns that could be walked to in a day. He'd done his duty and hadn't considered that there might be consequences, repercussions. 'Well, he is not,' he said again, with some attempt at firmness.

'Then, Mr Smith, you'd better turn about and find some place to hide unless you want a beating. For kidnapping. And dognapping. And soapnapping. And knapsacking. And walking out without your trousers on.' Again there was much laughter, though not from George.

Aymer put his hand up to his mouth. What did the sailors know? What had they seen? Was he observed when he pulled back the bolt, when he was masturbating in the alleyway, when he was peeping through the curtains at Katie's naked thighs? He coughed, and sniffed, but didn't chuckle. 'I cannot think,' he said, 'that this is any of my making . . .'

George put his lips to Aymer's ear, and whispered, 'You let that blackie go. You know you did. And, more's the point, *they* know you did, those sailors standing there.'

Aymer didn't dare to look. 'What do those fellows want? Do they mean harm?'

'They'll not do any harm themselves. They mean to be

spectators to it, though. It's the captain who will break your bones.'

'Captain Comstock?'

'He's the one. He is the only captain you've robbed, I hope.'

'Well, yes . . . well . . . no!'

'How many captains, then?'

'Good heavens, George, do you mistake me for a highwayman? I am not guilty of a spate of crimes. Or any crimes at all. No one could wish to break my bones. Besides, the captain is a gentleman, or ought to be, if he is worthy of command. He would not strike me. What example might that set? If he has grievances then he should settle them by law. This is not America, I hope. The law is clear. We have emancipated slaves and habeas corpus here. He will not strike me in my native land.'

'Who can tell what he might do? I just know this: you stick your bum in fire and you must sit on blisters. You interfere in someone else's life, and there's a price to pay. And that's the truth, for captains and for gentlemen, no matter what the law might say.'

George put his arm round Aymer's shoulder and led him into the blackness of a courtyard where they could not be watched or heard by the two Americans. Aymer couldn't see his face, so couldn't tell if there was any mockery in the new, honest tone to George's voice. 'The wisest thing for you is to let me find a horse and tackle, Mr Smith. Then hide yourself under my bed, or in the loft above the stables, until it's dawn. And then it's flesh and leather and you're away back home and no damage done to you excepting saddle sores.'

'I have no choice, you think.'

'You have a choice. It's blisters here, or saddle sores at home. If your backside's got any brain it'll settle for the sores. You put a sovereign in my hand to find the horse and it's as good as done, and done so cheaply on account of my esteem for you, sir. For no one likes to see a fellow black and blue for meaning well but doing harm. One sovereign ought to settle it. Though two would put four legs beneath the horse, instead of three legs and a limp . . .'

'Two sovereigns, George? I now begin to see your strategy . . .'

'Save yourself two sovereigns then, and you'll see this in't no strategy. It'll cost *ten* sovereigns for Fearful Phipps to set and mend your bones. Save yourself eight, Mr Smith, and do it quick because that is the captain I can hear and you'll be caught.'

They stood on tiptoe looking over the courtyard wall into the lesser, sloping darkness of the lane. Twenty or so crewmen and Wherrytowners were descending, clustered round two lanterns on a pole.

Their path was steep and slippery and dark, and women had to hold strangers' arms to stop themselves from falling in the snow. There was a lot of laughter, clutching, tumbling, apologies.

'He's there,' said George, pointing, 'and in good hands, poor man.'

The captain followed fifteen yards behind the rest,

almost out of lantern light. But there was no mistaking his square build, nor Mrs Yapp's oval one. She had her arm wrapped round the captain's waist. Her bonnet was inclined towards his chest. They were too engrossed and, like the Norrises, too impassioned by the warming congruences of church to pay much heed to anything but how they'd seal the Sabbath with a little commerce of the flesh. She had the captain's dollar in her hand.

'Stay still,' said George.

'I will not hide myself. This is a public place, and I am well within the law.' He was too frightened to stay still, or quiet. So Aymer Smith, with George and Whip on either side, stepped into the lane and stood beside the *Belle*'s fat mate and in the congregation's path. He had no plan, except to keep his dignity, tell nothing but the truth, and hide behind the law. Shipmaster Comstock would benefit, in Aymer's view, from some enlightenment. And some plain speaking.

Stand firm, he told himself. Though standing firm was difficult in his fine-weather boots. He'd put his feet too close together and too parallel. He lost his footing and he had to grasp the mate for balance. When he had regained his poise, he found himself surrounded by the crowd. The Wherrytowners amongst them raised their hats and said *Goodnight*; the Americans offered guffaws, whistles and expletives, and waited for their captain to arrive.

'Good evening, Mrs Yapp,' Aymer said, his voice uneven and a little high. 'I understand you have my clothes and other things in your safe keeping. If this is so, then I'd be obliged if you could let me have them back, and ditto sheets, as I am tired and not a little feverish and would be glad to go to bed . . .' He sniffed and coughed to illustrate his point.

'Dear Lord,' said Mrs Yapp. 'A ghost!' And burst out laughing.

Shipmaster Comstock let her go, and advanced to within a foot of Smith. Their gelid breaths made tiny, short-lived clouds, back-lit by lantern-light.

'Good evening, Captain Comstock,' Aymer said. 'I trust you had a halfways decent day.'

A *halfways* decent day? What should the captain make of such effrontery? What should he say, with his crew stood by, and people from the town? He had intended to intimidate the man and then to thrash him. He clenched his fist. The nugget of his ring protruded from his finger. He'd knock Smith to the ground with just one blow. And then he'd stamp on him. But he was now discovering what Aymer had discovered moments earlier, that icy snow on sloping stone without a woman's arm to keep you steady provides poor footing for a fight, or even for a dressing-down. He slipped, and Aymer had to – briefly – hold his hand. God Damn It that they had to meet like this, in public view, the captain thought. He'd like to hold on to the fellow's hand and break all twenty-seven bones. He'd like to have him in his crew, and flogged for mutiny. Alice Yapp tugged at the captain's coat: 'Don't get too wild.' Aymer Smith had backed away. For the moment Comstock was reduced to words. 'Good evening, sir,' he said at last, attempting something out of character, a note of irony. 'I understand you have *my* property in your safekeeping. I'd be *obliged* as well if you could let me have it back, as Mrs Yapp and I would like to go to bed.'

'I have no property of yours . . .'

'Well, then, I think you have.' He shook off Mrs Yapp and took two careful steps towards Aymer. He made a fist again.

'Then, search me, sir, and you will see I've not.'

Captain Comstock was infuriated now. 'My dear man Otto has been robbed from me! Do you deny that you pulled back the bolt, and sent the fellow out to die of cold?'

'I did not . . .' *Did not mean to leave the poor man cold* was what he meant to say. Instead he fumbled for the words. He wasn't rough enough for this. His eyes were wet. His chest was tight. His lip and voice were trembling. Was it the image of poor Otto, dead in snow? Or was it just that Aymer's fear was stronger than his dignity, and lies were safer haven than plain speaking or the law? He said, 'I did not pull back any bolt,' and sounded like a boy.

'You did, sir.'

'No, sir, you are mistaken. Nor do I understand what vexes you.' He stepped two paces back.

'It vexes me that you deny your meddling . . . that you have sent into this night of wind and snow a man who has enough misfortunes as it is.'

'Misfortunes of your making, Captain Comstock.'

The captain stretched and caught Aymer by the coat. 'No, sir! I rescued Otto from the fields. I paid good dollars for the man in open auction. He does not suffer from unkindnesses aboard my ship.' (His men grunted their agreement.) 'I work him no harder than any of my sailors here, and in the galley too, where there is always food and warmth for him. He is not muzzled like some black cooks. He helps himself. He eats at will. What kind of food and warmth will he find now that you have put him out of doors, like some poor dog? Like *my* poor dog indeed. Not only do you steal my man, you steal my dog as well.' He swung his arm and caught Aymer round the side of his head. Aymer hadn't seen it coming. There was a storm in his ear.

'*There* is your dog!' Aymer pointed to Whip, who, luck would have it, was sitting in the snow behind the captain. 'I will not press you for your apology, though it is clear to anyone with eyes that I have earned it.'

'You've earned yourself a beating, *Mister* Smith.' The captain let go of Aymer's coat and spread his feet in preparation for the knock-out blow which he now planned for Aymer's chin. The sailors clapped their hands and whistled. 'Defend yourself.'

The Wherrytowners were uneasy now. Bewildered, too. It wasn't long since they had been at prayer and sharing hymns with the Americans. It wouldn't do if bones were broken on the Sabbath. Blood on snow would bring bad luck, and who needs bad luck when their men would put to sea at midnight?

'Call Mr Phipps. He'll settle it,' one said. And even Mrs Yapp was alarmed by fisticuffs between her guests. 'Apologize or pay up, Mr Smith,' was her remedy. 'And then we'll put this little contretemps to bed ... For God's sake, find your tongue.'

Aymer kept his hands down by his side. He sniffed and

coughed and blinked his eyes. 'This is not just,' he said. 'What must I say to reassure you, Captain Comstock? I am a businessman, and well regarded hereabouts . . .' (There was no one to grunt agreement.) 'I am a son of Hector Smith & Sons. We have markets for our soaps in Boston, New Orleans and Philadelphia. I have no grudge against America. I have my errands here as well, in Wherrytown. Speak if you will to Walter Howells, who is our agent in these parts, and is acquainted with my standing. And should you doubt it that my errands here are innocent then you should talk with your own man, Ralph Parkiss. We were companions on the coast today and we have had no dealings with an African. I do not broadcast any views on slavery. I have no interest in your man. I did not put him out of doors, nor make the fellow cold. I did not pull the bolt for him. He is your loss, not mine. My loss is this. My sheets are stripped. My clothes and bag have disappeared. My books are seized . . .' He paused for breath.

Comstock's hands were at his side as well. He looked uncertain and diminished. There wouldn't be a beating after all. Aymer was – almost – believed. Perhaps he wasn't guilty of anything but hot air and timidity and tears. This much was obvious to everyone: he hadn't fled on the *Tar* with Otto and the dog as they'd all presumed. Here was the living – quaking – evidence of that. Here was the little dog. They had misjudged the man.

'You struck me, sir, in full view of all these witnesses,' said Aymer. He rubbed his face, and checked his hand for blood. 'I cannot think what recompense can settle this. Apologies are not enough.'

'Shake hands, the two of you,' suggested Alice Yapp.
'Then sleep on it. There's no use nursing it.'

'I am too bruised about my ears to sleep. I hope no
lasting damage has been done.'

'Well now, maybe we *ought* to sleep on it, like Mrs Yapp
suggests,' the captain said. He blew out cloudy air. He felt
he'd made a fool of himself. The Wherrytowners would
think he was a hot-head and a bully. They would not
mistake that for captaincy. The crew had seen him weaken
when they had hoped for bruises and broken bones. 'Well
now,' he said again.

Mrs Yapp stepped between the two men. 'Let's see the
pair of you shake hands,' she said again. She was getting
cold. 'We have been hasty, Mr Smith. You'll not be blaming
the captain, I'm sure.' She took him by the wrist and held
his arm up. She dug the captain in the ribs until he put his
hand out too and said, so softly that his men couldn't hear,
'Then, I am mistaken maybe, Mr Smith. I see I might
regret my hastiness . . .'

'And your bad temper,' prompted Mrs Yapp.

'I think I am man enough not to hold grudges,' Aymer
replied. 'Let this be but an episode.' The captain took his
hand, and stopped it shaking. How pleasant it would be to
crack some finger bones.

Many of the Wherrytowners hadn't known that Otto
had escaped, and now they were both angry and alarmed.
They didn't want an African at large, amongst their fields
and flocks and families. What kind of man was he, they
asked. Could he do any harm? What kind of flesh might he
hunt for? What magic did he know? Would it be wise to

send for soldiers, or could they hope the cold and snow had finished him, just like the captain said? Comstock was too angry and too thwarted to say much. He wanted just the privacy of Alice Yapp in bed. She held his arm again and they set off for the inn. But one or two of the Americans were quick to tease the Wherrytowners with tales of Otto's superhuman strength, his tiger temper and his monstrous appetite: 'I've seen him chewing leather boots.'

'*And* he likes human hams!'

'Flesh pudding.'

'Finger pie.'

And then another added, 'Make sure your daughters don't give birth to Africans.'

Aymer volunteered his expertise. He was recovered now, or, at least, he had stopped shaking and could pretend that Captain Comstock's odd outburst had caused him no embarrassment. 'The Africans are a noble race of men,' he said. Unlike Americans. 'They have their grievous faults, of course, and high qualities as well, much as the rest of us who are not Africans . . . There are as many saints and thieves in Africa as there are here . . .' He looked directly at the mate. And then he had an inspiration, one which should have been suppressed but which, if voiced, would clear his name, he hoped. Where was the harm in it? He called out to the captain's back, his voice a little sharper than he'd meant: 'Perhaps – and now this history becomes more clear to me – your African has stolen my affairs . . . my clothes, my few possessions. My sheets!' Everybody turned to hear. '. . . At least the man finds warmth in them wherever he might be . . . There is a staircase from the courtyard of the inn. It leads directly to my room. The coincidences of our two losses at one time cannot be dismissed. We can presume your African is well equipped against the night. If he were not, I think he would have crept back humbly to his lodging at the inn. No, he will have found himself some little snug, an outhouse or a stable. He has my carriage rug. Some decent clothes. A set of sheets. And soap to wash himself, fit for the aristocracy.'

'There's truth in that,' said Mrs Yapp. She couldn't laugh. She had to swallow it. Smith's clothes and soap and bag were on the settle in her room.

The Wherrytowners couldn't be blamed for their alarm. Not only had the African escaped, but now it seemed that he had burgled someone at the inn and might be hiding from the snow in Wherrytown. They wouldn't have been more worried if they'd heard a bull was loose. They understood the dangers of a bull. You could lock your door against a bull. But Africans? Lord preserve them from the savages. They might be raped and eaten in their beds. Some hurried off to check their daughters and their outhouses. Some looked uneasily into the shadows. How well would women sleep that night, with all their men at sea in pilchard boats and Otto on the loose?

A voice at Aymer's shoulder muttered, 'You are a provocation, sir.'

'Ah, George!'

They walked without speaking till they reached the lintelled door of the inn. Inside, Americans and Wherrytowners were waiting to be served with beer.

'No blisters! And two sovereigns saved, I think,' said

Aymer. He was delighted with himself, despite his throbbing ear. Ashamed as well. And then, 'I can rely, I hope, on your discretion?'

'Two sovvers buys discretion, sir, and also can provide you with some clothes that are a match for those the blackie stole. Such wickedness! And sheets and soap, if you require. And some very clever books from George's Lending Library. Do you begin to see my strategy?'

It wasn't long before Aymer was reunited with his property, and George (just a half-crown better off) was warming ale and punch for anyone with ha'pennies to spare.

Aymer took a candle to the room. How glad he was the Norrises were there, and still awake and talking softly to each other. He placed the candle on the sill and called to them behind the bed-curtain. 'I have my clothes. The parlourman has brought them back. There has been some misapprehension by Mrs Yapp and the Americans.'

He recounted to the curtains what had happened in the lane, and how it had required 'unusual restraint on my behalf, and dignity' to check the captain's temper. 'He spoke to me with a deal of freedom, and he struck me once, but did not dare to do it twice,' he explained. 'I could not admire it. But I am glad that my rebuttals were not expressed with any greater roughness than was absolutely requisite.'

His hands were shaking again. Retelling what had happened was reliving it.

'I cannot regard the captain as a man of much gentility,' he said. 'But it is good to share a room with people of distinction, such as you, dear friends. I hope I can regard you both as friends?' His nose was running now. He wiped it on the damp arm of his coat. He sniffed back tears as best he could. But soon he couldn't stifle them. The tears had let him down, and he was sobbing. 'I am not easy that the African is out in weather such as this.'

At last the curtain was drawn back and Robert Norris poked his head into the room. 'Don't upset yourself. Whoever set the poor man free could have chosen better times, it's true. But that's for *his* conscience, not yours.'

And then his wife, invisible behind his back, said, 'We should be grateful he's free from his imprisonment. It broke my heart to see him so derided in the yard.'

'You are so good,' said Aymer Smith. His sobbing now was unrestrained, and he was shivering. Katie Norris stepped across the room into the candlelight, and pressed Aymer's head against her stomach and her cotton nightdress as if he were a child and not a man.

'No, you are good to care so much for a stranger. You are a Good Samaritan,' she said.

'You think too kindly of me.' Aymer would have lifted up his hands and held her by the waist, and sunk his face more deeply into the cotton, into her mottled, salmon quilt of flesh, except that Robert Norris had crossed the room as well. He put his arm around his wife and placed his spare hand, like a preacher, on Aymer's head. 'Of course, we are your friends,' he said. They held each other for a moment, and listened to new noises in the courtyard, two flights below. Footsteps on the hardened snow. A wooden door banged shut. A sneeze. Had Otto come in from the snow? The parlour clock was striking twelve.

'It's only fishermen,' said Robert Norris. 'The Sabbath's over and they're going to their boats. But we must sleep.'

'I cannot.' Aymer's pulse was hammering.

'You must,' said Katie. But she was looking into Robert's eyes when she recited,

'Go to bed. Go to sleep.
Go all the way to the end of tired.
Sleep well. Sleep tight.
Don't wake up until it's light,
And all your heartaches have expired.'

8. Rankin's Dollar

THE DOLLY BOATS had no regard for Sabbaths. They'd rather catch the Devil's fish than none at all. They put to sea before midnight and took advantage of the snow-bounced moonlight and a little wind to shoot their unblessed net up-water from the *Belle*, two tons of it, a looping quarter-mile of rope and cork and lead, and every knot hand-tied. It curtained off the stem of sea beyond the Cradle Rock. Dollys had fished there for a hundred years at least. It was known to be an alleyway for shoals.

The larger boat, with Henry Dolly and his two younger sons aboard, rode on its anchor at the mouth of the net, with lanterns burning on both sides. They shared a pipe and, if they prayed, prayed only that the dawn or fish would come before they died of cold. They didn't speak. What should they say? That they would rather be asleep, farting supper in their beds? That they would rather they'd been born miles from sea and never had to smell or touch a fish again? They watched their boots, their knees, the backs of their hands, the final lamplit flurries of the snow. They listened to the wind, the distant flap of tattered canvas on the *Belle*, the grieving timbers of their boat, the never-ending tug of war between the granite and the sea, and

didn't for a moment feel bored, excited or afraid. This was
their life, and it was hard.

Their elder brother, Palmer Dolly – with only the old
man Skimmer as a mate – was master of their smaller boat,
fifty yards astern. He'd put it at the centre of the loop of
net, halved its sail and now was waiting at the tiller for the
call – *Tuck 'em in! And tuck 'em-IN!* – that fish were coming
through and that the tuck net should be dropped. And then
a night of labour, trawling pilchards from the curtained sea.
If there *was* a call, if any pilchards *came*, that is. He'd fished
this stem before, all night, all day, and netted nothing but
some kelp. But on this night he was an optimist. He felt
elated by the snow, the snubbing of the Sabbath and by
the *Belle*'s enticing, twiggy silhouette. The stranded ship,
he felt, had brought good luck. The *Belle* would bring the
pilchards in. The *Belle* would change – would *save?* – his
life.

Palmer Dolly was no gadabout. He'd hardly ever been
inland. He'd never seen the sea beyond Wherrytown. He
was a fisherman and not a mariner. But he was of an age –
at nineteen – when he could see his life mapped out, dry
ink on the page. He'd marry someone from the coast – 'We
weds wi' Dry Manston folk,' his mother said. 'We don't
have owt to do with Wherrytown.' He'd spend his life with
some girl like Miggy Bowe. She'd have the kids. He'd have
the boats. He would take his sons to tuck for fish and she
would keep their girls to help out with the kelp. A waste of
time, as kelp was worthless now. There'd be no strangers in
their lives, just cousins, neighbours, Mr Howells. And they
would sit, between their cottage and the sea, repairing nets

for Ever and Ever, World Without End. There'd been no prospect of escape until the *Belle* had come. But now he mapped a life out of his own. He could be a sailor on the *Belle*, and sail back to America to speak their showy, manly English baritone, and make his fortune in the sun. There always was a blue sky and a sun in Palmer's dreams. He only had to volunteer. Shipmaster Comstock, after all, already knew he was a willing and a useful hand. It had only been a couple of days since the captain had stood on deck and picked out Palmer Dolly to help with that 'one injured *party*, on the *orlop*' (remote, seductive, big-ship words). Palmer had been the first one pointed at, the first one chosen, the first one *favoured* by the captain.

Palmer hoped he'd proved himself a good man to employ. They'd gone below decks on the ship and seen the African. Nothing in the sea was quite as strange as that brown, bleeding man. But still Palmer had done as he was bid and put the fellow in a palliasse and hammocked him on deck and thence into the Dolly boat – the same boat, in fact, in which he and Skimmer were now waiting for the pilchards. The African had bled onto their boat. He'd marked their wood. Palmer couldn't see the bloodstain in the dark. But it was there, and probably would still be there when Palmer Dolly was elsewhere, a mariner, the optimist at sea, the emigrant, the escapee, the freeman in the Yankee sun.

'My money is we'll land a decent catch,' said Palmer. He stood and urinated off to leeward. He was in a rare and happy mood. 'Now, there's a bait'll bring 'em in.'

'My money is we're only netting snow tonight,' said

Skimmer. He spat into the sea: the Devil's brew of piss and phlegm and salt. He was not an optimist.

They didn't have to take a Devil's fish. It was gone midnight when the pilchards came. The snow had stopped, but there was now a storm of fish. The sea was drenched in fish. It was as if the water had lost its liquidness and was turning into solder. The pilchards winked and weaved their blue-green backs, their silver undersides, in teeming, wet stampedes. They trenched and ridged themselves between the deep-shore rollers. The solder boiled and swelled. Dozens of hake and some tunny fish, the smallest more than ten feet long, were at the pilchards' tails, herding them, and gorging on the ones they broke loose from the shoals. The pilchards bunched and fled into the in-shore pools. They stripped their rhombic scales and ripped their soft bellies on granite scree below the Cradle Rock. They banked up amongst the cattle carcasses in the shallows off Dry Manston beach, where tunny could not reach. They butted at the shoreline with their sulking lower lips. They threw themselves onto the beach. There was no need for boats or fishermen or nets. The Dollys could have saved themselves the trip, and come down to the beach with lanterns. They could have bucketed the fish by hand and carted them away by donkey-load and only got their ankles wet.

The pilchards seethed and tumbled round the Dolly boat, attracted by the light, and panicked by the dolphin-like clicks and whistles that the Dollys made.

'Tuck 'em in! Tuck 'em in! Tuck 'em in!'

They passed through the gateway of the net like one great metal eel, a half a mile in length, and twenty yards across. A giant could put a saddle on its back, and flank the shoal, and ride those pilchards like a horse. He'd not get wet. He'd not be ducked in Palmer's piss or Skimmer's phlegm. The shoal was solid tin.

The Dollys didn't close their net for fifteen, twenty minutes. Each wrap and fold of sea turned pilchards on their sides in heavy, silvered arcs. It was a blessing pilchards make no sound. If they could voice their bafflement at nets, then theirs would be the saddest lament in the world. The Dollys were no longer cold, and missing bed. They were too busy to be cold. If they worked hard and luck was on their side, they'd make enough on this one night to see them through to spring. So long as there was not a glut.

But there was a glut, of course. Too many pilchards. And far too many boats. Everybody had full nets. The thirty families or so who'd put to sea that night and worked their stem down-coast from Wherrytown were overwhelmed with fish. They'd brought as many pilchards as they could on board in baskets. Now the gunnels of their boats were so low that one good wave would flood their decks. They had to let their nets fill up, then herd the nets along the coast into the shallows beyond the channel buoys and harbour lights at Wherrytown and wait for day.

By four thirty in the morning there were forty-three nets bunched up like massive lily pads. The untucked pilchards tumbled in the water, struggling for their passage east, doing what they could to escape the hake which had been netted too. Those few that had the strength to leap over the nets only fell amongst the captive pilchards of a neighbour's net. The fishermen watched and waited in the melting darkness. A bumper catch. Not that that would do them any good. Mr Howells would shake his head and say, 'The fatter the shoal, the thinner the shilling. We'll not get rich from these.' Not rich, perhaps. But it was satisfying to have netted such a tumult. When dawn came, then the fun would start. They'd need a hundred volunteers to bring the fish ashore.

'We'll put those Americans to work,' said Henry Dolly. 'We'll break those jiggers' backs with lifting fish.' Again he shared a pipe with his two sons. It was all they had to keep them warm till daybreak. Monday would be fine and clear. There was no wind, and there were stars across the western, clearing sky. The paling and descending moon was touched with green. Good luck. Good weather. The seagulls didn't mind the dark. They shrieked like Saracens at such an easy feast of fish.

Skimmer in the smaller boat had made a canvas bed and – God knows how he managed it – was fast asleep, despite the cold and gulls. Palmer Dolly sank his head into his coat and pushed his hands into his sleeves, like a teacup Mandarin. He was Midshipman Dolly on the midnight watch. Crewman Dolly. Palmer Dolly, captain of the *Belle*. Mr Dolly and his dollars! He was dreaming distantly, though he hadn't got a landscape for America, or any idea how cruel the voyage there would be. He couldn't guess the span of the Atlantic, nor how the ocean, far from land, would scarp and dip like wolds, the *Belle* a wind-tossed wooden hut amongst the water hills. He had no proper sense of anything excepting Home, and three boys to the bed, and nets and nets and nets.

'Is that you, Palmer?' someone called.

Palmer looked out of his coat. He tried an American accent. 'What is it, then?'

One of the Dollys' neighbours was standing at the bulwarks of his boat twenty yards away and was pointing into the teeming semicircle of the Dolly net.

'What's that you've caught?'

'Too many bloody pilchers!' He couldn't get the accent's chesty resonance.

'No, that!' The neighbour pointed again. And then threw a broken end of rope to mark the spot. 'It in't no pilchard, that's for sure.'

Palmer couldn't make it out. There was a dark spot in the nets. A piece of wood, perhaps. Some matted kelp. The carcass of a porpoise. A tunny with a heart attack, from too much food. It certainly wasn't alive. It didn't move. It didn't absorb any of the little light there was.

'I don't know. We'll find out soon enough.' He couldn't give a stalk of parsley what it was. He put his head back in his coat, and crossed three thousand miles of sea, and was American again.

By six o'clock – with just a hint of Monday in the sky – they'd found out what was 'not alive'. Nathaniel Rankin bobbed and eddied closer to the Dolly boat, propelled by grazing fish. He was face down and so waterlogged that pilchards swam across his body. His clothes were shredded by the sea. Palmer poked him with a rigging pole. The body sank. The water blackened where he'd been, filled up with fish, and then was cleared again as Seaman Rankin floated back in view. Palmer's rigging pole had come out of the

water with a gluey tip. The body was as soft and decom-
posed as Bordeaux cheese. Palmer had to look away and
swallow hard on icy air. He called out to his father with the
news. 'Wake Skimmer,' he was told, 'and get it out of the
water. We'll not sell pilchards, else. Not with a taint like
that!' Together Palmer and Skimmer pulled Rankin's body
clear of the water by his open collar and his belt. They put
him on a piece of sail on deck. His clothes were tight. A
man who's marinated in the sea for two days is bound to
swell. His flesh becomes porous and water enters him. He
begins to peel and split. He loses shape. His margins flake.

They squeezed the water out of him, and threw the
tunnelling crabs and pilchards into the air, for gulls. At first
they thought it was the African. His skin, in that no-light,
was black. But once they'd got their lantern lit, they saw the
colour was a plum, a damson blue. His veins and arteries
had burst. His face and hands were bruised. His lips and
tongue were fungi. His eyes were gone. And he was
wounded on his forehead and his neck by gulls. He'd lost a
good part of his waist and shirt to a fish. A single bite.
There was – surprisingly – no smell, except the oily odour
of the pilchards. Skimmer searched the outer pockets of the
coat: more crabs, a blue neckerchief, a dollar and a swivel
knife. He bit the dollar, put it in his shirt. 'You'd better go
for help,' he said to Palmer. 'Tell their captain. Get Preacher
Phipps.' He shook his head as if to say, 'We've netted bad
luck here. I knew we would.'

For Palmer, though, the netting of Nathaniel Rankin
was not bad luck. It was just the opportunity he was hoping
for. 'Give me the dollar, Skimmer,' he said.

'Why's that?'

'Just fish it out. It in't yours to have.'

'Nor in't it yours.'

'You robbin' dead men, is it then? It in't no good to you, not hereabouts. Let's have it now. It's dead man's money, 'n' you in't dead.'

'Good as dead,' said Skimmer. He pulled the dollar from his shirt and slapped it into Palmer's hand. 'Palmer is the proper name for you. Picking pockets ... palming other people's tin.' Palmer didn't wait to hear the rest. He had to make his way to shore, through seven nets of fish. He dropped into the water. It was too deep to find a footing, though the pilchards kept him up. He slid across their tumbling backs, and pulled himself towards the edges of the net. His heart was battering his chest. He could hardly find the air to breathe. The water was so heavy and so cold that Palmer scarcely had the strength to move his arms through it. He had ten minutes at the most. More time and he would freeze. Then there would be two corpses and a mystery to bring ashore, for Rankin's dollar would be found in Palmer's mouth.

Once he'd reached the edges of the Dolly net, Palmer could use the surface rope and corks to pull himself more swiftly through the water. He could then transfer to the outer edges of a neighbour's net, and – half-circling that – bring himself into the shallow waters of the shore. He could hear his father and Skimmer calling to the nearest boats, explaining what they'd caught and why it was that Palmer was taking such a risk. It was a risk. But Palmer Dolly was a pioneer. He'd be the one to bring the news to Captain

Comstock. He'd die for it. His neighbours held their lanterns up and shouted their encouragement. They couldn't help in any other way. They watched him pull himself over the outer rim of the last net, into even colder water, where there were no fish – and fish, compared to this, were warm. Now he could find his feet. His upper body was clear of the water and he was wading, burdened with the weight of sodden clothes. What breeze there was was raw and aching on his skin. He gripped the dollar between his teeth and came up on the snow and sand. His boots were full of sea.

He walked – he couldn't run – along the backshore to the quayside where the *Tar* had docked. Thank God the lower entrance to the inn was open. It was quiet in the snow-packed courtyard, no wind, no gulls. Somewhere inside the inn a dog began to bark. There was no light. He had to find the narrow passageway by hand and by nose: the fish-head, urine, earthy smell of somewhere always damp and dark. The passageway was steep. Palmer was winded by the time he'd reached the raised front door. It wasn't locked against the night, or Africans. The handle turned. He knew it would. He didn't feel unlucky.

Perhaps he should have stopped to warm himself at the embers of the parlour fire, but he wanted to be seen as wet and cold and dutiful, a man who could be reckless if required. He found a candle on the mantel. He held it in the fire and blew into the ashes and the few remaining cherks of wood. His hand was shaking, and the candle wouldn't make a flame. He had to hold it with both hands. His fingers were both numb and throbbing as the fire revived. The candle lit. What should he do? Where should he go? He shook the parlour handbell, but its ring was far too timid and discreet. He'd have to find the parlourman or, better, Alice Yapp to ask where Captain Comstock was. He knew her rooms. He'd been there once. She was the only entertainment in the town.

Palmer hurried through the snug to Mrs Yapp's door. He rapped on it and shook the latch. The door was locked. 'Mrs Yapp. Wake up!'

'And who the Devil's that?'

'It's Palmer Dolly, Mrs Yapp. Where's the captain of that ship . . . ?'

'Why don't you scram, Palmer? What time is it?'

'We've got the body of the man who drowned!'

'Why wake me up, besides?'

'Tell me where the captain is. It's his man that's drowned . . .'

He heard some movement in the room, some heavy steps, and then the door was opened. The American captain was standing there, and naked too, but for the blanket round his waist and pillow cotton in his hair.

'Say all of that again,' he said.

Palmer Dolly stood to attention at the door, the candle held before him like a sword, a little shakily. The water ran off him and puddled at his feet. He couldn't stop the clatter of his teeth. 'We've netted the sailor, sir. The drownded one that's lost . . .'

'My man?'

'He's yours for sure.' He held the dollar up. 'I could've thieved it, sir. But that in't right . . .'

'Where is he?'

'On our tuck boat. On a bit o' canvas.'

'What state's he in?'

'Dead as stone.'

The captain turned, and spoke into the dark bedroom. 'Alice, did you hear? They've Seaman Rankin's body on their boat. Where do the bodies go in Wherrytown?'

'You'd better lay him in the stable block. The tackle room. Let Mr Phipps take care of it.'

'You hear that? What's your name . . . ?'

'It's Palmer Dolly, Captain. And I'm a sailor too.'

'So, Palmer Dolly. Put the body into Mrs Yapp's tackle room. And keep that dollar for yourself . . .'

'I'll hope to spend it in America, then.'

'You spend it how you want.'

'I mean, I hoped to ask if you were looking for a sailor for the *Belle* . . . you being one hand down.'

The captain closed the bedroom door. He should have dressed and gone down to the pilchard nets. He should have shown his *captaincy*. Instead he went to Mrs Yapp and took refuge in an hour more of sleep. His head ached badly when he woke. His shoulders were like wood. Hard winds, bad luck, a bar of sand had beached his ship. His masts were down, the cattle lost, the African set loose; the ground was deep in snow; and every half-wit in the land was either staying at the inn or banging at his door in the middle of the night with more bad news: damned Rankin had been found! What kind of day would Monday be? Oh praise the Lord if it could be a turning point! The *Belle* afloat. The cattle rounded up. The nightmare coming to an end.

9. Star-gazy Pie

WALTER HOWELLS had been sleeping unusually well, but he was woken abruptly before dawn. Someone with sopping feet was hurrying – too closely – past the window of his seafront home. Was *home* the word for where he lived? Or even *house*? *Warehouse,* perhaps. This was the man to see and bargain with if firearms were wanted. Or silk. Or books. Or laudanum. Or contraband. If anybody required horses, or had a letter to be sent, or needed to hire labour, acquire a wedding coat, buy shoes, a bed, a block of tea, some timber, a ticket for the *Tar*, then Walter was the man. He had the world beneath his bed in boxes, weighed and priced. 'Everything supplied,' he used to say, 'excepting payment on the slate. Or loans.'

Who could that be at such an early hour walking by his house? Not excise men or smugglers. They couldn't even sniff in Wherrytown without first informing Walter Howells and agreeing on percentages. Some filchers, then? Some early rising thief? He took his ancient German flintlock off its bedboard hook. Its ram's-horn butt was icy cold. As was the floor on his bare feet. As were the misted panes of window glass on his nose and forehead. He hadn't known that so much snow had settled. He'd been asleep too soon.

The seashore and the lane beyond the glass seemed inside out, the dark parts light, the ground much brighter than the sky. The sea was oddly matt. Its only scintillations came from the offshore lamps on the fishing boats, and the bobbing outlines of their masts and rigging, separated in the shallows by sparkling, turbulent circles of pilchards. No doubt the footsteps that he'd heard had been a fisherman's. He left the flintlock on the windowsill, and wrapped himself in the Spanish rug which he used as his bed cover. The rug caught on the flintlock's barrel and knocked it off the windowsill into the cushions of a chair, where it was lost. He wasn't sorry to be woken early. This would be a busy day, for Walter Howells and Wherrytown. Everyone would earn a decent crust. High tide, high times!

There was still a smoulder meditating in the bedroom grate. Walter Howells knelt down, his knees in ashes, and revived what heat there was with kindling and some pages from a used ledger. He lit a candle from the flame. He mixed and warmed a little ink and then stood at his high desk to write out his Monday tasks. Bring the catch ashore. Get the pilchards salted and barrelled up. Bring the cattle in. Refloat the *Belle*. He noted down how much salt he'd need, how many panniers and barrels, how many men and women, what weight of wood, what boats, what rope, what cattle feed. He wrote 'High Water – 2 p.m.?' and circled it.

There was a letter to be sent, on behalf of Shipmaster Comstock, to William Bagnall, debtor, rascal, bludger, footpad, horse-thief, pugilist. Walter chuckled to himself. The very thought of William Bagnall's many skills! He

smoothed a piece of paper and wrote with hardly any
hesitation and in high spirits:

My good friend Will,

    *You won't & can't deny you owe me favours. I wd. not
have you in my debt for ever. So I urge you, pay me off
thus, and easily, & let's be done with it. There is a man
who much deserves a beating & has quitt'd Wherrytown
w'out settling his accounts or providing for his Reckoning.
He is a fellow from yr. town. I cannot think it will be
hardship for you to find him isolated in some place & break
a bone or two, & well deserv'd. Some broken teeth wd. suit
my purpose also, to stay his conversation for a period. Do
this with trusted, vigorous friends to whom a sovereign
might be pay'd, & say no more, & you must count y'self
acquitt'd from my debt. His name is Aymer Smith, & you
will know him from the soap works of that name & family.
You shd. not stand in fear of him, but deal with him as you
might deal with what he is, a thief & not a gentleman.
Send proof of his misfortunes, & so we are confederates &
league'd together in good friendship, xcept my name shd. not
be known in this.*

    I sign myself on Monday 21st of November,
    Walter Howells

It was a fine start to his day.

Walter Howells was mounted on his re-shod horse and
organizing pilchards on the beach a little after eight. Most
of Wherrytown was there. The women too. And many of
the women from the coast had joined their husbands and

their neighbours for the landing of the catch. How could they resist it? Good pennies could be made that Monday morning by nimble hands that didn't mind the withering of salt or the rasp of fish-scales, that didn't care if their nails, softened in the brine, were ripped, or if their arms were pickled to the elbows. Why should they mind? This wasn't Paris, after all. This wasn't Lah-di-dah-on-Sea. They wouldn't need fine hands or perfect nails. They didn't spend their day in salons, waving Chinese fans, or playing cards, or offering their fingers for gentlemen to kiss. There weren't any Chinese fans or salons in Wherrytown. Nor any gentlemen either. But there was snow, and that was rare so early in the winter. Coastal snow does not last long; the Wherrytowners hurried out of bed to be the first to walk in it, to break its crusts, to roll it into balls. They gathered on the beach, made almost eager for the pilcharding by the crispy coverlet of white which hid the sand. It made them feel rosy with well-being. It brought the colours out. The blue and buff of the women's smocks and aprons seemed exotic, almost tropical, against the arctic white.

What would the sea make of the snow? They watched the tide swell up, curl its lip and skim the beach of snow like children skim the cream off cakes. Soon some crewmen from the *Belle*, too bored and restless to stay in bed, joined the Wherrytowners on the beach. Snowballs began to fly. The snow was mixed with sand, and was dangerous. Walter Howells decided it was time for pilcharding.

MIGGY BOWE had had her fill of fresh beef the night before. Her dreams were bilious. Her stomach wasn't used to large amounts of meat. She'd had to get up in the dark to pass an aching stool into the flattened heather behind their cottage. The night was cold and white. She squatted, shivering, and watched the lanterns of the fishing boats beyond the broken *Belle*. Her gut ached. It took its time. She didn't like the snow at night. It put her on display. She could be watched. She'd heard the movement in the undergrowth when she'd first hurried out of doors. She'd taken it to be the cattle or a fox. The dogs were barking and pulling on their ropes. They always barked when there were foxes near. But now that she was bent up double with her nightshift bunched onto her knees, scarcely balancing, and constipated too, the night sounds seemed more sinister. The undergrowth was not asleep. It fidgeted. It stirred. She heard the snap of wood, and then a chilling silence as if someone twenty yards behind her back were standing on one leg, mid-step, and watching her. She couldn't think that anyone would be about at such a time, on such a night, excepting fishermen, of course. Or Devils.

Miggy did her best to look around, to decipher all the darker shapes. But if she turned too much she'd topple. Was that somebody up against the rock, somebody large and shadowy? The shadow stayed as still and silent as a bush. But other shadows seemed to move and deepen. Again, the snap of wood, and silence.

Miggy was as quick as she could be. She didn't bury her waste. She had no light. The snowy earth was far too hard. She left it for the foxes and the crows. She shuffled back home. She didn't wait to rearrange her clothes. She untied the two mongrels and let them go to chase the Devils away.

The dogs went off, twisting like hunting eels into the snowy breakers of the hill, their barks abusive, their ears turned back like gills. She heard them growling in the dark, but soon they became quiet. There weren't any cries of pain. There were no Devils, then. Or else there was a silent Devil there. He had no tongue. He was half dog.

It was too cold inside the cottage to wash. But Miggy washed herself nevertheless in water from the pot next to the grate. It was a little shy of warm, but warm enough to take the gloss off one of the bars of Aymer's soap. She ran her fingers across the hard escutcheon of Hector Smith & Sons. She held the wet soap to her nose. Would she smell kelp from her own pits? She didn't recognize the smell. She'd not encountered almonds, oleander or eau de Sète before. But she was drugged on them at once. She would smell sweet for her sweet Ralph. She dressed in breeches and a wrap. She tied her hair back with a ribbon. She knotted the *Belle*'s red-patterned ensign at her throat – 'I need help' – and, as soon as there was any light, woke her mother. 'Come on, girl. Up. This in't the Sabbath. Let's not be idle, eh?' These were words her mother usually used.

It took the Bowes less than two hours to walk from Dry Manston to the pilchard beach. There was a quicker, more direct route than the coastal path. It was a wagon way which, though rutted, was flat, partly hedged from wind and shielded from the deeper, drifting snow. Miggy – far from mithering at every step – set the pace. 'Come on now, Ma. There's gonna be no work for us unless we stretch ourselves a bit.'

'What's biting at you, Miggy?'

'Nothin's biting at me, Ma. The quicker out's the quicker in.'

'Is that the truth of it?' said Rosie Bowe. She was no fool. She knew the signs. Her Miggy hadn't washed herself that thoroughly to please the pilchards. She had her hair tied back for some young man. It wasn't hard to guess which man that was, from amongst their new acquaintances. The windswept blond American? Or Mr Aymer Spindle-shanks, too nervous of a floating cow to get his ankles wet? To some extent she wished it was the spindleshanks. At least the man was educated, and wealthy. And *soft*, was that the word? She'd shouted at him at her cottage door ('A shillin' is a fine price to be paupered by!') and he had blushed and stuttered and hoped that they'd be friends, when all the other men she'd shouted at (and there'd been a few) had wagged their fingers in her face or turned away or laughed at her or knocked her to the ground. Rosie Bowe thought she could cope with Aymer Smith. He wasn't dangerous. But sailor Ralph? She saw the danger in that boy. At best he'd break her Miggy's heart, and leave her beached. That's what to expect from sailors. At worst, he'd win her heart and sail away with her on board the *Belle*. And that would be the last of Miggy Bowe.

So only Miggy ran along the path to Wherrytown. How long before she'd hold his hands again? How long before he'd run his finger down her spine, a bone, a bone, a bone, the hollow of her waist, his breath upon her neck? Her mother was less speedy in the snow, and for once in lower spirits than her daughter. She wasn't sorry for herself. She was too toughly made for that. But as she walked and watched her daughter hurrying ahead she had to face the truth of who she was: no one would hold her hand in Wherrytown, or try to count her vertebrae, no one would try to break her heart, or take her to America. She wasn't young or beautiful, she thought, or plump, and men and ships were not for her. She would be thirty-five at Christmas time. A modest age. Too young to feel so old and weathered. She watched her daughter on the path ahead. Miggy swung her arms as if there were no troubles in the world. Well, perhaps there weren't if you were seventeen, and there were lips to kiss.

'Go on, then,' Rosie said, to Miggy's back. 'Be happy if you can. It don't last for ever.' Nothing does, she thought. You can't rely on anything for long. Not even kelp. She smiled at that, and shook her head. But it wasn't kelp that bothered Rosie Bowe as she walked on her own along the wagon way. She could learn to do without the kelp. She hated it. How would she manage, though, without her cussed daughter to adore? Would it be long before she lived alone?

The shore at Wherrytown when they arrived was like a winter carnival, a hundred people at the very least with Walter Howells on his big horse as showmaster, and a leaping fire close to the water's edge to hold bad weather off. The townsmen and the fishermen and some Americans were already in the water, basketing the pilchards from the keepnets nearest shore with as much concern for their living catch as they would show for vegetables.

There were too many fish for sentiment. As each net was emptied and dragged up on the shore for gulls and boys to glean, so the outer nets were edged in by their boats until these pilchards were a gasping, thrashing multitude as well, maddened by the dipping baskets of the men and by the turmoil of air and sea and sand and snow. The tide was on the turn and so the water wasn't deep. But still the work was wet and cold. Men hurried to the fire, between each basketful of fish, to steam their knees and coax some blood back to their faces, hands and feet. Each filled basket was tallied by the agent Howells against the family who owned the net. He had a simple principle – he made no mark for every thirteenth load of fish. It wasn't superstition, but a sort of tithe, a fee for sitting on his horse. Less than eight per cent for him against their ninety-two. A fair division of the spoils, he thought. Walter Howells would make a lot of tithes that day, from pilchards and from ships. Who needed kelp? Who needed Hector Smith & Sons?

No one there resented Walter Howells. They cursed him, maybe. Wished he'd topple from his horse and break a leg. Wished – just for once – he'd get his trousers wet and find out how heavy a basketful of pilchards could be. But no one wished him dead. How could they manage without their agent with his peppery face and temper, and his good contacts to the east, his wagons and his warehouse home? He was worth his eight per cent. They didn't have to like the man. They didn't have to speak to him. They only had to concentrate on the strenuous joy of dipping baskets into, fish and swinging them onto the shore until the sea drained out, and know that Walter Howells would turn their efforts into cash.

The Americans would not get any cash from Walter

Howells. He regarded them as volunteers, free labour, and not worth a fourpenny fig between the lot of them, despite their noise and swaggering. They were too clumsy with the fish and were a hindrance rather than a help. They teased each other and flirted with the working women. They splashed their skirts, or dropped a pilchard down their apron fronts, or touched the younger and prettier women unnecessarily while they helped to put the baskets on their backs. The women, happy to be flirted with, on such a high and zesty day, carried the pilchards through the snow and sand up to the salting hall, next to Walter Howells's house. Their baskets filled the lane, the yard, the courtway to the hall. Any living fish that jumped free of the baskets didn't stand a chance. They suffocated in the icy air. Or they were scavenged by cats and gulls and by the little girls whose job it was to grill them for breakfast on the beach fire. There wasn't any idleness. This was a working hive.

Up at the salting hall some of the older women were as panicky and breathless as the fish. They tipped each basket-load of pilchards onto the sloping flagstones and sorted them with brooms and wooden spades. Most were sent slithering down lead-lined chutes onto the cellar floor for balking with layers of rough salt. There'd be no waste. Farmers boasted, when pigs were slaughtered, that they had a use for everything except the squeal. The pilchards though were better than pigs: even the smell of fish was put to use – it kept the Devil out of town. Their fins, the flesh, the scales, the eyes, they all had purposes. Their blood and oil would drain into the cellar tanks for sale as cheap lamp fuel. Their flesh would end up, thanks to Walter Howells's hogsheads and his wagons, on tables in London, Bristol, Liverpool and even in the sugar plantations of America, on nigger bread. The badly damaged pilchards – torn scales, ripped fins, their bellies gaping – were flipped aside. They were fit only for manure on a farmer's field. The second best were packed on woodweave trays. They would be hawked and jousted inland while they were fresh. The remainder would be potted with vinegar, bay leaves, spices or pickled in jars with brine, for the spring. But the largest and the very best of the fish were put in panniers and covered by damp cloths. These were the ones that would be cooked to celebrate the catch. No table in Wherrytown would be without star-gazy pie that night, with pilchard heads protruding from the brown sea of a pastry crust, and pilchard eyes recriminating in the candlelight. A comic meal, and one that recognized how farcical it was to have a town so occupied by fish.

The Bowes were given jobs as basket carriers. Walter Howells was glad to see them there. They were strong and used to lifting heavy loads of seaweed and so could be expected to shift a decent share of fish. He noted down their names. He'd pay them later on – in pilchards and with a promissory note. There'd be no pennies till the fish were sold, and he could calculate his own cut of the profits.

Rosie Bowe was frozen from her walk. She warmed herself at the fire. She greeted her neighbours from Dry Manston and tasted her first roast pilchard of the season – not a touch on beef. But still she savoured it. It would be a long and arduous day, an aching day. She meant to pace herself. But Miggy didn't wait to warm herself or taste the fish. She was already hot. She had seen Ralph Parkiss, thigh deep in the sea, basketing the pilchards with Palmer Dolly and his brothers. He would hand his next full load to her, and no one else. She'd see to it. Palmer Dolly – that idiot! – tried to put his basket on her back. 'Come on, Miggy Bowe. Let's see you give the pilchards legs.' And then, 'I got myself a dollar here . . .' But she was deaf and blind to him. When Ralph stepped across the net, a wriggling basket on his shoulders, she paddled in to meet him. 'That's one for me,' she said.

'It's heavy, though.'

'So what of that?' She took the weight of it. Her hand held his. Her lower lip turned in to check her smile. 'Ma says I'm stronger than a horse . . .'

'Giddup,' Ralph said.

They worked in concert then. He kept the baskets light for her, and every time they met at the water's edge, they touched each other's hands. Their fingertips were lips.

Where did Aymer Smith fit in? He was, of course, the Smith & Son whom Walter Howells no longer needed. Whom Rosie Bowe would learn to do without. Whom Shipmaster Comstock took to be a kidnapper. Who was a coward and a weeper. Who was (his own assessment now) an apostate not only to God but to himself. Who had abandoned Otto to the snow.

He hadn't slept too well, and little wonder, given how his ear and self-esteem had taken such a bruising. His nose was blocked. His throat was sore. The muscles in his legs were torn. He should have stayed in bed. But he didn't want to wake the Norrises with his offensive cough, or with his sniffing. Sea air, he thought, might clear his passages and lift his spirits, a little exercise might be his remedy. So he'd followed everybody else down to the shore and stood, his back against the fire, observing 'all the colour of the scene', the spectacle of one small, single-minded, unremitting town at its busiest. This, certainly, must be the point of travel, he was sure, to see the different tribes of humankind, at ease with themselves. Perhaps he ought to travel more, to Edinburgh, say, or Paris or Florence, to see the greater works of man, the castles and the statues and the churches. Though what greater work of art than this live pageant might he see abroad? He rehearsed (not quite aloud) his 'philosophic certitude' that a traveller should leave himself exposed to humankind, not art or landscape. Just for the moment, though, he preferred not to expose himself too deeply. He wasn't tempted to wade in amongst the pilchards. He wasn't well enough. He must stay warm.

He nursed his sore chest at the fire. He waved at his good friend, Ralph Parkiss, and nodded dutifully, but nothing more, to agent Howells (who seemed both startled and amused to see him). Aymer couldn't like the man, his red shock hair, his redder face, his unbecoming leather hat, his gracelessness, his ostentatious horse. But even greeting enemies was better than the desolation of being the only person on the beach without a job.

'Good morning,' and, 'A wonderful sight!' he said to any of the shivering fishermen that he recognized from his Sunday walk to Dry Manston as they came up to thaw out at the fire. 'An exemplary spectacle ... A feast for the eyes ... What better work has man than this?' Some

Wherrytowners and some of the Americans who had wit-
nessed his public dispute with Captain Comstock came to
warm themselves as well. Aymer treated them with equal
cheerfulness. He made them look him in the eye. He made
them reply to his 'Good morning' and his comments on the
weather. He wouldn't be discomfited. He would put last
night behind him. The morning was too fine for melancholia and self-consciousness. He belonged, he told himself;
he was entitled to be there. Hector Smith & Sons had had
dealings with Wherrytown for forty years. Who could say
the same for Captain Comstock? Or his crew? They'd
be come-and-gone in two weeks at the most, and couldn't
count on much respect for that.

No, Aymer need not defer to the Americans. He had his
tasks – to make sure that all the kelping families were
properly informed of their new circumstance, and to carry
out his promise to take care of the Bowes. He had been
wrong to think there was no job for him in Wherrytown.
He owed a duty to the Bowes. He might that day walk out
to Dry Manston with some provisions for their home. They
would appreciate candied oranges, perhaps, a yard or two of
twill, some sweeter-burning candles. There would be the
opportunity to enquire of Rosie Bowe if Miggy, Margaret,
her daughter, might benefit from marriage to an older,
wealthy, educated man. He hadn't yet spotted the Bowes at
work among the pilcharders. Nor had he noticed George.

The parlourman approached him from behind: 'Have
you had breakfast yet, sir? Try one of these.' He offered
Aymer a grilled pilchard on a stick. Beneath the charcoal
skin the flesh was white and succulent. Aymer burnt his lips

on it. He was more hungry than he'd thought; the fresh air and the smell, perhaps. He pulled the burnt skin off with his free hand, and picked off fingerfuls of flesh. The fish juices ran onto his chin.

'An oily fish,' warned George. 'Take heed you don't grease up the lappets on that coat.'

'The pilchard is a surface fish,' replied Aymer, picking knowledge from his memory as clumsily as he now was picking bones from between his teeth. He was delighted to see George. 'Pelagic is the term. You know the word?'

'Don't know the word. I know the fish well enough. There's nothing else this time of year, exceptin' pilchers.'

'Demersic is the other word, I think. The twin of pelagic. It speaks of fish that live upon the ocean floor. I see a parallel with people here. Those shoals of common men who live near the surface, and those solitary, more silent ones that inhabit deeper water. I count myself to be demersic, then. You, George, can I describe you as pelagic, a pilchard as it were? You would not take offence at that?'

'You're talking to a pilchard, then?'

'Well, yes, I am, within my metaphor . . .'

'Mistaking a man for a fish is madness, I should say. It in't what I'd call deep and solitary. What was that word you used?'

'Demersic, George.'

'Now, there's a word! What do you say I'll never have to use that word again?'

'Do not hold words in low regard. Words have power, George. Words are deeds . . .'

'Oh, yes?' said George. 'And the wind is a potato, I

suppose. If words are deeds, then I'm the meanest man in Wherrytown. There in't a sin I won't have done.'

'No, what I meant to say is this, that words and deeds should be the same. You make a promise, you should keep it. You hold a view, then you should stand by it. You should say what you do: you should do what you say.'

'Well, there's the difference,' said George, evidently losing interest. 'People in these parts in't impressed by words. They don't mean what they say. They only mean what they do. And that, I think, makes better sense.'

This was a conversation Aymer liked: witty, schematic, circular; thrust, riposte, touché. 'Deep and solitary', indeed! That had a chilling edge to it. He had to credit George with some intellectual energy, a rarity in Wherrytown where ideas were not valued, it would seem, an even greater rarity amongst parlourmen where brain was less admired than brawn and impudence. George was an equal in some ways. In wiliness at least. And oddly democratic for a serving man, not deferential. Aymer – quiet for once – threw his fish-bone to the gulls and rubbed the oil into his hands. 'What better work has man than this?' he said to George, and turned his attentions once again to the dealings on the shore. Miggy Bowe, a basket of pilchards on her back, was coming up the shore. He couldn't miss seeing her. George was saying something, but Aymer waved him quiet and walked away from the fire in pursuit of Miggy, Mrs Margaret Smith. He wouldn't speak to her. He only wanted to remind himself what she looked like, what kind of girl she was. He meant to rediscover that extravagant and rushing inspiration that, yesterday, had cast this young woman as his wife. He found her coming back down to the beach from the salt hall, empty-handed. She seemed immensely joyful. There was more expression in her face than he had noted on the previous day. She was more colourful, and smiling even. Her hair was tied back prettily and was flattered by the low and sunny winter light. The red kerchief around her neck was dramatic; alluring, even. Yes, she'd do well. Aymer was more certain now. She made good sense to him. He'd seek her mother out. He'd talk to Rosie Bowe at once.

'GOOD MORNING, Mrs Bowe.' She didn't seem to want to stop and talk. Her smile was wintry, but she was cold and tired and shy, no doubt, and keen to get the pilchards off her back. 'I trust you suppered well on that beef-fish you netted yesterday.'

'A tasty fish,' she said, and took a further step towards the salting hall. She hadn't liked to smile too freely; he had an oily scab of burnt fish-skin on his nose. A comic beauty spot.

'You might remember, Mrs Bowe, my parting words to you yesterday when you were kind enough to entertain me at your home. I promised to devise some ways in which I might alleviate your loss of kelping for a living . . .' (she took another step, and moved the basket on her shoulder) '. . . for which, alas, my family firm owes some responsibility.' He closed the gap between them, and whispered, 'Your daughter, Mrs Bowe. Now I might help you both through her, though I would not wish to separate a mother and her daughter unless . . .'

She looked at him and nodded. She understood. 'You mean to take my Miggy as a maid?'

'No, no. I would not take her as a maid. Your daughter is too fine.' He swallowed deeply, blushed, and spoke almost inaudibly, his lips six inches from her ear. 'I hope to take her as a wife.' Rosie Bowe was startled now. She couldn't think of a reply. She nodded. Shook her head. Raised her eyebrows. Smiled. 'My Miggy get wed to you?'

'You might not know of it, but I am yet a bachelor . . .' He blushed again. She didn't notice it. She'd turned away from him. She pulled a face.

'You must regard me as a friend who wishes simply to enhance your lives,' he said. 'Consider, if you will, the benefits . . .' He counted seven on his hands, and ended with 'the benefit of some prosperity, not only for Margaret, but for all those who love her . . . She will regard it as an opportunity, I am certain of it, Mrs Bowe.'

She shook her head. 'I couldn't say,' she said.

'You might like to join your daughter in my house.'

'No, I in't leaving here.'

'There's nothing here for you, not now.'

'It's home, is what it is. A bit o' kelp don't make the difference. At least my heart is fixed.'

'Mrs Bowe, we need to talk of this at length. You might consider me an unexpected son-in-law. Indeed, you have a right. There is the matter of my age, my class, my sensibility. I am unlike your daughter, it is true. I might not make a pattern husband for her. I owe no debt to Beauty or to Youth. But I am earnest, Mrs Bowe, and trustworthy, and diligent. My motives are sincere and simple. You will not find me stained by that Humbug which is the besetting weakness of our age. I ask you and your daughter to consider me as if I am the continent of Canada, an unknown land, perhaps, but one of opportunity to which you might set sail with trepidation but an easy heart, and, on arriving there, discover unexpected rewards. And joys. Can I say more?'

'I wouldn't want my Miggy to go to Canada,' she said. 'America neither.'

'She does not need to emigrate, Mrs Bowe. That was not my proposition.'

'I hope you're right.'

'Well, then, what do you say?'

'What do I say? I don't say anything. It's her you want to carry off, and so it's her you'll have to listen to. And she'll not marry you. Now then, and that's the truth of it . . .'

'Listen to me,' Aymer said. He needed Rosie on his side.

'No more. Not now.' She put her basket at her feet, and pointed down the beach. 'Don't talk,' she said. 'They's bringing that poor sailor in.'

'What sailor's that?'

'What's drowned on Saturday. They've netted him.'

They watched in silence – embarrassed by each other's company – as the Dolly net was tugged into the shallows and Nathaniel Rankin's body was lifted off the deck of the tuck boat. All work stopped, to show respect. The men left the water. The women put their baskets down. The older ones came out of the salting house into the foreshore lane and muttered prayers. Walter Howells even dismounted from his horse. He could supply a decent coffin for the man.

JIM CRACE

Palmer, Skimmer, Henry Dolly and his second son carried the body in its canvas sling. They ducked it once in sea water, to wash the briny residues away, and clean his clothes and skin of wet, dark blood and pus. A few stray pilchards slithered out of his shirt. They put the body on a cart, and let Nathaniel's shipmates from the *Belle* say their prayers for him, or touch the canvas or the cartwood in farewell. Then everybody else jostled for a brief and queasy look – and Miggy, she couldn't think why, was the only one to touch. Aymer was quite proud of her. She put her little finger on Nat Rankin's leg. She'd never seen a corpse before. She then stepped back, put her head against Ralph's chest, and let him put his arms around her waist. She let him kiss her hair. Where was Palmer Dolly? She looked for him. She wanted him to see her body wrapped in Ralph's. She wanted everyone to see. Her mother, too. Here was a girl intended for America.

Aymer wasn't watching Nat. If he was breathless it was not because the corpse had winded him. He watched his new friend Ralph clasp Mrs Margaret Smith around the waist and put his fine young nose into her hair. Aymer took his spectacles off and wiped his eyes. 'Too late to talk, I think,' he said to Rosie Bowe.

'She's only but a girl.' Rosie put her hand out and touched him on the arm. 'She in't for you. You must know that.'

'I *in't* for no one, Mrs Bowe.'

He bowed. No one had ever bowed to her before. It wouldn't do to laugh. Instead, while he was stooped in front of her, she brushed the fish skin from his nose. 'Pilchard

154

tears,' she said. He turned and followed Nathaniel Rankin into Wherrytown, with the heavy head of a mourner.

So Nathaniel Rankin came ashore with ninety tons of pilchards. The Dollys put him in the tackle room where Otto had slept. The Americans came in ones and twos to peek at him, and count their blessings. The captain ordered John Peacock, the *Belle*'s sailmaker, to sew the drowned man up in the piece of canvas he'd been carried in. George hovered at the door and watched. John Peacock smoked his pipe, and hummed to himself. He didn't seem to mind the work. 'You lose a man, you lose a piece of sail,' he said. 'This ain't the first I've stitched. Nor will it be the last.'

'What was that tale you told in the parlour the other night?' George said. 'The iced-up man from Canadee that ended up in Liverpool, and never died at all? They thawed *him* out. You think I ought to fetch some towels and grog for this one?'

'Nat Rankin won't see Liverpool,' John Peacock said. 'He won't be calling out for grog. I've stitched him in for good. There now.' He'd wrapped his shipmate out of sight. 'And that's the end of it. Except for digging him a hole. And prayers.'

'And worms,' said George.

THE PILCHARDS had been brought ashore before midday, and though the townswomen still had several days' more work to do in the salting hall, the men were free at last to take advantage of the heavy, flooding tide and get the *Belle* clear of the bar at Dry Manston. The fishermen took in their nets, and made the best of a modest breeze to get along the coast before high tide at a quarter after two. Their task: to put a dozen towlines on the *Belle*, and steady it from drifting further inshore once the keel was floating free of sand. The Americans and another fifteen willing hands from Wherrytown were hurrying along the coast by foot. The snow was slush by now. The day was mild. And they could make fast progress. Ralph Parkiss pointed out the Cradle Rock as they passed by. His comrades teased him endlessly about the girl he'd found. 'Dump her, Ralph,' they said. 'We don't want ballast on the *Belle*.'

Walter Howells had got the Monday organized with military precision. He loved to be the mounted major-general, deploying men with stabs and swipes from his riding crop. He would have had his flintlock in his belt if only he could have found it in his house. He would have fired it in the air to start the men off on their journey down the coast. 'Not now. No time,' he said, when anybody threatened to delay him with questions or pleasantries. He heeled his horse from shore to inn and back. He might seem bad-tempered to those he shouted at. But Walter Howells, in fact, was happy with himself, and red-faced only with high hopes and skin that didn't like salt air. His day was going well. And it was fine, thank God; no awkward wind, no squally sea. He'd have no trouble with the *Belle of Wilmington*, so long as he made haste. There was no time to waste. He found a birchwood coffin and took it from his storeroom to the inn, balanced across the saddle of his second horse. He leant it up against the tackle-room door, and nodded at the corpse and at John Peacock, the sailmaker, within.

The agent marked the coffin price on his pocket ledger against the *Belle*'s name, called George to mind the horses for a moment, and went in search of Captain Comstock. He didn't have to hunt. The captain was exactly where he'd been the morning before; in low spirits, sitting with a bottle in the snug.

'Now, sir, to horse,' Howells said. 'There's work that must be done if you're to see America again.' He put the stopper in the bottle, and pulled the captain from his chair. 'What did I say about we're partners now? I never meant that you'd sit idle while I did all the work and worrying . . .'

'I worry, Mr Howells, because I have one seaman dead and needing burial, and another man gone missing in this wretched land . . .' He recounted, as he pulled his deck boots on and hurried down to the courtyard, how they had wrongly blamed 'that Smith'. He'd not stolen Otto after all. 'We could have blacked an innocent eye.'

'Too late, too late,' said Mr Howells. His letter to William Bagnall was signed and sealed. The sovereign was put aside. 'So where's your blackie, then, if not with Soapie Smith?' Shipmaster Comstock shrugged. 'He won't have gone far, Captain. He'll have found some little nest, and rats and grass to eat. Let's bring the *Belle* around to Wherrytown today, and then I'll organize a hunt to track the fellow down, or find his body at the very least.' And then he said, 'Let's put a sovereign on his head. Whoever finds your blackie gets the prize! That's an entertainment for your men.'

George steadied their horses in the courtyard while Howells and Comstock mounted. He watched them go down to the quay, then turn westwards along the coast. A comic sight. The American did not sit squarely on his horse. He didn't match his bottom to the rhythms of the horse's back. The mare would do her best to kick him off.

'There's a man who'll be bringing blisters home tonight,' he said. 'Prepare the poultices!'

Now the only living men in Wherrytown, apart from George, were Aymer, Robert Norris, Mr Phipps, John Peacock, the undertaker-cum-sailmaker, and those few gouty veterans too stiff and ailing to step out of doors, except for funerals.

It was a lucky day for everyone except Aymer. By the time the riders had arrived at Dry Manston beach, the landlubbers and gangs of boys had found and roped eighty of the cattle from Quebec. They'd made rough fencing out of gorse where they could keep the herd until they could be loaded on the *Belle*. 'There's plenty more,' they reported to Walter Howells.

'Keep thirty separate,' he ordered them, and winked at Captain Comstock. 'A little candle-end for us,' he said.

They rode down to the shore. The captain jumped onto the sand. His thighs and back were stiff and bruised. He'd never been so tossed about, not even by the ocean off the Cape. He stood amongst his men and watched the fishermen attach their lines to the *Belle*. The smaller boats came into the shallows. Palmer took the captain's arm and helped him climb into the Dolly boat, and at last Captain Comstock and his crew took to the sea again. Quite soon, and hardly dampened by the spray, they were aboard the *Belle*. America!

First they had to reduce the ship's draught at the bow where it was held most firmly. The rigging and the masts were wrecked, the decks were broken through, but – thank the Lord and Neptune – the ship was savable. They cleared out the bilges, and examined the inside of the hull for signs of cracks and movement in the frames and planking. The larboard bow was holed. The outer planks on the orlop deck had sprung. The captain ordered that they should be patched and braced immediately. All the loose gear – lockers, broken timber, equipment and supplies, the mounted double-barrelled cannon – was taken on deck, and loaded on the smaller fishing boats, then put ashore above the high-tide line. Quite soon the beach at Dry Manston, despite the one or two remaining carcasses of cows, began to look like the landing point of some immigrant community in Canada or in Australia. How long before a settlement would spring up amongst the dunes? How long before the natives came with spears?

By two o'clock the *Belle* was stripped, and it was sitting higher in the water. Some of the crew took to the beach. The stronger ones remained. No orders were required. They knew what they must do and they were happy doing it. They worked the pumps and put bilge-water back into the sea. At ten past two they laid out kedge anchors on the seaward side, attached by cables to the one working capstan and to windlasses. Some anchors didn't bite, but those that did were firm enough to take the winch. The barrel of the capstan groaned. The captain too. He thought the wire would bite right through. But, to cheers from the beach, the stern was lifted and the bow was pulled around. The kedge anchors and the lines from fishing boats tied to the waistings of the masts were now enough to hold the *Belle* secure while the sea came upon its highest autumn tide. And how the sea came up! Not swelling, but flat and deep and strong, shouldering the beached ship's keel and hefting it, unshakingly, free of the bar. The sand released its grip. The *Belle* was afloat. It lifted off the bar and slipped into the channel with the resignation of an old and wounded seal. Now it was ready for the towing back to dock at Wherrytown. The tide rose up against the stern. It gripped the ship in foaming chevrons of water. It pushed. It was as if the ocean had wearily reclaimed the *Belle*, had reconciled it to the water, as if the sea were saying to the ship – and what sailor does not think the sea can speak? – 'Enough's enough. You must go home.'

WALTER HOWELLS put up some kegs of beer for everyone that night. There were too many people for the inn parlour, and so despite the cold they lit and warmed the courtyard with lanterns and braziers, and sat around on barrels and bales of straw with star-gazy pie and hot beer. The out-of-towny women hadn't walked back to their cottages. They'd sleep in the agent's salting hall. There'd be work for them until the pilchards were balked and packed, and all the unfit fish carted off by farmers as manure. They sat around self-consciously. They'd had nowhere to wash. They had no change of clothes, and couldn't match the fine, embroidered smocks that the townswomen had put on, or the dresses and the shawls that Katie Norris and Alice Yapp were wearing. They watched the men consuming too much drink too quickly. It wasn't a comfortable mix – town and parish, off-comers, emigrants, the preacher. There was something deadening about the agent's generosity. He gave them beer; he made them wait for cash.

The American sailors were, of course, the first to break the ice. Outsiders are always reckless. No one's watching over them. They were exuberant. The *Belle* was off the bar. They would be going home, huzzah – but not quite yet! There was a little time for fun. They drank the health of all the fishermen whose boats had towed their 'darling *Belle*' back into town. Again, they flirted with wives and daughters. No one was too old or plain for their attentions, and that was charming. When 'Captain Keg' attempted a silent plantation dance with the portly daughter of the Wherrytown shipwright, the cry went up for music. John Peacock brought a damp and battered fiddle from the *Belle*. Another sailor fetched his bellows box. And soon there was a lively jig to dance away the cold. The women danced amongst themselves at first. Even the married ones. They didn't simply foot the measure in their seats. There wasn't any city etiquette in Wherrytown. Then, when all the beer had gone and they'd started on the punch, they let the men lay hold of them and danced in drunken pairs. The captain partnered Alice Yapp until Walter Howells intervened, and then they shared her, jig by jig. Ralph Parkiss showed Miggy how to step, then held her waist and showed her how to kiss. Her mother Rosie even took the hand of, first, old Skimmer, and then her neighbour Henry Dolly. Henry, she thought, was either clumsy from the drink or getting too familiar.

Katie Norris danced with all of the Americans. Her

husband did not dance. He hadn't got the frame for it, he said. He sat at the trestle table that had been carried from the inn and talked with Aymer Smith (with Mr Phipps the preacher eavesdropping) about the age and provenance of Earth, but kept an eye on his wife. He was happy to see her so admired and animated.

'I can recommend a volume for your journey, Mr Norris,' Aymer said. He didn't even want to catch a glimpse of Miggy or her mother. He turned his back on all the dancing and the music. 'It is the work of Mr Lyell. *The Principles of Geology.*' He stole a glance at Preacher Phipps. 'He proposes a world with no vestige of a beginning and no prospect of an end. It is a scientific world. Not one that owes itself to some Creation. An interesting book.'

'It sounds so, Mr Smith.' Robert Norris watched his wife pass from the hands of one sailor to another. He waved at her.

'You wish to ask, I know, what geology might tell us about our moral world. I have considered it. And that is why I am a convinced Amender. I will throw light on that. You know the term?'

'An interesting book,' repeated Robert Norris. His wife's skirts were swinging in the dance, billowing with air then wrapping round her legs.

'Amendism is the scientific view that every offence – Mr Phipps might call it sin – should be settled only by reparations of an equal force.'

'An eye for an eye,' said Preacher Phipps absently. 'The Bible precedes you.'

'Not that. No eyes and teeth. I am talking of self-discipline. Those sailors who are drunk tonight on Mr Howells's beer, for instance, would need to make amends tomorrow by fasting, say, or imbibing some unpleasing liquid, or buying but not drinking beers of equal value to those that have intoxicated them. There is a calm to be maintained between oneself and one's behaviour . . .'

'Indeed there is,' said Robert Norris. Where was Katie?

'Mr Phipps might recommend a different course – that it is enough to confess one's sins and seek forgiveness. Amenders do not hold to that. It is our understanding, should we transgress, that there is, implicit in the sinful act, a second act of amends to balance out the first and re-establish calm. And so we labour to avoid the making of amends by controlling our offences.' He looked Mr Phipps directly in the eye. 'Amends are better than Amens, I think.' But Mr Phipps would not be drawn. He was watching Katie Norris too. He was debating sin, but silently.

'I see that I have silenced you,' said Aymer. He'd had a beer too many. His tongue was hurtling. He tipped a chair up. It toppled to the ground. He'd make them concentrate. 'Take this example, then. Should I, in a temper, upset a chair, I upright it to make amends. Like so. I put it in its proper place and restore the harmony I squandered . . .' The music stopped, and so did Aymer Smith. It had occurred to him that George would have found a shorter way of explaining Amendism: 'You stick your bum in fire, and you must sit on blisters.' What would the preacher make of that?

By now John Peacock had run out of jigs. He played the bass stringed introduction to a round dance. 'Form two circles; the gentleman should take the outer ring.' Reluctant dancers were pulled up and dragged into the ring. Katie Norris ran up to the table. She knew her husband wouldn't dance. She couldn't ask a preacher – though this preacher stood and showed his readiness. She put her hand out for her roommate, Aymer Smith. 'Step up,' she said, flushed, irrefusable. She held his wrist and pulled. He stood opposing her until the music began. She spun twice beneath his arm. They back-to-backed. They swung. But then the partners changed and Aymer had to hold the hand of Amy Farrow from the town; then Nan Dolly (whose hands were briny from the fish), then Alice Yapp, then Miggy Bowe (she blushed, he blushed), then on through grandmamas, and fishing wives, and ten-year-olds, and Rosie Bowe. They didn't have the breath or chance to talk; they had to spin and whirl and stamp, and then move on. At last he faced Katie Norris for the second time. The music stopped. They bowed. Her hair touched his.

Then Robert Norris sang: 'Old Faisie-do', 'The Ballad of the Greenwood King', and 'The traveller is far from home, and lost, and lost, and lost'. His voice was thinner than in chapel. The cold night air reduced it. There was no roof to give it resonance. But still it reached the darkest corners of the courtyard, where Whip had taken stolen fish, where Ralph and Miggy were embracing, where some young men who'd drunk too much were being sick or sleeping, and filled them with that mesmerizing, odd conjunction, both sad and hopeful, which is the human voice in song. Everyone was hot from dancing, and everyone was full of beer and pie. His songs were sobering.

It was too late and cold to linger in the courtyard. To bed. There was a lot of work to be done the next day: a funeral, some carpentry and sail repairs, the further balking of the fish, amends to make, harmonies to restore. But, at least, the *Belle* was docked, the cattle fenced, the pilchards in, the seaman Rankin cleaned and in his box, the world in order for a change. When the candles were snuffed out at the Inn-that-had-no-name, the travellers there could dream of home, in Quebec, in Wilmington, at sea, and know that home was within reach at last. America and Canadee. Nobody thought of Africa that night, except for Aymer Smith. His head was aching from the dancing and the beer. He lay awake and tried to picture Otto going home, the stone and sand of Africa, the moon and sun, the trees perspiring in the night.

10. The Faintest Voice

IT WOULD HAVE been wise for Aymer Smith to have listened to the message swelling from the sea, 'Enough's enough. You must go home.' Unlike the *Belle* he didn't need his rigging fixed. He could go now. He only had to have a word with George and pay two sovereigns for the day hire of a horse. He could reach the Seven Springs by evening, spend the night in civilized company at the Cross and Crown Hotel, and then secure a place, first class, *inside* the mail coach going east. Three days and he'd be back where he belonged, amongst his books, with good acquaintances, fellow Sceptics and Amenders to converse with, and his work at Hector Smith & Sons to take his mind off Wherrytown.

So what if he didn't know the way to the Seven Springs? Or if he was too timid for the horse? Or if he was nervous of travelling on his own across moors where there were highwaymen and bridgeless rivers? Then he could go home in company. There were a dozen wagonloads of salted pilchards leaving on the Wednesday morning. If he could only tolerate an exposed place amongst the hogsheads and put his shoulder to the wheel when there was mud, or a heavy hill, then he'd be back with the Sceptics by the

Sunday night. His duty would be done. More to the point, he would be free of Wherrytown and all of its embarrassments. Nobody at home would know what a mighty fool he had made of himself.

He'd had a dream that Monday night, made turbulent by pilchard oil and too much beer, in which he danced a jig with Miggy, Katie and Alice Yapp as his three partners. He had no trousers on. The captain punched him on the chin, but no one tried to intervene. Otto shouted at him, pointing at the door, 'Go! Go! Go!' The sailors pelted him with kelp.

Aymer woke to daylight and an empty room. The Norrises were out of bed. Either they had gone to breakfast or they were on their morning walk. His throat was dry and sore. His head ached. Whip was stirring in her sleep at his side. He stretched his hand and stroked her ear. Was she the only friend in Wherrytown, this scraggy, undiscriminating dog? He feared, he *knew*, she was. And that was why he wouldn't take the wagon or the horse. He had to put the world to rights. *His* world, that is. He wanted to be liked. He wanted to regain his dignity before he left. He couldn't fool himself that he still had any tasks in Wherrytown. He'd paid his shillings to the kelpers. He'd spoken to the agent Howells. His work was done. And any foolish hopes that he might find a country wife had – just in time – been dashed. Otto haunted him, it's true. But surely Otto would be far from Wherrytown by now. And surely in good hands. Aymer wouldn't allow himself to consider the bleak alternatives. His conscience was too bruised already. Still, he was persuaded he must stay in Wherrytown, but not for Otto's sake. Good sense dictated it. He couldn't go back home just yet. After all, he had a chesty cold. He couldn't travel in this weather until the infection had eased at least. It would be suicide.

Instead? Instead he'd stay on till the Wednesday week and take a passage on the *Tar* on its next return along the coast. That was a symmetry worth waiting for. And in the meantime he'd have seven days to know the countryside. He'd always been an admirer of the Picturesque. He could take George as his guide, perhaps. And Whip, of course. There might be antiquities to see. He'd botanize. He'd read. He'd try a little poetry, and begin a diary of his observations. He might attempt some sketches, too: the Cradle Rock, the harbour boats, the charming, unconceited cottages above Dry Manston beach. His health would benefit from rambles and diversions such as that. At night he wouldn't be able to avoid the company in the parlour, of course. But he would be a *mended* man, keeping his own counsel and maintaining an educated distance from the conversations of his fellow guests. He knew that he had *volunteered* himself too much. Had been too generous and too exotic. Had interfered. He had seven days to be more reticent, more taciturn, more worthy of respect. He would be reckless with his reticence, a pleasing paradox.

There was no one in the parlour. Nor was there any fire. He didn't ring the handbell. He helped himself to a cold breakfast from what had been left on the side table: potted hare, a dish of plain pilchards, oat bread, some cheese, some lukewarm grog. He didn't touch the pilchards or the grog. He put his nose into a book – Emile dell'Ova's *Truismes*, in French – and ate just bread and cheese. Surely it wouldn't be long before someone came, and could encounter him sitting quietly at the table, preoccupied, contained. But no one came for half an hour, and Aymer soon grew bored of dell'Ova's company. He hand-fed the dog on potted hare and pilchards and then, when she wouldn't stop wimping at the outer door, he took his coat and went into the lane.

Here was a town more preoccupied than Aymer could ever hope to be. He walked up towards the chapel first. He nodded gravely at a balding, elderly woman spinning in her outhouse. Hanks of flax hung from a beam between the hams and herbs. A pig, tied by the leg, sent Whip away. The woman didn't look up from her wheel. One nod and she might snap her yarn. There wasn't anybody else to be *grave* with, or to show the new, forbidding brevity of his conversation. The lanes and yards were quiet and empty, and all the windows shut. The chapel door was open, though, and there were two old men digging in the chapel green, with Mr Phipps the preacher looking on. Aymer might have found some company there – another man who loved debate, who took his pleasures from a book – for Mr Phipps was Aymer's twin in many ways. Both were prisoners of priggishness, and dogma, and vocabulary. Both had Latin. Both were smitten by Katie Norris. They were two peas, except they disagreed on everything they had in common. So Aymer didn't catch the preacher's eye but persevered with his walk, following the path round to some rough-cut steps in rock behind the chapel. They led up to a muddy overhang which opened out to flat, high ground and a patchwork of stone-walled fields. Aymer turned towards the sea. There was a perfect panorama of chapel, town and harbour, with thinning wraiths of smoke haunting the sky in silent, crooked unison and the last remaining smudges of the snow slipping down those roofs that had no warming chimneys.

Was this worthy of a sketch, a verse, an observation in his diary, Aymer wondered. What was that phrase he'd read that morning in dell'Ova? He took the book from his pocket and found the passage: 'The solitary Traveller has better company than those that voyage in the multitude, for he has Nature as his best Companion and no man can be lonely in its Assemblies of sky and earth and water, nor want of Friends.' Aymer read this passage several times. It ought to comfort him, he thought. He was one of life's 'solitary travellers' after all, a Radical, an aesthete and a bachelor. He didn't voyage in the multitude. He knew that he was destined to a life alone. He looked for solace in the Assembly of sky and earth and water that was spread out before him. But there wasn't any solace. He couldn't fool himself. He'd rather be some cheerful low-jack, welcome at an inn, than the emperor of all this landscape.

Thankfully the sound of Wherrytown at work disturbed his *Melancholia*. The two men on the chapel green were striking granite with their shovels. Nathaniel Rankin's grave already had collapsing sides. Down on the shore and all around the salting hall, the local women shouted to each other and clattered barrels. And from the harbour there were the sounds of distant carpentry, of mallets hitting nails, and saws in wood. Aymer could see that there were men hauling recut spars and repaired masts into place on the *Belle* and much industry on deck and on the quay. But he

would need an eyeglass to decipher who was who. Was
that a couple arm in arm, standing partly hidden by the
ship? Was that the Norrises? The only figure he could name
for sure was sitting on a horse and waving his arms like a
general.

Whip didn't seem to like the height. She snapped at
Aymer's shoes and barked.

'Good morning, Mr Smith.' Preacher Phipps was standing fifteen feet below the overhang and looking up. 'What
brings you to my chapel? You come to be baptized, I hope?
What Scriptures are you holding in your hand?'

Aymer resisted the temptation to summarize his views
on God and churches. 'I came only to admire the outlook,'
he said.

'What do you see then? A man of God engaged in God's
good work.'

Aymer couldn't stop himself. 'I do not see you working,
Mr Phipps. You do not seem to have a shovel in your
hands. I did not spot you yesterday amongst the pilchards.
Nor do I expect to see you tomorrow labouring with wood
and rope.'

'I was not sent here to labour with my hands, but to
grace the pulpit. The Good Lord chose me for my Morals
not my Muscles. And which of those do you excel in, Mr
Smith?'

'I do not aspire to either.'

'Then I will pray for you.'

'What will you pray? That I should be more muscular?'

'More muscular indeed. But hot in body, sir. More
muscular in Spirit. More muscular in Faith.'

'I thank you for your kind concern. But I have walked here simply for the view and not to join your congregation.' Aymer looked out once again towards the quay. Why hadn't he been 'more reticent, more taciturn'? It wasn't dignified to be caught in debate above an open grave. 'I thank you, Mr Phipps,' he said again. 'I only wish to see what progress they are making on the ship and then I will vacate this lookout and leave you to your holy duties.'

'See if you can spy your African from there and earn yourself a sovereign.'

'What do you say?'

The preacher explained how Walter Howells had put a sovereign up for anyone who brought the slave back to the ship. 'Warm or frozen. The reward is just the same. There is to be a party organized to search for him tomorrow morning after we have put the sailor to rest in this grave. We'll sniff the fellow out.'

'Why don't you leave the man at liberty?'

'Come, come. We cannot let the man roam free. He is a savage. Dangerous. Unbaptized!'

'You are a Christian, Mr Phipps. You should concern yourself with his emancipation, not his capture.'

'We must first capture the body, Mr Smith, and then we can make amends for that by attending to the emancipation of his soul. Is that not your philosophy? Or have I misapprehended it?'

'Amenders are opposed to slavery. But you are not, it seems.'

'No, sir. Nor are the Scriptures or the saints. I might

refer you, sir, to Moses. And to St Jerome, "Born of the Devil, we are black."'

The preacher beamed at his two gravediggers. 'We will dig a grave for him in holy ground if he is found and he is dead. You cannot say my heart is closed to him.'

'Well, he in't dead, and that's for sure,' one of the old men said.

The second one agreed. 'He in't. He's up to mischief though.'

Between them they recounted all the evidence that they had heard that morning from their neighbours: the theft of clothes and bedding from the inn, the outsized footsteps in the snow, the wind-like, wolf-like howling in the night, the dismembered cow that had been found by the Americans on the beach at Dry Manston. ('Ripped apart it was. By human hands. And nothing left excepting hoof and bone.' 'Not human hands. Not human, anyway, like us.')

'I can assure you, gentlemen, that Negroes do not howl at night, nor do they tear up cows like tigers, nor do they have the six-inch remnant of a tail,' said Aymer, addressing the two gravediggers with what he meant to be a kindly and a patient tone (and an example for the preacher). 'If they are distinguished from the European then it is by their virtues, not their savagery. It is true that the Negro has great strength and must have if he will toil beneath the blazing sun of Africa. But he also has these further strengths of character, that he is cheerful, loyal and does not harbour grudges for the sorrows and the cruelties of life. I do not speak from theory only. I have met with the man. His name is Otto and I promise you, there is no cause to fear the African . . .'

'Not when the blackie's got a pistol in his hand?'

'He does not have a pistol in his hand.'

'Well, that in't so. He's broke into Walter Howells's house and made off with a pistol.'

'I cannot think that that is true . . .'

'And so it is. Mr Howells's place is only two spits down the lane from me. I'm locking up my doors at night, until the man's chained up again . . .'

'*Save a stranger from the sea*,' his friend recited, in his wisest voice. '*And he'll prove your enemy.* They should've let the bugger drown. He in't worth the sovereign.'

AYMER HURRIED BACK with Whip to the inn. Again there were no signs of life. He put his warmest clothes on underneath his tarpaulin coat. He filled his pockets with the half-stale breakfast bread that was still on the side table. He wrapped some pilchards and some cheese in a napkin. Where should he go? He headed out of Wherrytown on the path that he knew best, the one that met the Cradle Rock. He had an image in his head of Otto sitting on the rock, becoming stone, his blackness camouflaged by sea salt and by lichens the colour of mustard. Aymer's legs already felt like pease pudding. His heart was beating like a wren's. He knew his duty now. He knew why he had stayed.

When Aymer was out of earshot of the town, he started calling 'Otto! Otto!' and then 'Uwip! Uwip!' but only Whip responded. His trousers and the skirt of his coat were soon muddy from her front paws and his patience with the dog was exhausted. After an energetic, breathtaking half hour of walking at a speed more suited to a horse, Aymer slowed. He stopped calling out for Otto. He stopped expecting a reply. He didn't even search the countryside for distant, single figures, or giant footprints, or wolf-like cries. He concentrated only on the path. Come what may, he told himself, he'd reach the Rock. And if the African was there? His plan was this: he'd bribe the Bowes to take him in, hide him till the Wednesday dawn, and then bring him – disguised in a dress and bonnet – to the quay at Wherry-town and the safety of the *Tar*. He'd give Otto a job at Hector Smith & Sons. The plan was not preposterous. He'd dress him well. He'd mould him into shape. Otto would learn to read, write, cypher, be a gentleman, and enjoy the status and emancipation that otherwise could flourish only in his dreams. If he was not at the Cradle Rock? What then? Aymer could do little more than leave the meal of bread and cheese, protected from the gulls by stones. That wasn't much of a rescue. But at least Aymer wouldn't have abandoned his freed man for a third cold night entirely without provisions. He must make some amends for the haste and carelessness of *emancipating* Otto without a scrap of food. Without a hat, a weathercoat or money. He wondered if there were a sign that he could leave, a simple warning that Otto would be hunted down and put back on the *Belle* unless he ran and ran and ran.

Of course, there was no sign of anybody at the Cradle Rock, not even fishermen at sea. Something else was odd, too, an absence from the scene. At first Aymer couldn't say quite what. But then he saw the cabin lockers, the seamen's

chests, the double-barrelled cannon, the ship's supplies, the
stacks of timber partly covered in tarpaulins and left for
safekeeping above the tideline amongst the salty foliage of
the backshore dunes. There, too, were the cattle from
Quebec herded in two gorse-fenced compounds. He
remembered. That then was the oddity. The American ship
had been removed. The sea was more remote without the
Belle, as if now its only urgency was moon and tide. Two
days before the *Belle* had seemed to be a solid fixture on its
sandbar. More solid than the Cradle Rock.

Aymer climbed up to the rounded platform, found the
spot that he had shared with Ralph Parkiss on the Sunday,
put his back against the granite mass again and pushed.
How had it ever moved? Its weight seemed anchored to the
coast. A third Ice Age might move it from its pivot stone,
but not a man alone, not Aymer, not a thousand Aymers.
He might as well have put his back against the door of a
great cathedral and hoped to shake the pigeons from its
spire.

He called 'Otto'. Just once. Whip turned and growled.
But no one came to help him with the Rock. He went back
up the narrow path onto the headland and sat down on the
wooden bench where he had rested with Ralph Parkiss
before they'd grappled – together – with the Cradle Rock.
Ralph's initials were freshly carved on the seat, the splintered wood still fleshy brown and free of timber mould.
Aymer put the cheese, the bread, the pilchards on the seat
where they couldn't be missed. He covered them with the
napkin and weighed the corners down with stones. The
walk had made him hungry, and thirsty too. He lifted up

the napkin edge and broke off just an elbow of the bread and one small whang of cheese. The gulls came down to watch him eat. It wasn't yet one o'clock. There was no hurry to return. He took a sharp stone and scratched a careless A.H.S. in the wood. He added Otto's name beneath. And then he circled Ralph's carving with a heart, and added Miggy's initials, M.B., below the deeper, more painstaking R and P.

He walked down to Dry Manston beach, nosed amongst the loose equipment from the *Belle*, walked to the water's edge to see what kelps and carcasses there were, threw scraps of broken timber for the dog. He watched the dunes and the path beyond for anybody passing by. At last he was so cold and thirsty that he found the courage he'd been waiting for. He walked up past the Bowes' kelping pit, along the track where Miggy had refused to shake his hand, until he reached their cottage yard. He didn't have to knock at the door. The two Bowe mongrels leaped up on their ropes and barked. Whip's tail was uncontrolled. The Bowes had returned from pilcharding, it seemed. Thank God for that. The curtain cloth was pulled back and Miggy's face was pressed against the bottle-glass, her red kerchief refracted in a dozen glassy crescents, her cold face flushed with tears. Aymer raised his hat. He mouthed, 'Good morning, Miss Bowe.' She did not move. Her mother opened the door.

Why had he come? He didn't know how to explain except to say, rather lamely, 'I was passing by, and thought I might impose on you.' Again he had the only chair, but on this Tuesday there wasn't any warm mahogany to drink, nor any fire, nor any bending flattery of light except the thin, cold, steady light of day which came in through the window and spread its square and chilling carpet on the earth floor. Should he, perhaps, explain he had the influenza and was merely seeking some respite from the weather? Or that he hoped to gain permission to sketch their cottage at some later date? Or tell the truth, that he was looking for the African, the African that in a day would be brought back as a slave? Was that the truth? Had Otto brought him to this door, this dark room? Or was it that he simply liked it there, its smell of fish and half-dried clothes, its lack of ornament, its womanly silence, its calm?

He watched the women's silhouettes as they made room for him and cleared some floor space for his legs. They gave him water flavoured with a little mint, and bread with beef. Rosie Bowe sat in the corner on a box. Miggy went beyond the sacking curtain, lay down on the box-bed and soon was talking to herself, like young girls do when they are full of hope and tears. Aymer's eyes were soon accustomed to the light, and he could see the room more clearly and just pick out on the chimney breast the few embroidered lines from Jeremiah. 'Weep sore for him that goeth away . . .' he began to read out loud, and meant to say something about Otto. But Rosie Bowe interrupted him. 'Not that!' she said, and stood to turn the embroidery around, so that the letters were reversed and all the working threads revealed.

'She says she's going to America.' Rosie pointed to the bed. 'She says she's going to be with that boy Ralph.'

'I am, Ma. Yes, I am.'

'He hasn't asked you yet?'

'He will, though. He says that's why he came here. So's me and him could meet and be together.'

'He din't choose to come here, girl. He was brought here by the sea.'

'That's why the sea has brought him, then.'

'You think that husbands get washed in by storms, is that it?'

'I do think that. I do.' She hadn't thought it, up till then, in fact – but the image of her Ralph delivered to her in a storm was like a fairytale, and she the princess in her hut. 'Why should I stay here any more?' she said. 'I'm seventeen. There's Oxy Hobbs, she went away when she was only fifteen, and married since.'

'She's gone ten miles, that's all.'

'Well, Mary Dolly, then. She's gone to London . . . That in't ten miles.'

'Gone to be a chambergirl and not to wed, and not gone to America . . .'

'She don't have Ralph, though, and I do. If he goes off without me, Ma, I'm going to drown myself from swimming after him.'

'You're talking wild and silly, Miggy Bowe.'

'I in't.'

'She in't, she says.' She spoke to Aymer Smith. 'She don't know what it means, America. She thinks it's down the coast. She thinks they'll walk back here on Sundays for a bite.'

'I know better. Ralph has said.'

'Has Ralph said how you'll never see your ma again?'

'I'll send you word.'

'How will you send me word? Who's taught you how to write since yesterday?'

'You can't read in any case.'

'So that's it, then? I might as well be dead to you.'

'Oh, Ma, don't start.'

Rosie Bowe sighed loudly, shook her shoulders and her head, stood up, sat down, sighed deeply once again. 'Well, then . . .' she said. She'd have to settle for it, she supposed. She'd never known her daughter so implacable.

Aymer hadn't said a word. Had Rosie Bowe expected him to repeat his offer of yesterday, his promise to 'enhance' their lives by taking Miggy as his wife, in lieu of kelp? She'd said, 'My Miggy in't for you. She's only but a girl.' But had she staged this public argument with her daughter so that Aymer could intervene, and count off the seven certain benefits of being Mrs Margaret Smith? He couldn't speak. He couldn't try to take this girl from Ralph. She would flourish in America. He had no doubt of it. At last he could admit it to himself – her country face would not transport so well to Aymer's home. She'd never be a Margaret. Look at the way she sat, her manly breeches and her busy legs. Listen to her breathing through her mouth, and speaking in an accent full of wind and salt. See, in that half light, the narrow tightness of her face, the unsophisti-cated hair. She wasn't Katie Norris. He wouldn't wish to travel *to the end of tired* with her. She didn't even have her mother's virtues, a kind and ready smile, good, open, unem-barrassed eyes, a spirit made from weathered oak.

'If she must go,' he said at last, 'then, I hope, you will

allow me to . . . to make your new lives less uncertain. I can provide a little money for you both . . .'

Miggy came down off the bed, and stood beside her mother.

'. . . Before I leave, or Miggy leaves, I will arrange a . . . small payment.' He was embarrassed by their stillness and their silence. 'I must leave now . . .' He stood up hastily. He was so clumsy in their house, both in his body and his speech. 'I mean, I must go back.' He shook both women's hands and fled into the cottage yard. He almost ran away. Whip barked and followed him. The two roped mongrels growled as he passed. The sea air slapped his blushing, sweating face. Betrayed, betrayed, betrayed. He didn't stop until he reached the path above the Cradle Rock.

There wasn't any sign of Otto's food or the napkin on the seat. They'd disappeared. One of the stones Aymer had used to weigh the napkin down had rolled, almost, onto the heart scratched in the wood, obscuring Ralph's and Miggy's initials. A heart of stone, Aymer thought. He looked beneath the seat. He pushed the grass aside with his boot. No crusts or fishbones there. No snubs of cheese. There were seagulls about, one-legged on rocks, their necks tucked in. Had they the strength to pull the napkin free of stones? He called out Otto's name again. Then Miggy's name. Then Katie's name. Then all the swear words he knew. He was uncontrolled, despairing, angry, faint, ashamed. He'd missed Otto by a half hour at the most. He kicked the seat. He threw the napkin's stone onto the ground. He banged his forehead with his fist. He cursed himself, out loud. Whip and seagulls echoed him.

If he hadn't been shouting, perhaps he would have heard more clearly what he took to be a distant voice, coming off the land. He called again, 'Otto! Otto!' and yes, there was the faintest voice. It was the echo of his own, rebounding off the rocks. He climbed up off the path onto the headland until he had a decent view inland. The coastal granite bluffs; the bracken and the gorse; a narrow wind-break of stooping skew and thorns; the first low wall; the salty grazing land; the miles of distant fields; the moors. He ranged from left to right, searching for some sign of human life, some moving shadow. He only spotted birds and something that might have been a bending man but turned sideways to prove itself a tethered goat.

At first he thought there was a single, cussed wedge of snow, surviving in the shadows of a thorn which grew behind the nearest drystone wall, a hundred yards away. But when he saw it for the second time, it appeared to lift and change its shape, then drop and hang like washing on a line. Was that the missing napkin from Otto's meal? It seemed to be. Its weight looked right for cloth in that low wind, and it was white and square. Its corners showed against the darker branches of the tree. Surely, Aymer thought, it didn't walk there on its own. And it couldn't be carried by the flimsy wind that had been blowing all that day. He wet his index finger in his mouth and held it up. What little wind there was was heading east. The napkin had gone north. 'We have him, Whip,' he said. 'He's there.'

The going wasn't hard at first. The land was wild and wet, but Aymer made stepping-stones of granite, and even though he slipped from time to time, and had to slither once on his haunches down a mossy outcrop, he found a route towards the cloth, that white and flapping signal of distress. When he reached the dip beyond the headland though and the sea was out of sight, the soil was deeper. There were no granite stepping-stones. The ground refused to take his weight. His boots sank in. The earth expired its brackish coffin smells. His ankle turned. He fell again onto his outstretched hand. He sank up to his cuff. Aymer headed for the bracken to his right, and found firmer footing there, though the gorse that grew beyond was thicker than it looked. He had to force his way through. His trousers and his legs were spiked. The gorse snapped. The air about him smelled of coconut. Whip wasn't happy on this walk. She barked that they should go back to the path. She ran away. She waited. Barked again. But finally she followed Aymer through the bracken and the gorse to the dry, slight rise beyond, to the thorn tree and the wall.

Aymer wedged his foot into the wall, pushed himself up on a low branch, and pulled the white cloth free. His hopes were dashed. It was too big and flimsy for a napkin. He recognized it, though. It was the sling he'd had for his bad arm. He'd flung it to the ground when he had needed both his hands to help Ralph move the Cradle Rock. He remembered how the heavy wind that Sunday had picked up the sling, turned it once or twice, then took it on a seagull flight inland.

He called for Whip. But Whip had gone. She'd scaled the wall and run across the pasture in its lee. When Aymer called she barked for him to follow her. He climbed up on the wall, and clapped his hands. Whip had her chin pressed to the grass. Her tail was wagging heavily. She rolled on her back. What had she found? Rabbit droppings, probably. A rotting crow. Manure. Something irresistible and smelly to mark her coat with. Aymer followed her. At least the pastureland was firm. He held Whip by her collar. She had rolled in something dead. The smell was unbearable. He flipped her over by her legs and wiped her back on the grass. And then he wiped his own hands on the grass. They were as smelly as the dog.

They walked up to a second, higher wall, climbed over it and then headed eastwards towards Wherrytown. To the north there was a lonely curl of smoke, a second lonely curl of hope that Otto might be found. There was a rough gate in the corner of the pasture. It led into a rutted wagon way, the quicker, more direct back path from Dry Manston which the Bowes had used the day before. Their footprints could be followed in the mud. Aymer would be happy to get back. He'd had a disappointing, empty day. Nothing he had done would change the world. The hunting party would go out the next day, and Otto would be carried back, at best half dead. Aymer Smith of Hector Smith & Sons, the meddler, the emancipationist, would be to blame. They'd shared the moment when the bolt was pulled, and he was pointing at the open door and telling Otto, 'Go! Go! Go!' Now they'd share the moment when the bolt was shut again.

The light was fading on that Tuesday afternoon, but Aymer was not concerned. The wagon way would lead to Wherrytown if there was any logic in the world. He only had to stumble on and run the history of the last five days through his mind; the storm, the inn, the salmon flesh, the country wife, the Cradle Rock, the African, the bruising innocence of people far from home, the transience of life and snow, the permanence of all the damage done, and finally the distant curl of smoke which beckoned to him from the north. He didn't know what made him leave the wagon way as soon as he heard the chapel foghorn sound for Tuesday evensong. Except this was his final chance. Go now, while everybody was at prayer. Or be too late.

He concentrated on the curl of smoke, a dozen fields away. There was what looked to be a small stone hut nearby. The smoke belonged to it, it seemed. He'd walk that far, and then give up. Otto, surely, would have sought some shelter, away from the town. He would have lit a fire – and Africans were good at lighting fires from stones and bark. They hadn't lost their ancient skills. Aymer had read the travel journals of men like Bruce and Soules, how Africans could navigate by stars, make light with bones, catch fish by hand, skin cattle with a sharpened stick, survive for weeks without a drink, speak with the birds, protect themselves from wounds and fevers with potions made from leaves. There was a narrow track which led off from the wagon way and skirted three small oblong fields before it disappeared in mud. Aymer checked the mud for footprints. There were none. Or none so far as he could see, because there was a sudden dusk and nothing could be certain in that light. *Get to the smoke*, he told himself. *If he is anywhere, he will be at the smoke.*

He climbed on to the wall. It was wide and flat enough on top to be a path. Someone had walked that way before,

and many times. The undergrowth was flattened. Roots
were snapped. The loosest rocks had been knocked on to
the earth below the wall-top path. Aymer followed it,
leaping over branches, glad to be out of the mud, and
benefiting from the last of the daylight and the low light of
the moon. The whole length of his body was reliefed against
the sky. He looked as if he was ten feet tall, a comic, skinny
stilts-man at a fair, with performing dog. A stringy hedge-
row ghost. A diabolic scarecrow on the move. He found a
route around the patchwork of the fields towards the smoke
and hut, and came at last into the corner of a field that had
been tilled and turned for winter. It looked at first like a
landscape of ten thousand lakes; the mountains were the
ridges in the earth; the valleys, furrows; the narrow pools,
each shaped like icy mouths, reflecting all the silver in the
sky. Again, it looked as if some fairy silversmith had
dropped a cargo of brooches, or tried to plant the soil with
polished, metal leaves. Was Aymer looking down on shards
of ice? He walked along the wall a little further, so that the
shards, the lakes, the leaves, the brooches, could be seen
more clearly. He focused on the smell, before he focused
on the ground. He knew it well. The field was full of fish.
The sea was taking everyone away, and putting fish on
land. There were no leaves or lakes or brooches, just one
star-gazy pie with a four-acre crust of earth and a shoal of
pilchards staring at the moon, their eyes as dead as flint,
their scales like beaten tin, their fraying fins and tails like
frost, their flesh composting for the next year's crop. The
field was absolutely still. The fastest movements were the

snails and slugs which were enamelling the fleshy silverwork with their saliva trails.

Whip and Aymer jumped into the field. Whip nosed about, then started eating. Aymer squatted on his heels, and backed against the wall. The fish had frightened him. Where was the order in the universe? How long before the sky was tumbling with frogs and rats? How long before the ears of corn had fins? He'd never known such superstitious, concentrated fear, nor ever felt so far from home. He thrust his hands into his coat. He shut his eyes. He hung his head towards his knees. This expedition had been mad.

A scuffle thirty yards away made him look up once again. At first he thought it was the dog. But Whip was standing in the middle of the field, her nose pointing, her chin greasy with pilchards, her neck hairs hackling. She'd heard the scuffle too. There was some movement on the far side of the field, ten yards below the little hut and its twist of smoke. Some shadows shifting. Some interruptions to the glinting silver of the fish. Aymer could convince himself he saw someone, crouching in the furrowed soil, pushing pilchards in his mouth. Aymer could convince himself by now that there were wolves or hobgoblins or sharks. But Whip wasn't afraid. She sped across the moonlit pilchard pie and gave chase to a feeding nest of rats.

Aymer found himself a broken length of branch and followed Whip. The smell of rotting fish was soon displaced by that of wood smoke, drier and more bitter. What fire there was hadn't been fed for quite a while. Its fuel was mostly root and bark and tough billets of thorn. Its grate –

hidden up against the north side of the hut – was made from slates and stones that had been dislodged from the roof and walls. There was a flat slate in the ashes, with fish bones. Someone had cooked a meal. It was instinctive: Aymer crouched again; he blew into the fire to try and raise a flame. He got the embers to glow, but there was nothing for their heat to curl and burst around. He searched his pockets, took out the book, and fed some of the *Truismes* by dell'Ova to the fire. The pages lifted, stiffened, blackened, smoked. He tore more pages into tiny shreds, like kindling. He blew again until the hot eye of the fire lifted up its lid and winked a tiny flame. The fire grew strong on aphorisms, epigrams and teasing ambiguities, in French. Aymer's face and hands were glowing now. His pulse had slowed. His blood was warm. He added more wood to the fire. The smoke was damp.

He rolled the last remaining pages of his book into a torch. The ink burned blue. He held the torch up to the broken wall of the hut. It might have been the refuge from the rain a dozen years before for cattle boys. It might have been a winter sty for pigs. Or some hidden place that smugglers used. There was a tiny room inside, not five feet high, not six feet long, not fully roofed, no proper floor, but snug. Half of the ground was covered in dry bracken. There was a cup, a metal box, a demijohn, some more fish bones. Aymer stooped and went inside. He opened the metal box: some candle ends, an apple core, some cheese, some hard-bake, a button, a teaspoon, an empty pot of Dr Sweetzer's Panacea for Salving Wounds and Burns. No pistol. Aymer lit one of the candle ends, and stamped his torch out on the earth. He put the candle on the metal box, and searched the bracken bed. No pistol there. No body warmth. No blood. No anything. The blanket hanging from the wall was invisible, until Aymer almost fell and had to steady himself. Then he felt the cheap perpetuanna of the woollen cloth, and took it down off its twig peg. It was a horse blanket – and like the ones used in the stable and the tackle room at the inn.

Aymer went outside, stood straight, and slowly turned a full circle, looking for the outlines of a man. He dared not call. The landscape of his circle ducked and ridged and plunged as walls gave way to trees, and trees arched weatherways towards the moors, and moors descended into fields and back again to walls and down onto the galaxy of fish. The only light was moon. The only life was Whip's.

Aymer waited for an hour, the horse blanket wrapped around his shoulders and his head, until his fire was almost dead. He tried to find a place for Otto in his life, to make amends inside his head at least, to revive the harmony he'd squandered. Whip snoozed, one-eyed, her fur just inches from the embers. It seemed much later, but it wasn't yet eight o'clock and he might still be back in time for supper at the inn. He woke the dog, found his broken branch, returned the blanket to its peg, put all his change into the metal box – three shillings and a farthing – and climbed again onto the highway of the wall. The moon provided enough light, if he was careful. The branch was helpful as a walking stick. He wasn't certain of the way. There were too many crossroads in the walls. Too many junctions. And, this time, no wisp of smoke to mark his destination. He tried to listen for the sea, but it wasn't as noisy as the wind. At last he found a policy. The wind would come up off the sea at night. The warm attracts the cold. If he could follow routes that led into the wind then he must come finally to the wagon way. Then turn left for Wherrytown.

He found a wall that ran into the wind. He hadn't taken more than a dozen steps when he saw a light ahead. Was it a building on the edge of town? A marker on the chapel? He waited and watched, holding his breath, holding his cudgel-branch. The light was moving parallel to him and in a straight line. And then it took a sudden right-angled turn and was coming, more or less, towards Aymer. It moved from side to side, like a porch light swinging on its hook. Aymer made himself as small as possible. He pushed Whip down onto the wall and held her muzzle and her back. Again the light went right, and then resumed another path towards Aymer and the dog. Someone else was walking along the network of the walls, with a lantern. It wasn't bravery, but cold and cowardice that made Aymer stand up and call out, 'Who goes there?' Such a foolish and dramatic phrase! He even blushed. There was no reply. Perhaps the wind had shredded his words and scattered them inland. This time he called out, 'Hello. It's Aymer Smith,' and then, 'I'm only lost.' He could now make out the silhouette of a small man, walking on the wall with the certainty of a goat. The lantern was fifty yards away when Aymer recognized the busy and ironic walk of George the parlourman.

'Ah, George.' Ah, George, sweet George was carrying a half loaf, some apples and a ripped kerseymere jacket.

'Ah, Mr Smith. Moon-hunting or rabbiting tonight?' George sounded uneasy – and embarrassed – for once.

'Neither, George. I'm fishing in the fields.' He was delighted with his joke, and happier than he could say to have the parlourman and the lantern as companions home, and to have his conscience liberated by the happy certainty that Otto had an unexpected friend.

11. Gone to Ground

THAT NIGHT a chicken disappeared. Amy Farrow found some feathers from the missing bird and the shells of two eggs, eaten raw, next to the coop. There were more feathers outside, in the lane. Had Otto taken the chicken? Was he the beak hunter? Or was this the work of foxes? The older Wherrytowners who had time to gather in the inn's courtyard for sailor Rankin's funeral were in no doubt. If there had been a fox prowling through Wherrytown at night then there would have been a din of squawking, and barking dogs. But no one had been woken. The Farrows' bedroom – an open stage of boards across the roof beams – was above their yard and Amy Farrow said she slept 'with one ear cocked, and never heard a thing, excepting Mr Farrow, wheezing like a steaming pie'.

'It had to be some mighty clever fox,' her husband said, 'to climb our wall and smash the coop door open. And then he puts a spell on both the chickens and the dog and sends 'em dumb. If we had foxes sharp as that we wouldn't have no need of folk. Not womenfolk, at least.'

'I never knowed a fox before shell eggs. They eat the lot,' a neighbour added. 'It's only men and monkeys can shell eggs. And I suppose we know it in't a monkey, unless it was the Devil's monkey. My wager is it was the Devil's *man*.'

They all agreed it *was* the Devil's work. The sooner that they brought the blackie in, the safer they would be in their beds at night and Mrs Farrow wouldn't have to sleep with one ear cocked.

George and Mrs Yapp brought beer and mugwort tea into the yard to warm the mourners while Nathaniel Rankin, still stitched in his piece of sail, was boxed in Walter Howells's birchwood coffin and carried out from the tackle room. Mr Phipps placed a wooden cross on top of the coffin, smiled bleakly at his parishioners and raised his eyebrows for a moment too long when the Norrises and Aymer Smith came down the outer staircase from their room. He would, he thought, require the man (if he were bent on coming to the burial) to stand outside the chapel grounds with his Unholy Scepticism for a companion. He sent George down to the quay where the captain, his crew and the local artisans were working on the *Belle*, and making better progress than they'd dared to hope. They'd have to spare an hour for their shipmate's funeral. Mr Phipps was hoping for another large congregation, and had prepared a careful sermon and found the perfect hymn. He was pleased to see the Dollys from Dry Manston arrive – the parents, three sons, two daughters, Skimmer. They weren't usually a chapel-going family. They didn't even, he suspected, observe the Sabbath if it suited them. He shook the hands of the two older men and nodded impatiently while they explained – in unnecessary detail, he judged – how it was the Dolly nets that had brought the sailor in, and how it was their duty now to see their 'catch' put to rest.

Mr Phipps was glad when the Americans arrived. He was in a hurry to begin. The sailors were happy to have a break from the tedious and unexciting work of ship repair. Their lungs were trained for salt, not sawdust. They were even more content to have the offer of some beer so early in the day. They drank too much of it, too quickly, and when the time came for the four bearers to lift their shipmate to their shoulders in his box, they mismanaged it. The body in its canvas shroud could be heard buffeting the wood. He'd been dead since Saturday, but still the bruises came.

The pebbled passageway which led up through the inn was too slippery with mud, too narrow for the bearers and the coffin, and too steep. They had to put the coffin on the ground and drag it up the steps.

'Shake out his bones, Onto the stones, He's only a sailor, Who nobody owns!' the mate sang, and didn't care who overheard.

When they'd finally got the coffin into the lane, kicked off the mud and hoisted it once more onto the shoulders of men of roughly equal height, they set off to the chapel at such a pace and in such high spirits that many of the older mourners were left behind. The bearers waited at the chapel gates for the preacher and their captain to arrive, and then put the coffin in the graveyard shelter on a slate table. They only quietened down when Captain Comstock threatened them. They plunged their hands into their pockets and smirked into their chests.

Mr Phipps stood at the gate and greeted all his congregation as they arrived. The fittest sailors first, including Ralph Parkiss. Then John Peacock, the sailmaker, and the older crew. Then the Dollys, with their boy Palmer executing an untidy and unnecessary salute at Captain Comstock like some raw volunteer, and offering an awkward 'G'day, Captain' in what was not a local accent. Alice Yapp came next, alone and out of breath. (A wink for Captain Comstock.) The Norrises then. Katie − in her blackest bonnet − was quite beautiful, Mr Phipps thought. He'd make a point of comforting her when the burial was over. Her husband had a halfways decent voice and could be asked to lead the hymn. Aymer Smith was with the Norrises. He even gave his hand to Mr Phipps. The preacher pressed his fingers on to Aymer's chest: 'And have you come to be baptized at last?'

'No, sir. I come . . .' Aymer was alarmed. The preacher's fingers had been hard and hostile.

'No, sir, indeed! Will you then tread on blessed ground?'

'I come only for the burial, to pay respects.'

'Then pay respects to God and stay beyond His wall. You can attend our holy interment, Mr Smith, but from a distance.'

'Come, Mr Phipps . . .' said Robert Norris, taking Aymer by the arm to demonstrate their friendship. 'I see no harm in it . . .' He looked to Katie for some help.

'We would not like to leave dear Mr Smith outside.'

'No, Mrs Norris. Do not speak for me. I am content to be a distant witness.' Aymer wished the ground would open up and swallow him. Already he was close to tears. Why was he always close to tears?

'But, Mr Phipps . . .' she said.

'You see, he does not want to trespass here. He has no interest in Morals, and boasts of it. He told me only yesterday that he nurtured not a single aspiration to stand amongst my congregation. He paraded himself above the chapel . . .' (Mr Phipps pointed at the muddy overhang, fifteen feet above) '. . . and he holloa'd it, as my gravediggers are my witnesses. Now, Mr Smith, do me the courtesy of stepping back. There are chapelgoers at your shoulder who would appreciate an easy entrance to the chapel green.'

'Allow me this indulgence, Mr Phipps, that our good friend should be allowed to stand with us,' Katie said.

'I cannot, madam, no. I am the instrument of God, and have no freedom to indulge, but . . .' But could he reject so pretty, so black-bonneted a request? He turned to Captain Comstock, who was standing just beyond, with Alice Yapp at his side, and Palmer Dolly, hovering. 'What do you say, Captain? It is for your man that we're gathered here. Do you request that Mr Smith should join you?'

Alice squeezed his hand. 'I see no call for it,' he said.

Aymer had already turned his back, and would have hurried out of sight. He would have sought the refuge of an empty room or the company of gulls. But Robert Norris caught his sleeve. 'We'll stand with you,' he said. They led him down a path along the chapel wall, and found a place where they could overlook the grave. They stood on either side of him, white-faced and angry. Aymer's face was red, red not only from embarrassment but from a hardly comprehended joy. What was the song? *For once. For once. For once, at last, he did not stand alone.*

The congregation gathered at the grave and Mr Phipps began his sermon. He wasn't happy – he was furious, in fact – to have lost the Norrises. Especially the wife. She wouldn't let him comfort her now. What could they see in that fool Smith? He put on his Holy Face, his Holy Voice, his Holy Grief, and spoke about Nathaniel Rankin as if they had been friends. 'We must not forget that Death is a visitation of God Almighty. To have the breath of life taken from you is to have your body touched by God. His is the Gift of Life. So when we think of that dark storm when our brother Nathaniel passed from us and his dear face was chilled with the salty dew of life's last struggle, we should not grieve; we should rejoice, because the child of God is back with God, and all is well within His Universe.' He nodded that the coffin should be lowered. Then he read a passage from *The Navigations of the Saints*, threw granite pebbles on the birchwood lid and asked them all to sing 'For Death Is But the Shaded Sea'. Robert Norris's voice was strong enough to cross the wall, and lead the hymn. The congregation parted for his voice. They let it in and did their best to match his perfect pitch. Aymer sang as well. He would have danced a jig.

> 'For Death is but the shaded sea
> Let every lost ship, in the deep,
> Rejoice. Our Saviour's at the helm.
> And He, our pilot Lord,
> Will keep
> The midnight watch
> On Death and Sleep.
> And He, our captain Lord,

Will give
The tidings
That our souls will live,
And oceans, overwhelm.'

When the hymn was done and the shovels were at work, rattling earth and stones on Nathaniel Rankin's coffin, Aymer could have volunteered a hug, at least, to these two allies at his side. He was the handshake not the hugging sort. He wasn't used to taking people in his arms, not since he'd been small and in the care of Granny Todd, his parents' housekeeper. He had, it's true, hugged Ralph Parkiss. That was in an empty parlour, though, and comradely, a manly thing. Here, there was a congregation looking on. He should have lifted up his arms and put them round the Norrises, his hands upon their shoulders. He should have hugged them so tightly that they fell against the wall and toppled onto holy ground. He volunteered, instead, a tiny inclination of his head, and said, 'I thank you for your kind interference.' He added something, too soft and muttered to be understood. But he was hugging in his heart, and both the Norrises knew it. It hardly mattered that they didn't touch. What mattered was that they had stood in line.

They had to touch the preacher, though. He made them shake his hand. He held Katie's hands too long, and squeezed Aymer's hand too tightly. He hoped they had not misunderstood the fierceness of his Faith. How 'generous and Christian' it had been for Mr and Mrs Norris to offer Mr Smith their company while Mr Phipps's solemn duty was performed. Both he and Mr Smith were men of principle and Mr Smith, he was quite sure, could not respect a man who was not 'a Moral rock'. The chapel was for Christians. He did not imagine Mr Smith would wish to make a pilgrimage to Mecca unless he were a Mussulman. Or hope to find a welcome in the sanctums of a synagogue. Though if he did, he would not chance upon such singing there as he had heard today. 'Our Mr Norris has an angel's voice,' he said. 'And Mrs Norris too, of course.' He took their hands again, and clapped Aymer on the shoulder. 'We'll have you yet,' he said. 'I urge you, sir, to read the Scriptures, and you will, I think, find both Faith and Reason satisfied.' By the time he had convinced himself that his reputation was not damaged but enhanced with the Norrises, the mourners from the funeral had dispersed, and Nathaniel Rankin's grave was almost full with earth.

Aymer and the Norrises descended through Wherrytown by empty lanes, except that halfway back a reproachful-looking Whip accosted Aymer and wouldn't settle for a tiny inclination of his head. She wanted him to scratch her ears and rub her chest.

Mrs Yapp gave them lunch, though Aymer had little appetite for fish. When they had eaten and – frankly – needed some respite from Mr Smith's addresses on Mahom-etans, the 'native' ways of making fire and 'the habit in the East' of burning the dead, Katie and her husband walked down to the quay to see what progress had been made on the *Belle*. How long before they could set sail for Canada?

Aymer took a book into the parlour, persuaded Mrs Yapp to revive the fire and wet some tea, and settled to the

Common Sense of Thomas Paine. When his tea was brought, he asked for 'a less idle light'.

'If you want better light for reading by, you'll have to shift yourself to the window or go outdoors,' Mrs Yapp said. She wasn't servant to the man. Why couldn't he take five paces to the side table and find a candle for himself? 'I'm on my own, with George not here, and haven't time to fetch and carry all day long. I saw you wasn't welcome in the chapel, though.' She hoped he'd say something indiscreet about Mr Phipps.

'Where *is* George, Mrs Yapp? You have the oddest parlourman in the land.'

'There's odd, and there's odd,' she said. If George was odd, then what was Aymer Smith?

'Where is he, though?'

'He's volunteered as guide.'

'As guide to what?'

'As guide to hunting down the captain's African. There's no one knows this corner of the world like George. He's better than a hound. He'll sniff him out. He'll have that sovereign off Walter Howells.' She watched as Aymer leaped up like a man who'd sat on pins. He ran out into the lane without a hat or coat. Then she sat down by the fire, tossed *Common Sense* aside, and drank his tea.

AYMER WAS too late to find the hunting party or its hound. They had assembled in the courtyard as soon as the funeral was over. Five sailors from the *Belle* with Captain Comstock. A dozen Wherrytowners armed with sticks and scythes and one old musket which the owner said had 'seen the Frenchie off at Waterloo'. And Palmer Dolly, who had volunteered, and hoped not for the sovereign but for a hammock on the *Belle* as his reward. Walter Howells attended on his horse. He sent the Wherrytowners off to search every outhouse, coop and sty, to check behind wood piles, in net stores, underneath the upturned hulls of boats. He sent the sailors and Palmer, under George's command, to search the local fields, ten deep, and anywhere 'that's big enough to hide a man'.

Howells went with the captain to search the salt-hall and the shore. The salt-hall only took five minutes, and Otto wasn't there – unless he'd been balked and barrelled along with the pilchards. They spent a pleasant afternoon in Walter Howells's room, with good Jamaicee rum. They could watch the shore from there.

'They're bound to bring your Otto back, don't give it any thought,' Howells said. 'We have to think about ourselves a bit. There's matters need discussing, if we're to turn a little black luck into profit.' He outlined for the captain how he would present a bill of repairs that 'would not run amiss with those good gentlemen who'll have to settle it. Let's not pretend we've mended what was never broke. The greedy piglet soon gets pushed out of the trough. The cunning, patient one gets fed.' They'd quickly re-equip the *Belle*, a patch-up job, he said: 'I've put good timber in, of course. Watertight. But not the best. Masts and rigging ditto, Captain Comstock. No harm in saying that you had to lose a few possessions overboard. There's all that stuff we stored down in the dunes. I'll get a decent price for that. And we've some cattle set aside. It's fifty-fifty all the way, if I'm a man to trust.' He poured the captain a fourth tot of rum. He put a purse of sovereigns in Captain Comstock's hand. 'There now. We'll have you back at sea within the week, and nothing to regret from your short stay in Wherrytown.'

Captain Comstock settled back into the cushions of his chair. 'It's turned out well,' he said. He put the purse out of sight, beneath his thigh. The sovereigns hit something hard. He pulled a pistol out from underneath the cushions, a German flintlock with a ram's-horn butt.

'Well found, sir,' said Walter Howells. 'I'd marked it down as being lost or stolen.' He hung the flintlock on its bedboard hook. The two men shook hands, but didn't meet each other's eyes.

GEORGE THE parlourman, meanwhile, had got the five Americans and Palmer Dolly knee deep in mud in fields just to the east of Wherrytown. There'd been reports, he said, of 'trespasses': an open gate, a disturbed turnip clamp, a light at night, goats with burgled udders. At first their search party had been high-spirited. This was more fun than mending sails. They whistled as they walked. They called out Otto's name, and some names that George and Palmer hadn't heard before. The mate began a plantation song and all his shipmates joined the chorus:

> 'Run, nigger, run,
> The day is come,
> The wind gonna ketch you.
> Dat nigger run,
> Dat nigger flew,
> But still we comes to fetch you.'

Once the song had ended, though, the wind began to bite, and legs that were at ease on tossing decks grew tired and heavy in the steadfast, frozen fields. By now the sailors didn't give a damn if Otto were caught or not. He wasn't worth the mud. We're going back, they said. This wasn't mutiny. The captain wasn't there. And George was not an officer, and this was not the *Belle*. George teased them for their lack of fortitude until it was suggested, by the mate, old Captain Keg, that he'd be wise to give his mouth a rest unless he wanted mud in it. He led them into Wherrytown, in an unusually silent and cheerful mood. They went back to the *Belle*.

George and Palmer found the Wherrytowners gathered at an empty cattle shed, on the leeward side of town. Someone, something, was in the loft, they said. No one – not even the veteran of Waterloo – would volunteer to climb up the ladder and search the straw. They were convinced that Otto was hiding there, a pistol in his hand, a head full of mischief, black magic at his fingertips. They'd either smoke him out or wait until he starved. It might be amusing, George thought, to let them try and starve him out. It could take a year or two, before the siege became a bore. But he was more amused at the quicker prospect of being mistaken for a hero. 'He'll never starve,' he said. 'Those Africans can live on straw. Here, let me take a look.' He wouldn't take the musket or a stick or let Palmer, keen to be a hero, too, accompany him. He climbed up into the straw, threw bunches of it through the loft trap, made a din, made choking noises, went quiet, and finally came down with an injured pigeon folded in his hands.

'There, Otto, there,' he said. 'We're going to put you somewhere safe, where you can't do these people any harm, nor steal their chickens, nor rip the meat off cows, nor go howling like a wolf all night. We're going to put you in a pie.'

12. Amor

How DULL it was in Wherrytown. Even the weather was dull, a leaden sky, no wind worth spitting at. And mild! November must have lost its gloves and gone back to October to look for them. The townsfolk – gloveless, leaden too – went about their business making pennies, making pies, helping out with pilchards and the *Belle*. Otto only bothered them at night. Each banging gate, each barking dog, caused wives to wake their men, and men to take a nervous look outside, expecting worse than ghosts. Nathaniel Rankin settled in the chapel green. He was not the haunting kind. The weight of stone and earth splintered the cheap wood of the coffin lid. The mound that marked his grave collapsed and sank. As soon as there was any light two robins gleaned the open earth for worms; a dog hawk gleaned the sky for birds.

Along the coast at Dry Manston there were nets to be mended, sails to patch, peat to cut. No one bothered with the kelp. The high-tide mark was hemmed with it. It was as worthless now as sand. Miggy Bowe had too much time. She didn't want to stay at home. She was uncomfortable there. She hated every stone of it. Her mother hardly had the heart to speak. She just watched Miggy, constantly, and took every chance to kiss her daughter, hug her, wish her well. Miggy fled each day to Wherrytown and idled around the quay, watching as the ship was mended, and provisioned for the voyage with salt meat, potted pilchards, orange preserve in stone jars, dried raisins, blocks of portable soup. She looked seasick already. The sailors nicknamed her the Ghost: the white, unsmiling face, the red kerchief, her haunted, lovelorn voice. Ralph Parkiss slipped away from work at every thin excuse. He gave her one of his best shirts, and promised her a silver wedding band as soon as he could find the money. He'd already signed away his next month's wage to pay for Miggy's passage to America. The captain said he'd marry them at sea and let them have a cabin for a night. He'd take down a side of bacon for the wedding feast. Everyone was fond of Ralph. He wasn't calloused yet.

Ralph walked to the shore with Miggy, and took her out of sight between beached fishing boats. He kissed her on the neck, the mouth, the ear. It was too cold and open for much more. But Miggy was prepared for more. What would it be like to be touched and kissed by Ralph when he was her husband, when they were bucking on the sea with bacon on their breath? Why wait? Why not go off and find some barn where she could throw away her clothes, undress herself from this dull place, and be a naked child again? She wouldn't throw away her neckerchief, though. Ralph said he liked it at her throat. It made him passionate, and she should wear it on their wedding night, and nothing else. She thought that making love was lying still. They'd be like two caterpillars, softly wrapped, and hanging motionless from a fern on one thin, breathless thread. Or like two boats at anchor in the same light breeze, tethered on a single line, and calm. She'd have her body matched to his, his chest against her back, their flesh mollified not made hard by passion, their breathing slow and unified. The love she felt for Ralph would somehow – on their wedding night, or in some barn near Wherrytown – become as tangible and soft as thistledown. No matter what her mother said.

She wasn't pleased to see that Palmer Dolly also hung around the quay, offering to help with any heavy load or fetch some tool or timber from Mr Howells's store. Palmer was too intimate. He called her 'Mig'. He pulled her coat. 'I got a dollar,' he said. 'You want to see it, then?' He put Rankin's dollar in her hand: 'There's fifteen stars on that,' he said. He pointed out the harp-winged, bowered bird on the reverse, and the date of 1794. 'It's old, in't it? It's older than my ma and da.'

Miggy didn't care about the date, the bird or fifteen stars.

'So what?' she said. But she liked the dollar's bust, so unlike the bull's-head portrait of the King on English coins: it was a girl with flowing, unconsidered hair, slightly parted lips, and eyes raised to the sky.

'Don't that look like you a bit?' Palmer said. 'It's Liberty, she's called.'

'So what?' Miggy's lips were slightly parted, too. Her hair had not been combed, it seemed, since 1794. 'Where d'you get it, though?'

'The captain give it me.'

'I bet he didn't. What for?'

He made her listen to his boasts that Captain Comstock

meant – if he were asked – to take him on as a sailor. Miggy was not pleased. She and Palmer might have been sandmates when they were small. But now she was a woman, promised to another man, and ready for the voyage to America. She wanted no one in the rigging except the real Americans. Palmer ought to leave her well alone. She didn't even want to speak to him.

Nor did she really want to speak to Aymer Smith. But he was so insistent with his greetings and his enquiries on her welfare when they coincided on the quay that she had little choice. Besides, hadn't he promised her 'a small payment'? She didn't like to mention it outright. But when he asked how she was looking forward to America, she said, 'I'm looking forward to it well enough, so long as we have pennies for our supper.'

'You'll not find pennies in America,' he said. 'The coin there is called the dollar, Miss Bowe. You will not discover the sovereign's head on it, nor will you find it divides into farthings. The farthing in America is called the cent, though the *scent* of money is the same, both here and in America . . .'

'I've seen a dollar.' She didn't look at him. He wasn't thistledown. This man was badger hair. She knelt and stroked the little bitch which – God knows why – had taken quite a fancy to him. It seemed a lifetime since the dog had first come up to their cottage, the ship's ensign in its collar.

'You've seen a dollar? So then you understand, Miss Bowe.' He stood back to let a length of timber through. 'I see the *Belle* is getting shipshape. How soon before she leaves?'

'Ralph says three days or four.'

'So Tuesday, then? Are you prepared for your encounters with the sea? I promise you – and I have voyaged both in tranquil waters and in rough – that there is nothing you must fear except, perhaps, unsteady feet. Keep your stomach full and sickness will not bother you.'

Seeing Ralph up in the renewed rigging of the *Belle*, she walked away and said (she hoped, she feared, that Aymer overheard): 'It's only money'll keep our stomachs full.'

Aymer hadn't forgotten his promise to the Bowes. But he would wait until the day the *Belle* set sail. Then he could make his payment to this girl and her mother in public view. He might be required to stand beyond the chapel wall in Wherrytown, but they would see who was charitable and who was not. He didn't think that Mr Phipps would hand out coins on the quay. He might hand out tracts. Or New Commandments for America. And Mr Walter Howells, on all the evidence, was more likely to collect than give: a penny tax for walking on *his* quay, a halfpenny for breathing *his* salt air, another penny for the screaming concert of *his* gulls, a shilling for the hire of sea.

Aymer felt unusually well, apart from aching legs. His chest had cleared. His throat was sweet. And his greatest fear, that Otto would be found and sent back to America, had disappeared, now that the hunting parties were returned with nothing but a pigeon, and now that he'd discovered George with his lantern, walking on the walls towards the little hut. Aymer was in a celebratory mood. 'There is no better doctor than the sea,' he told himself.

And he was getting all the sea he could. Katie Norris

had expressed a plan to put the voyage to Canada to good use. She'd make a two-loop necklace from the shells near Wherrytown. She'd have to bore a needle hole in each and then work through the thread. That would keep her busy on the *Belle*. And then she'd always have a little bit of home to wear around her neck in Canada. She and Robert could be seen each morning with their backs bent, searching along the shore in front of the salting hall for matching, tender-coloured shells. If the Norrises were there, then Aymer was as well. He used Whip as an excuse. She had to have her exercise. She loved the beach. So while the dog played in the surf or made life difficult for crabs and sanderlings, Aymer joined the Norrises and made life difficult for them. He had the name of everything. He knew his winkles from his whelks. The pink and glossy chink-shell that she had chosen for her necklace, he explained to Katie, was *Lacuna vincta*. No, he didn't know the common name. Nor did he know the common name for what it was brought him and Whip down to the beach. He might pretend it was *Amicitia platonica*, and that his affections were directed equally at both of the Norrises. But there was a simpler word, as ever. Even in Latin. It was *amor*.

So Aymer picked amongst the seaweeds for her, glad of every chance – when he found an unblemished chink-shell for her throat – to put his fingers in her palm. She would reward him with a smile: 'I thank you, Mr Smith. A lovely one.' Sometimes a strand of sandy-coloured hair would lift up from her forehead in the breeze and reach across to Aymer's face. Sometimes the breeze would sway her skirts at Aymer's legs, or tug the ribbons on her shawl. He spoke most to her husband, but hardly took his eyes away from Katie. He didn't want to miss those times when she bent down to search the sand and displayed her ankles, petticoats, her clothy, apple thighs, her willow back.

His love for her was undeclared, of course. She wasn't like a Miggy Bowe, uneducated, immature, unlovable, within his reach. Katie was a distant star. Aymer wouldn't force his lips on hers, nor write her sentimental letters, nor even make her blush with any open display of his feelings. There wouldn't be a duel between Aymer Smith and Robert Norris, at dawn, with swords. There wouldn't even be a duel of words. They weren't the personalities for that – a chilling thought. There wasn't time. She'd be off to Canada within the week. What Aymer wanted, in these final days in Wherrytown, was simply her proximity. He wanted to store her up, like Rosie Bowe was storing Miggy, to load himself with images of her, to have, if not a country wife, then some lasting, dark companion of the heart. When he was old, the greying bachelor, they wouldn't look at him and say he'd never loved. They would instead remark on how his silences were *her*, whoever she might be, however far from home. What would Fidia and Matthias make of brother Aymer sighing?

The Norrises regarded Aymer as a nuisance. Katie threw his shells away where they would not be found again. The whole point of the necklace was that she would only thread the shells she'd found with Robert. She might wish her husband were a little 'fuller' in his conversations. She might snub him once in a while, out loud. But that was just to show her power. She loved every blink of his eye. When the necklace was finished, she could tell a rosary of love on every shell, his, hers, his, hers, their lives looped round her throat. She didn't want a stranger's shells to interrupt the chain.

By Saturday she and her husband had had enough of Aymer Smith's unrelenting company. They avoided the nearest foreshores and walked instead along the coast towards more subtle coves. But hardly had they found the path down from the cliff and reached the pebble beach than they heard Whip barking at them from above and turned to find their room companion waving at them with his hat. They were still fond of him, despite his oddities. He was too vulnerable and headlong in his dealings to be disliked entirely. And he clearly regarded them as his friends and equals. That was both flattering and charming from such an educated man. He and Robert had a lot in common, Katie thought. Yet she could not imagine two men less alike in their attractiveness. Aymer wasn't resolute like Robert. He wasn't wise. He had, in fact, become an irritant for both the Norrises. They did their best to hide their impatience, though. They didn't want to be impolite. He meant well, after all.

And surely it was only loneliness that made him hunt them down, that made him join them over breakfast, lunch and dinner, that made him sit on his bed at night, a candle on his knees, engaging them in conversations that had no consequence or end, or reading to them from his book, and asking them to comment on his Mr Paine or Mr Lyell or Mr Know-not-who. He seemed to watch them all the time, and be too ready with his feeble, reedy laugh. Katie didn't even want to make love anymore. She felt their every movement could be heard and, if she and Robert whispered in the night, the words would bounce around the room and Mr Smith would hear. She wondered if he ever slept. Was that him wheezing, or the dog? She worried that the man was watching her when she took her clothes off for the night, when she crept out for the pot. Did he stand with his candle, looking down on her, when she was unconscious in her bed, her hair across the pillow and her nightdress disarranged? How could she now get pregnant for the *Belle* with Aymer Smith just yards away?

When Sunday came, despite Mr Phipps's disapproval, the work continued on the *Belle*. 'You will bring God's damnation down on the ship,' he warned. 'Betray the Lord's observances and you will pay the price.' But Walter Howells thought God had all Eternity for His observances, and Sabbaths till the end of time, while he had promised Captain Comstock that the ship would sail at high tide on the Tuesday morning, November the 29th, 1836. That was a day that wouldn't come again. To start the voyage in December, when the sea was at its most unforgiving and the polar ice was sending its outriders south, would be a day too late. It had to be the Tuesday, Comstock said, or it would be next year. So Howells had every hand on deck, tarring timbers, knotting canvas, dislodging barnacles. Most of the Wherrytowners wouldn't work, of course, not even for the extra fourpence on the day. The Americans might leave on time, they judged, but Preacher Phipps would not. And his memory was long and unforgiving. They didn't want to find themselves made to stand outside the chapel walls, or be buried on the common land without a prayer or hymn, or be told their sons and daughters couldn't marry on holy ground. They went to all the Sunday services and made certain they were seen and heard. But there were some who thought it worth the fourpence to risk a stay in Purgatory and help out with the ship. Palmer Dolly, for example. Some of the coastal fishermen, who lived outside Mr Phipps's rule. Together with the sailors, there were more than twenty men. When the chapel foghorn was blown for matins, the hammers on the *Belle* called back and didn't stop for prayers.

Walter Howells couldn't ride his horse down companion ladders nor canter between decks. He had to swagger on his feet, directing what repairs should be completed, often as not with unseasoned, shrinking wood and cordage that was badly chafed. He pointed out what minor leaks or springing planks or damage from marine worm should be disguised with gobs of tar, or battened down with strips of wood. The Dolly boy, he had discovered, would do what he was told, no questions asked. Howells worked him all the time. That ... Palmer? Was that his name? ... might prove to be a useful man in future. Palmer had asked Walter Howells to recommend him to the captain. The boy wanted, it would seem, to be a sailor and go off to America. But Howells considered him too handy and too willing to lose so soon. He needed him in Wherrytown. He'd warn the captain that Palmer Dolly could not be trusted. Light-fingered, maybe? Clumsy? Daft? The captain wouldn't want the risk. Who'd ever know? Who'd ever learn the truth?

That afternoon, when dusk had put a stop to work,

Palmer Dolly did ask the captain for Nathaniel Rankin's place. He was, he said, a willing hand, and strong, and young, and used to boats. He'd been the one, he reminded the captain, to bring the dead sailor ashore. No one had worked harder on the *Belle*. Surely Captain Comstock had seen him work? But it was too late. Walter Howells had already said the boy had fits. They couldn't take a boy with fits on board. The captain shook his head, 'No, sir. Your place is here, amongst your own,' and went to spend his last night at the inn in Alice Yapp's good care.

That Sunday night, they all sat down again to pie. Not squab. Not star-gazy. But good beef pie. One of the cattle in the dunes had 'died', and Walter Howells had given the flank to Alice Yapp. She'd pay him back somehow, when her captain had departed. Again, the young Americans were sitting at the softwood trestle in the Commercial, raucously excited by the prospects of their voyage home, the wives and lovers they might see in the New Year. They envied Ralph. He would be the first to have a woman in his arms.

The large oak table in the parlour was a squeeze. There were two extra places set. Mrs Yapp and Walter Howells wouldn't miss out on beef. They sat with Captain Comstock by the parlour fire. Only George didn't have a knife and plate. He had to serve. And only Otto wasn't there.

'Not pie again!' said Aymer Smith, down at the cold end of the table with the Norrises.

'It's always pie,' said George. 'Be glad of it. That's why the Devil never comes to Wherrytown. For fear we'll put him in a pie.'

At this, John Peacock took up his fiddle and played the

Devil's Jig at George's shoulder, serenading every steaming
plateful in the parlour. When George placed the servings
for the Norrises on the table, John Peacock put down his
fiddle and sang in Robert's ear:

> 'Put the Devil in the pie,
> Hot coals, hot coals,
> Put the Devil in the pie,
> Hot coals hot.
>
> Dish the Devil to your wife,
> Hot coals, hot coals,
> Dish the Devil to your wife,
> Cut his tail off with a knife,
> Run away to save your life,
> Hot coals hot.'

Katie hoped that Canadians would prove to be a little
more self-conscious than these Americans. The fiddler had
almost put her off her meal. She didn't like the way the beef
had whistled when George had spooned it on her plate. She
didn't like the way that Aymer Smith was watching her, as
if she had the Devil's gravy on her chin.

Elsewhere in Wherrytown, the more observant families
had already finished their pies and had climbed the lanes to
chapel. The Norrises wouldn't go. They couldn't condone
the preacher's fierceness at the funeral.

'Master Sacrilege and his bloody uncles, Mr Cant, Mr
Sin and Mr Cynicism,' Preacher Phipps told his smallest
congregation for more than a week in his toughest – and
most alliterative – sermon of the year, 'are not amongst us
with the Lord this evensong. They do not hear the Sab-

bath's holy horn. They do not lay their cups aside, they do
not hand their hammers down, they do not pause in their
profanities. These gentlemen and their dark friend are not
content with building Pandaemonium for six days of the
week, and doing Devil's work amid our harbours and our
homes, amongst our barley and our beans. Now Master
Sacrilege is roaming free in Wherrytown and he is intent
on breaking up the one day in the week when we can give
our thanks unto the Lord, Amen. These freethinkers, the
Devil at their side, are lodged in Wherrytown and they are
labouring against the Lord our God and His Observances.'

His congregation couldn't think where the beans and
barley were. The best they had was thistle-rye. But they
enjoyed this sermon more than most. It cracked with piety
and spleen. And it was thinly coded. They could tell whom
Preacher Phipps was lamming from the pulpit – anyone
who hadn't come to chapel. He thrashed the sailors and
the Sabbath-breakers. Master Sacrilege was 'surely' Agent
Howells (the preacher's most long-standing foe). And that
dark stranger doing Devil's work was, no doubt of it, the
African. The congregation was, for once, excluded from his
disapproval. It was a happy sermon then. They couldn't wait
to sing.

So when Mr Phipps called the first note of the hymn,
the congregation did its best. They sang more loudly,
more zealously, more fearfully than they'd sung for weeks.
They sent the African away with verses beating at his
ears. They drove him back to Hell with choruses. This was
their battle hymn. They'd save their daughters and their
chickens from the Devil's work with euphony. They'd scarify

the night with noise. Their voices could be heard at sea. But Mr Phipps was not entirely pleased. The hymn seemed thin. So did his flock on that chilling Sunday night. He should have been elated. He was not. He missed the finest voice. He missed the finest head of hair.

When Mr Phipps's flock departed for their beds, his eyes were fiery at the chapel door. His goodnight handshakes were hard and purposeful. And unforgiving. But the preacher's fires were dull. He was cold inside. He put the chapel candles out and went back to the chapel house. Usually he was proud of the simplicity of his two rooms, the hardness of his bolster, the bareness of his unplanched floor, the plain wooden cross, the water in the jug. He wasn't lonely with the Lord as his companion. How could he be? That was the choice he had made when he was only seventeen, that he should embalm himself in God. But today he hoped the Lord had not been his witness, had not heard him preach so icily, and did not see him now retrieve the brandy bottle from its hiding place. He warmed his teeth and chest on it. He said his prayers. He could not sleep. His sermon haunted him. Had it been too venomous? It had, it had. It had no warmth, no Christian charity. It was not kind. He was a snake, he thought, a hornet. No wonder people flinched when he shook hands with them. No wonder Katie Norris had not come to chapel. He warmed his teeth again. He was used to dealing with self-pity. He lay, fully clothed, on his bed. He dreamed up better times in Wherrytown; he made amends. He and the Norrises – and even Mr Smith – were spending pleasant evenings in the chapel house. They made a decent four at whist. He called them by their Christian names. They called him John. They put the world to rights over cups of tea. They lodged with him, and somehow he refrained from feeding them on Buttered Tracts or Bible Soup or Hebrewed Ale, or dishing up the Word Made Flesh for supper. And Katie, Robert, Aymer, John were fond companions for the night.

13. Cradle Rock

THE AMERICANS had slept their last night at the inn. That was the end of mattresses for them. They'd spend the Monday night in hammocks on the *Belle*, roped to the quay at Wherrytown but ready for the Tuesday's swelling tide and for the eight hard, pieless weeks at sea which separated them from home.

Their ship had been refitted in a breathless seven days. It would have taken seventeen – or seventy? – if Walter Howells hadn't been there, with his quick eye and his belief in shaving costs rather than shaving badly fitting wood. Was he their captain on the land? Their own Captain Comstock hardly bothered to speak. He still seemed beached. Dry-docked. An Admiral Driftwood who had turned green and queasy as soon as he'd come ashore. But Walter Howells was a Napoleon: shorter, fatter and more demanding by the day. He'd told ten of the younger, fitter sailors that they had to get out of their beds at dawn that Monday morning to fetch the cattle and the stores from Dry Manston beach. He should have sent ten older, calmer men. They would have done less harm. He woke the Americans himself; he never seemed to sleep. The sailors only had to pull their boots and surtouts on. They slept in shirts and breeches. They didn't wash themselves. Tobacco took the smell away.

Walter Howells provided two narrow, open wagons and a pair of nags. He told them not to touch the smaller herd of cattle, but to drive the larger group back to Wherrytown for re-loading on the *Belle*. He gave them two black bottles. 'Keeps you warm,' he said. 'And quiet, I hope.' He winked. He put his fingers to his lips. The sailors didn't give a damn what Walter Howells was up to. Fewer cattle, less work, was all that bothered them. What mattered most, once they were up and out, was that they were freed from the dullness of the town and not yet prisoned by the sea. Two nags, two wagons, two bottles, and the whole day to themselves. They would have a high time on the coast. Still farting Sunday's beef and beer and creased with sleep, they left the courtyard and made a noisy exit west.

Ralph Parkiss was their guide. He knew the coastal path. He led them out of Wherrytown along a half-flagged lane. Some of the sailors sat on the wagon ends and smoked. Some walked ahead with Ralph. They only had to give the horses gentle tugs at first, but once the lane and flagstones ended and they had to climb on softer ground into the wind the horses became obstinate. They dropped their heads, and tried to back the wagons home.

How should the sailors navigate a horse? They tugged the ropes as best they could, but made no better progress than an ostler would if he were put behind a ship's wheel and told to sail it to America. It would have taken them all day to reach Dry Manston beach, if Palmer Dolly hadn't come by on his way to the quay. They pressed him into helping them. He showed them how a wagon horse was like a fishing boat, steered by the rudder, from the back. He found two sticks, and beat the horses on the flanks. They soon put up their heads and rattled off along the paths. Once they'd reached the granite levels above the town, the walkers had to run to keep up with the wagons, and the riders had to put their pipes away and hold on with both hands.

'In't there no horses in America?' Palmer Dolly wanted to know. And, 'What will a dollar buy?' And, 'Has Captain Comstock got a man to take Nathaniel Rankin's place?' The sailors amused themselves with lies. No, they hadn't any horses in America, not yet. The farmers there rode goats. One dollar bought one dozen goats, and there was money left for saddles. No one with any sense would want Nathaniel Rankin's place. His place was up the topmast with a stick, night and day, knocking seagulls off the rigging, 'for no one travels free on board the *Belle*, not even birds'. Palmer knew they were teasing him. He didn't care. He was happy to belong, and to prove how useful he could be, even if there weren't any horses in America, even if the captain had already said he couldn't crew with them. He had a better plan. He'd stow away. He'd take his dollar on the *Belle*.

The riders were numb to the bone with cold when they arrived on the bluffs above Dry Manston, late in the morning. The walkers were as warm as toast, except their faces and their hands. Ralph Parkiss went across to the bench where he'd carved his initials, nine days before. Had they survived the snow? Someone had ringed his carving

with a heart and inexpertly added more initials: M.B. Miggy
Bowe! Ralph blushed with pleasure. She must have come
and seen his name carved in the wood. She'd found a stone
and scratched her love for him. A heart, containing both of
them. He ran his fingers around the heart. He kissed his
fingers and he pressed them to the wood. He would have
put his lips on to the wood if he had been alone, and
tongued the letters of her name. If only he could slip away,
and hold his Miggy in his arms.

He rejoined the wagons and the sailors as they began
their descent to the beach. The tide was high up on the
shore. The strongest waves fell just short of the dunes. The
horses were not happy going down. The rocks were steep
and slippery, and all the sailors had to hold the wagons
from behind or let them tumble with the horses onto the
beach. It took them more than an hour to negotiate the
rocks and reach a wider and less steep path. First came
grassy heathland, then salty flats littered with the flotsam
of the winter tides, and then the shifting dunes, so flimsy at
the edges of the sea that even the roar of breakers, eighty
yards away, and the rattle of the tide throwing pebble dice,
were all it took to make the dune sand blink, and separate,
and slip.

The wagons sank into the sand. They'd have to leave
them at the edges of the dunes and lug the ship's stores over
by hand. Unless the horses could be forced, of course.
Palmer shook his head. 'They in't gonna shift,' he said.
'They've had enough for now. Leave 'em to their bit o'
grass.' Ralph Parkiss thought he knew better. He tried to
pull one of the nags by its head. He held it by the headstall.

And tugged. Perhaps there really weren't any horses in America, thought Palmer. Ralph didn't seem to know that horses could nip. And hard. He watched the old horse nuzzle Ralph's shirt. He saw it bite. Ralph could hardly breathe for pain. When he opened up his shirt, there was a bleeding four-inch bruise in the soft flesh of his stomach.

His shipmates made the most of it. 'Don't let your Miggy see that, Ralph, not on your wedding night.'

'A horse had its mouth inside your shirt? Oh, yes! She'll think you've found another girl.'

'She'll think the mare was Mrs Yapp. She's got the teeth!'

They poured a drop of spirit from one of Walter Howells's black bottles onto the wound. Ralph could hardly breathe again. The pain came back. 'That's firing stuff,' he said.

'Let's taste it, then!' They passed both bottles round.

'It's bottled tar,' one man suggested.

'It's pilchard gin!'

'It's Devil's piss and vinegar.'

Palmer Dolly told them it was treacle rum. He'd never liked the taste of it, but still he drank and passed the bottle on.

'Dear Lord, it's firing stuff,' Ralph said again. 'I need a bit of air.'

'There's air enough out here to last a lifetime.'

'It's not this air I want,' Ralph said. 'I want some air down there.' He pointed along the coast towards the cottages at Dry Manston. It was half a mile to Miggy's home. He could run along the beach and be with her, and then be back within the hour. 'I'll not be missed, I hope.' His shipmates jeered when he walked off – 'Go on then, boy. Don't let her get inside your shirt' – but it was only jealousy. If each of them were young and had a girl a half a mile away, they wouldn't feel so wild and mischievous. Perhaps if Ralph hadn't been the greenhorn of the crew they would have mocked him more cruelly. Seasoned sailors didn't lose their hearts to girls like Miggy. They couldn't marry every girl they kissed. But Ralph was still a novice. That was his charm. He gave his heart quite readily.

The sailors didn't wait for Ralph. Their muscles itched. With treacle rum inside of them, the job of loading the wagons with the loose gear from the *Belle* seemed almost enjoyable. They packed the gear as tightly as they could, but there was hardly space for all of it. The wagon wheels sank into the ground a further inch or two. Water puddled at their rims. They should have brought three wagons and six horses. They'd never get this load up onto the headland without an act of God. They had to half unload again and waste the best part of an hour carrying the smaller and the lighter stores up to the headland by hand. They let Palmer take charge of the cattle. He was less nervous of cows than the sailors were. He went into their makeshift pen and roped the biggest with a length of bowline. He tempted it with grass. And when it came, the others followed, single file, as orderly as ants. They had eaten all the hay that Howells had left and then had cropped their pen back to the sand. They'd put up with anything so long as they could reach the untouched grass. When they had grazed for a while, Palmer held the lead cow by the bowline and led it

up the path to the headland by the Cradle Rock and tied it
to a boulder. The others followed, encouraged at first by
Palmer's sticks. Then the hullabaloo of the Americans
behind them was so alarming that they clambered up
between the rocks like goats.

The sailors had to make a noise. They put their
shoulders to the half-loaded wagons and pushed, and
when they pushed they had to shout the effort out. Even
then they only managed to move the wagons one yard at a
time. It had been easier to shift the *Belle*. They missed their
capstans and their windlasses. They couldn't rest between
each push. The wagons and the horses would roll back,
down hill, to join the debris in the dunes. They wedged
large rocks behind the wheels of the second wagon, and
concentrated on the first. They anchored it with ropes to
boulders at the top of the path. Two men stayed with the
ropes and took up the slack; the other eight stayed with
the horses and forced the wagon forward. The earth was
loose. Cascades of rocks dislodged and bounced downhill.
The Americans muttered every foul word that they knew.
They put their shoulders to the wagon back and screamed
it to the top. Then they cursed and screamed the second
wagon too. Palmer Dolly made the loudest noises of all.
'Tuck 'em in!' he shouted, every time the wheels began to
move. 'And tuck 'em in!'

The sailors spread a canvas on the grass and lay down
on the headland. Their backs and shoulders ached. Their
hands were trembling. They shared tobacco and what
pipes there were, while Palmer Dolly pointed out the Dolly
home, the cottage where the Bowes lived, the Cradle Rock,

the moors and, finally, a tiny figure on the beach – Ralph Parkiss – running along the water's edge, to catch them up. The cattle spread out along the path. The two horses steamed. Palmer Dolly searched the wagons for food. Perhaps there'd be a side of bacon or some sacks of ship's biscuit amongst the gear. 'I can't find anything,' he said. 'There's only brandy.'

'*Only* brandy? How much?' One of the Americans stood up and walked across to Palmer.

Palmer pulled the cases out. 'There's four-and-twenty bottles, at least,' he said.

'And two of them is broken, ain't that so?' Palmer checked again. 'No, there in't one broken . . .'

'And I say two of them has broken in the storm. Now that's a shame! What a bugger storm that was. Brought our rigging down and smashed the captain's brandy. Don't tell me life ain't cruel.' The sailor winked, took two bottles from the case and rejoined the other Americans on their canvas mat. He shook the bottles, pulled the corks. 'Gentlemen, the captain sends his compliments.' They mixed the captain's brandy with the treacle rum already in their stomachs. They were revived and warm and dangerous.

'Another bottle, then?'
    'And how!'
    'The captain'll be hogged.'
    'He's always hogged.'
    'What'll the captain know? If two's got broken, why not three?'
    'Or four?'

'We'll drink the bloody lot of it, for all he knows.'

'I couldn't drink another drop, unless you offered it.' This man had got an empty bottle balanced on his chest.

'Don't drink it, then. Just rub it in.'

'No, throw it over me. I'll smell it when I wakes.'

'*If* you wakes.'

'How many, then?'

'Just one more for the journey back?'

'And another for the voyage home.'

'And a couple for the horses.'

'Don't bloody count. Just drink.'

'We're dead men if the captain knows. He'll put the whip on us.'

'Don't breathe on him, he'll never know.'

'Don't waste a fart on him.'

'Another bottle or not?'

'For God's sake, pull the cork. I'm dying here!'

'Spin a coin. Take a risk. Heads we drink. Tails we spin again.'

'No, I'll throw my hat. If it lands we'll wet it home with two more bottles. If it don't come down again, then what to do but go back sober?'

'Now that's the sort of risk I like.'

The hat came down two yards away. To cheers.

'Go get 'em, boy! Two bottles of the best.'

'Bring six, or I'll crack your head!'

Palmer did as he was asked. He pulled the corks out with his teeth. 'I'll never breathe a word of this,' he said. 'Not to the captain.' They looked at him with narrowed eyes.

'You do, and we'll throw you off that cliff.'

'Let's throw him anyway.'

'No, what I mean is . . . I'll stay quiet . . . I'm . . . hoping you'll stay quiet for me, an' all. I mean to ask you, if someone in't a proper passenger and tried to hide away on the *Belle*, then would you breathe a word of it, if, say, you found him hiding?'

They laughed at this. 'Now, that depends on who it is.'

'If it was that Mrs Yapp . . . Well, she'd be welcome on my yardarm anytime.'

'I'd come abeam for her, that I would.'

'No, say it might be me aboard, suppose . . .' said Palmer.

'What, you the stowaway?'

'I never said.'

'Well, is it you, boy, or not?'

'I want to leave this place, that's all. I want to go to America. I've got a dollar, see.' He held his dollar up.

'Toss it over, then.'

'It's mine.'

'You toss it over, Palmer boy.'

'It's mine to keep.'

'It ain't. Not unless you want to starve. A dollar pays for board and lodging on the *Belle*. It's a fair shake. Ain't that the case?' The sailor's comrades nodded their agreement. 'We'll give you meat and drink all right.'

'Raw rats, Adam's ale . . .'

'Except you'll have to catch the rats yourself.'

They suggested twenty places he could hide: in the bilges ('Plenty to drink down there'), on the anchor deck, between companion plankings, in the canvas store, in the jib-boom housing, in the pilchard kegs, 'up the mate's backside'. It would be fun to have a stowaway, they decided. They were too full of brandy to be rational.

'You're in good hands,' they said, when Palmer parted with the flowing hair of Liberty and threw Nat Rankin's dollar to them.

'I'll drink to that!'

'Let's break another bottle for the stowaway!'

'Let's break it on his head!'

WHEN Ralph Parkiss reached his shipmates on the head-land, there was not a cow in sight, except the bow-roped one. The sailors looked as if the plague had come. Their faces were both red and pale. Their eyes were wild and dead. Their greetings didn't make sense. Their gestures were obscene.

'Hoy, Ralph. Have you come back without your stick?'

'Any more mare bites to show us, sailor?'

'Meet the stowaway.'

Ralph saw the empty bottles on the grass. So what? He was drunk himself. A heart was scratched around him. Miggy had been in the cottage with her mother when he arrived. He'd had to play the model son-in-law and talk about his family and his prospects in America. But then they'd walked behind, into the fields, while Rosie baked the bread. And there he'd kissed his Miggy on the mouth.

'I saw your bit of carving on the bench,' he said. She didn't understand. She blushed, and shook her head. But Ralph adored her shyness. He kissed her mouth again. He kissed her tunic, over her breast.

'Tell me how it'll be when we get to America. Tell me, Ralph.' She let him guide her hand onto his trousers. She frowned, more baffled than afraid. She knew it wasn't right. They held their breath. She rubbed. Was this lovemaking, then? Was this as soft as thistledown?

'America . . .' he said. 'It's hard to think of anything to say . . .'

He didn't tell the sailors what she'd done. He didn't need to. They could tell. He was in a restless mood. 'Come on. Who'll help me swing the Cradle Rock?'

He got four volunteers. But when the others saw the massive rock in motion, they all got up and ran, as best they could, along the grassy path up to the hollow bowl below the tonsured granite of the Rock. They climbed between the arrowed slabs onto the platform where their comrades stood, watching the Cradle Rock dipping on its pivot stone. They whooped like Indians. It was a giddy sight; the drink, the rapid clouds, the undulating rock. They couldn't tell what moved and what was still. One sailor wedged an empty brandy bottle underneath. The Rock descended on the glass, and powdered it.

Palmer Dolly hadn't run along the path to help them with the Rock. He stayed with the wagons, and he watched. He was superstitious. Cradle Rock could bring good luck, and bad. He wouldn't risk the bad.

All ten Americans put their backs against the Rock. They'd see how far and quickly they could move it. 'And push! Let-her-go. And push! Let-her-go.' The eighty granite tons were rocking at their own pace. But the sailors didn't step away to watch. As each decline reversed into ascent they put their hands and shoulders underneath the rock and hastened it. Each time the Rock lifted on its pivot, they looked into the damp and darkness underneath. No one said anything. But they felt stronger than the rock. They could bring it down.

Four men went back to the wagons and returned with iron bars, and lengths of hardwood. They knocked away the loose stones underneath the Rock on the seaward side. They undermined the earth, so that the Rock could fall and rise a few more inches at its outer edge. They tested it again. It made more noise. Its rise and fall expanded on each push. Again they knocked away more stones and earth. They levered with the iron bars.

Of course ten men, no matter what they'd drunk, could not send the Cradle Rock crashing into the sea. It was a hundred times their weight. All they could do was displace it from its pivot stone, so that it slipped an inch or two and rested on its seaward base, to rock no more. They put their ten backs against it when it fell, but they might as well have tried to knock a mountain down. 'And push! And push! And push!' There was no 'Let-her-go'. It was a disappointment then. The Rock had beaten them. The Rock had sobered them as well. The sweat was gelid on their foreheads. The air was icy. Their breaths were sugary and high. What could they chew to take the smell of drink away before they got the wagons – and the cattle – back to Wherrytown?

It was early on the Tuesday morning and still dark, with the sailors nursing headaches and sore backs in their hammocks, when the earth below the repositioned Rock gave way. It could not support the weight. There was an avalanche of stones and earth, which bounced into the sea. The Cradle Rock fell fifteen feet from its platform. It was too big to bounce. It dug into the ground and stopped within two seconds of its fall. Its underside, revealed at last to moonlight, was black and glistening, and barnacled with snails. You couldn't see it from the path. Its eminence was now declivity. Palmer Dolly, on his last night at home, heard the distant impact of the Rock and trembled in his bed. The Rock was down. The coast would never be the same again. He didn't care.

Miggy would have trembled, too, if she had not been dreaming of the sea and how a girl with unkempt hair might flourish in America.

14. The Last of Wherrytown

THE NORRISES weren't the only ones to pack their bags that Tuesday morning and say farewell to Wherrytown. Lotty Kyte was emigrating, too. Her brother Chesney had paid the seventy shillings for her passage, second class, on the *Belle*. Chesney had been a cabinet-maker before he emigrated with his bag of tools. Now, 'after just seven years in Canada', as Lotty explained to everyone she met, he had a wife called Maisie and a factory in Montreal. 'You can't take beds and tables with you. Not all the way to Canada. Too far,' she said as she was led, blindfolded, down to the quay a little after ten. 'The land of freedom it is. Clear a bit of ground and put a cabin up. That's all you have to do. But still, for all the freedom in the world, you haven't got a stick of decent furniture. You can't sit down, except on logs. You're sleeping on the floor. What can you do? Speak to my Chesney, of course! He has the furnishings, and you don't have to pay till harvest time. It's made him rich in seven years. He sends for me. He tells me, Sister, put your blindfold on and come to Canada.' She shook the letter and the ticket which she had received from him two months before. 'He wants his sister by his side, no matter what. To help out with his books. To be a friend for Maisie. A sister can't refuse. My Chesney's odd, but he *is* family, when all is said and done. So I must make this little sacrifice, and blind myself with cloth.' What, her challenge was, could be more logical, more natural than that?

They found a wooden box for her to rest on by the quay. They dusted it, and cushioned it with folded sack, and helped her sit. At first the sailors, stowing stores and luggage on the *Belle*, thought Lotty Kyte was pregnant. The only softness to her long and angular body was her stomach. It seemed distended. But she wasn't fat from pregnancy. She wore an opium bag, tied round her waist, to ward off seasickness. She had three travel chests and a carpet bag at her feet. Every few minutes she touched them with her toes to check they'd not been stolen. She kept her head bowed and her hand across her blindfold for a while, keeping out the harsh sea light. Then she pulled a knitted scarf from her bag and tied it round her head. The extra darkness seemed to comfort her. She was less frightened, and sat quietly, fingering her ticket and her letter. The Wherrytowners who came to stare at her could see a chin, some bonnet and an inch of hair. They morning'd her. 'Who's that?' she asked. They gave their names and wished her luck in Canada. 'You don't need luck in Canada,' she answered. 'My brother says.' They didn't have to hide their smiles. Now here was something they could tell their grandchildren – the blindfolded emigrant!

Lotty Kyte, who lived only two parishes from Wherrytown, had never seen the sea, and never would. When she was born, some Madame Haruspex from a travelling fair had warned the family that if Lotty ever saw the sea she'd die, 'and not by drowning'. So that is how she'd lived her life. She'd stayed inland for thirty-seven years. It wasn't hard – until, that is, she received the ticket from her brother and she was taken to the quay. And then it wasn't even hard, just dark and inconvenient and itchy. She'd take off the scarf and her blindfold when she was in the *Belle*. She didn't have to go on deck. She didn't have to press her nose against a porthole. And even if the sea galed up and lashed the porthole glass, she had simply to pull her bonnet down or hide under a blanket. She would sit as quietly as a mouse for six or seven weeks, hugging opium, and then go blind-folded into Canada.

Aymer Smith, with Whip on a length of rope, had walked down to the quay ahead of the Norrises. He got a short good morning and an even shorter, nervous smile from the preacher, and no reply at all from Walter Howells, who was waiting on his horse at harbour end. Miggy and Rosie Bowe rewarded his greetings with red-eyed, ghostly smiles. He wouldn't present them with their stipend yet.

He'd not expected such a crowd, nor so much noise and jollity. He joined the queue of onlookers, and listened to a dozen versions of Lotty Kyte's life story. Someone, he thought, should tear her blindfold off and let her see salt water. There wouldn't be a flash of lightning or a heart attack. She wouldn't choke on it. At worst she'd die of fright. 'Blind superstition,' he muttered to himself, but loud enough for Mr Phipps to hear. When he saw Robert and Katie Norris arriving on the quay with George as porter, he walked over and repeated it out loud, 'Blind superstition, nothing more.'

'What is?' asked George. 'What isn't, too?' He winked at the Norrises, took the pennies they offered him and said, 'Here's better recompense than soap.'

'No, Mr Smith's soap is very fine,' said Katie. 'I still have a cake of it untouched. It will serve me well in Canada, though I suppose they must have soap in Canada as well . . .' She smiled at Aymer. 'And when I use it I will think of you and these amusing days in Wherrytown.'

Aymer couldn't find an amusing reply. He wasn't looking forward to the loss of Katie and his soap to the colonies. At last, to break his silence, he pointed out Lotty Kyte for them, and retold her story. 'She is your fellow passenger,' he said, 'and she is, I might suggest, a parable of sorts, for emigrants. A poet could not better her. She goes blindfolded into the future. She travels with her vision blocked, but her hopes intact. Are not your situations similar, except without the bindings on your eyes?'

'Oh, Mr Smith, will you not simply wish us God's speed?' said Katie. She didn't want to listen to his lecture. She wanted to sit quietly on the quay, with Robert's hand engaged in hers, and feel the solid stone beneath her feet.

'Of course I wish you speed, dear Mrs Norris,' Aymer said. Her hair was pinned and out of sight. She wore a warm grey cloak with long, loose sleeves. He noted all of it; the rising colour of her face, the laces of her shoes, the 'Oh' before she said his name, her frown. 'And furthermore I wish you every fortune on your arrival there. I would not want you, though, to miss the aptness of the parable.'

'We are not seeking parables in Canada, but three good meals a day, and work and advancement for ourselves,' replied Robert Norris, diverting Aymer from his wife. 'We want only to live plainly and wholesomely, and to find a welcome there.'

'There can be no guarantees of those,' said Aymer. 'No one can guarantee the heavens in Canada will have more stars . . .'

'Of course, but . . .'

'. . . or that the skies will display a deeper blue, or that the soil of that uncharted wilderness will be as rich as cake, or that you and Mrs Norris will step ashore to a spontaneity of well-being and abundance . . .'

'We hope, at least, for better than we have.'

'Yes, Hope is guaranteed . . .'

'Blind superstition, nothing more,' said George. Katie couldn't stop her laugh.

'. . . No, Hope will flourish as you sail further from our shores. Hope is what will greet you when you land. And Hope is blindfolded; her eyes are bound. This is what I mean to say.' The Norrises were hardly listening. Mr Phipps had joined them and had taken Katie's hand. He smiled at Aymer once again. What could he mean by it? 'Yes, this is what I meant to say,' continued Aymer, hurriedly, attempting to insinuate his shoulder between Katie and the preacher. Whip, made nervous by the tightness of the rope, had the good judgement to growl at Mr Phipps's shoes. Aymer lowered his voice for Katie Norris: 'Forgive me for my parables,' he almost whispered. 'I wish to speak as plainly as I can. May all your Hopes come true.'

'And yours, of course,' said Katie Norris, though she couldn't imagine that a man like him had Hopes of anything. 'And we will pray for you.' The preacher beamed at her.

'And I will think of you. From time to time,' said Aymer.

'You will not *pray* for our brave pioneers, I hear,' said Mr Phipps, doing his best to strike a note of irony and not of irritation. 'But, then, you would not claim to understand how little Hope there is without Prayer.'

'Blind superstition,' Aymer said. He was surprised that Katie didn't squander a laugh for him as readily as she had done for George.

'Indeed, indeed,' the preacher said, and arched his eyes. Comically, he thought. 'So Prayer is superstition? And Hope is blindfolded, is it, Mr Smith? And Canada, I heard you say, a wilderness without a chart? I have better news for our two voyagers by sea.' Again, a disconcerting smile for Aymer Smith. Then he turned away and fixed his gaze on Katie's face. When would these men leave her at peace? He said, 'I have the chart to guide you through the wilderness. The Bible is your chart.' He took a small Bible with a brass clasp and green leather covers from his coat and handed it to Katie Norris. 'God's speed,' he said, and would have taken her hand again and forced a Christian parable on her. But Alice Yapp had joined them on the quay and Alice Yapp was the one person in the town who silenced him.

'I have a useful gift,' she said. More useful than a Bible or a bar of soap, she meant. She gave the Norrises a pot of arrowroot for the journey and a stoppered jar: 'Six-Spoon Syrup. That's against the seasickness, Mrs Norris.' She turned and shook the jar to mix the brew. 'Two teaspoons, essence of ginger. Two dessert spoons, brown brandy. Two tablespoons, strong tea. A pinch of cayenne pepper. Now let old Neptune do his worst. A sip of that and I defy you to be sick.'

In fact, old Neptune was in a placid mood that day. The sea was welcoming, with just sufficient wind to fatten up the sails. The sailors came ashore for their farewells. George seemed especially popular. He received a dozen slaps across his back, and twice as many ha'pennies for services and favours at the inn. The captain kissed Alice Yapp full on the mouth and bunched her skirts up in his hand. He waved at Walter Howells, who kept his distance from the crowd. He shook Mr Phipps's hand. He even smiled at Aymer Smith. Then he put his hand out for the dog. Aymer pulled the rope away. 'No, no.' This was not expected.

'She is the *Belle*'s, I think. We can't abandon her.'

'I cannot let her go.' How many days had passed, he wondered, since he'd last squared up against the captain, in the snowy lane above the inn, and been accused of theft? ('Not only do you steal my man, you steal my dog as well.') This time he wouldn't hide behind a lie. He'd take the beating if it would rescue Whip. 'It is not possible,' he said. 'No, no.'

'Must I ask half a dozen of my men to take her off you?'

'No, sir.'

'Then let me have my dog. What, would you have us settle here and not go home? We'll not go home without our property.'

'I'd pay ten shillings for her, happily, or twelve,' Aymer said. Would Whip abandon him, if he let go of the rope? 'I beg you, leave her in my hands. She has quite adopted me.' His voice was calm; his thoughts were not. Would he go home without a single friend? '*Twenty* shillings, sir.' He'd liberate the dog. He'd snap her chains of slavery. The thought was not preposterous.

The captain laughed at Aymer's shillings ('A ship without a dog?') and shook his head. He took hold of the rope and snapped it out of Aymer's hand. Whip didn't seem to mind. She liked the smell of shoes and legs, it didn't matter whose. The captain shook George's hand. A sixpence passed between them. 'Good man, George. And if you ever want a place at sea . . .' The captain put his arm round Mrs Yapp again. 'Next trip,' he said. 'We could be back within the year. Now, let's aboard.' He tugged at Whip. Aymer should have snatched the rope and run. At least he should have stooped and rubbed Whip's head and wept into her hair. Instead he stayed as stiff as pine, between the preacher and the parlourman, and watched the ship's dog disappear for good.

They rang one bell to call the crew aboard. Three men were sent to load the passengers' bags and boxes. Palmer Dolly, 'unremarked amongst the crowd', ran forward to lend a hand. He lifted Lotty Kyte's heaviest box onto his shoulders and carried it on to the *Belle*. No one challenged him. And no one missed him for a while. He hadn't said goodbye to anyone. He simply disappeared into the shadows – and the bloodstains – of the orlop deck. He'd have the salvaged cattle for company at first. And then he'd have their straw bedding to himself, until America. Soon the sound of falling lightlines and hoisting canvas filled the air. 'And pull! Let-her-go.' The sailors were a team again. The captain was Napoleon. The mooring ropes were loosened, the fenders lifted and the jib sail set to take the port tack out of Wherrytown for the emigrant ports of Fowey and Cork before the weeks in open sea. They rang the final bell, this time for paying passengers to come aboard.

Aymer would have liked to hug the Norrises, but he could only shake their hands. They walked away towards the *Belle*, and joined their two fellow voyagers, Lotty Kyte and Miggy, at the bottom of the ship's gangway where Ralph Parkiss was waiting for his bride. Katie Norris went ahead, keen to get away. Robert Norris took Lotty's arm and guided her onto the *Belle*. Her hands were shaking from the dread of it. Her eyes were hot and watering. 'My brother can supply your furnishings when we arrive,' she said, just to hear a voice.

Rosie Bowe had Miggy in her arms. She planted kisses on her neck and face. Her sobs were animal, a seal. She didn't have the breath to speak. Her throat was aching from the tears and cries she had suppressed all morning, all week. Her eyes were raw. Ralph put his arms around them both and made promises: he and Miggy would find someone to write a letter if Rosie would find someone to read; they would send for her when they were rich; they would name their first daughter Rosie Parkiss; and, come what may, they would return one day before she died. But Rosie Bowe did not believe in that. She only knew that all the bone and sinew of her life was leaving on the *Belle*. 'Be good to her,' she said to Ralph. She gave her gifts to Miggy in a straw bag: some salted beef, the petticoat her sister had made, a baby shawl, one of the bars of soap that Aymer Smith had left, and the embroidered passage from the cottage wall, 'Weep sore for him that goeth away . . .'

'Oh, Ma, don't fret,' said Miggy. 'I'll end up crying too. And that's bad luck. That in't the way to go.' She put her arm through Ralph's and took her first step on the *Belle*. She didn't look at Rosie Bowe. Her eye was caught by Aymer Smith approaching from the crowd. At last. She'd almost given up on him.

Aymer ran up to the gangway. He stood between Rosie and her daughter. He took his purse out of his coat. And handed three bright sovereigns to the girl. ('What's going on?' said Alice Yapp out loud. 'What has old spindleshanks been doing with the girl that's worth that weight of tin? Now there's a tale. I'll find the bottom of it, don't you worry.') There wasn't any time for Aymer to make a speech. Miggy took his money without a word of thanks, though Ralph shook his hand. The captain rang the final bell, to pull the gangway up. And that was that, and nothing much to celebrate.

The *Belle* had soon left the perils of the shore. It slowly dropped down-channel against the tide and waited on capricious winds to take it out beyond the harbour boom and between the channel buoys. It idled there, in the offing, for half an hour. The quayside crowd could pick out Lotty Kyte on deck, still blindfolded, and the Norrises. Then the light picked up, and with the light the sea, for light can energize the sea and make the waves more spirited. The wind did not diminish as they feared. It held – and more than held. The ship turned stern to Wherrytown and beat a passage through the bay up to the Finters, those final, storm-racked morsels of the land where there were only cormorants and kelp. Within the hour the *Belle of Wilmington* had dissolved into the fog-veiled precipices of cloud, and Rosie Bowe, heartbroken on the quay, had nothing left to do but set her face against the wind and walk the six miles home.

If she had waited for ten minutes more – as did Aymer Smith – she would have noticed the fog-cloud thicken where the *Belle* had disappeared and a yellow twist of smoke make smudges on the white. The coastal steampacket, *Ha'porth of Tar*, passed within fifty yards of the *Belle*. They rang their greetings across the water, and Lotty Kyte, reluctant to abandon the sea air and the deck, waved both hands into the darkness and had no fear. It seemed to Aymer that the tussling spirits of the age were passing on the sea; the old, the new, the wind, the steam, the modest and the brash. The future would be driven by steam, he was sure. It was a more compliant slave than wind. Already there were steam coaches, steam looms, steam threshers, and he had heard of a machine that could hatch eggs by steam. 'There'll be no need for men and chickens soon,' he thought. 'There'll be no need for sails on boats either. A shame.' And such a shame as well that there wasn't anyone to share his observations with. The quay was empty now. Aymer went in search of educated company, George, perhaps, or even Mr Phipps.

The *Tar*, its progress simplified by steam, put into Wherrytown with no one there to watch – unless there was someone, lost behind the town, with nothing else to do but stare and wonder if the *Belle*'s departure was a liberation or a curse.

Aymer Smith didn't find educated company. He went back to his room. His own bed smelled of Whip. He lay down on the Norrises' double bed, his boots still on, his face pressed into the mattress. He smelled where Katie Norris had been, and would have masturbated there and then had not Mrs Yapp come in on some thin pretext and plagued him with her nosiness.

'In bed? Are you not well, Mr Smith?'

'I am entirely well, despite a malady of spirit.'

'What's that then? Fever? I'll bring you a pennyworth of something for it, if you want.'

'I suffer from a sentimental malady, Mrs Yapp. A penny-worth of peace and quiet is all I want.'

Mrs Yapp was not the sort to take offence. 'Don't suffer for that Miggy Bowe,' she said. 'She's gone and in't worth the fever.'

'I have not got a fever, Mrs Yapp. Nor do I suffer anything for Miggy Bowe . . .'

'I think you have been singed by her, though. You can say.'

'Good heavens, she's a country girl! What dealings could I have had with her?'

'Now there's a question to be asked, and asked by anyone who saw you handing money to the girl.'

'Phaa, Mrs Yapp!'

'I'm only mentioning . . .'

'Then please to mention nothing more. I have no head

for it.' He stood up and looked out on to the courtyard, with his back to her. 'I have business dealings with the Bowes, the younger and the elder both, regarding the manufacture of our family soap. As you well know. Those coins that I gave were kindly recompense for their loss of kelping. My pocket has been singed by her and nothing else. I aim to give some coins to the mother, too. And so you see there is no gossip to be brewed from it.'

'That is uncommon kindly, sir. For Rosie Bowe will want a little helping, what with her Miggy gone, the kelping finished with and bad luck all along the coast. You heard the Cradle Rock's pushed down?'

'The Rock pushed down! And how is that?'

'That blackie done it, Mr Smith. Pushed it halfway down the cliff.'

'Then it's the work of Nature. Otto would not have the strength for that.'

'He must've done. It's him, all right. He signed his work. They say he's put his name to it, scratched in some piece of benchwood that they found . . .'

Aymer walked out of the room and pulled his coat on as he ran along the inn's odd levels to the parlour and the lane. No Ralph. No George. No Whip. He had to walk along the coast alone. He hadn't known he had such energy or speed. His coastal walks had made him healthy. Now he could almost run. Six miles was not a trial.

Mrs Yapp had not exaggerated. The Cradle Rock had fallen on its side, and where the rock had once pivoted was now a newly opened cave, musty, colourless and wet, with streaks of bird lime and the bones of rats amongst the debris of the stone. When Aymer came, a group of fishermen were standing where the rock had been, talking in low voices with their hands across their mouths, as if they feared the wind would take their words away. Walter Howells was standing on the pivot edge, looking down on to the toppled Rock. He had his pistol in his jacket belt. 'That's never coming up again,' he said. 'That's going to end up in the sea. A thousand shillings wouldn't put that back in place. Don't even ask.'

Skimmer and two of the Dollys climbed up from the headland rocks and joined their neighbours.

'There in't no sign of him,' said Palmer's father, Henry.

'How long's it been?'

'Most half a day. He wasn't there when we put up the nets. We sent the dogs out looking for the boy. And we've been hollering his name all morning.'

'He'll show up,' said Skimmer.

'Bound to.'

No one dared say 'cannibal'. Palmer would show up all right, his bones picked clean, his blood drunk dry, his sable hair as lifeless as a mat. They blamed themselves. They'd had Otto almost in their hands. They should've tossed him in the sea. They should've kept him chained and gagged.

'You'll have to put a bullet through the bugger's heart, Mr Howells,' one fisherman said. 'Or else what? If he can down a rock that size and on his own, then it'll be our cottages next. He'll snap our boats in two. He'll rip the country up, so help me God.'

His neighbour stooped amongst the bones and lifted up a piece of broken glass. He put it to his nose. 'That's brandy

I can smell,' he said. 'And fresh.' The fishermen looked nervously inland. What now? They even turned to Aymer Smith for his advice, but he had none, or none at least that they would want to hear.

Aymer went down to the beach, past the thirty cattle from the *Belle* which were still fenced off by snaps of gorse amongst the dunes, awaiting agent Howells. The tide was high, almost on the turn, and heavy with weed. The kelp! He had forgotten it though it had brought him there. In that tumbling clarity of water, the weeds were as vibrant and seductive as a satin-merchant's shop. The mustards and the crimsons he had seen when Ralph and the Bowes were fishing for their cow were no longer there. The seaweeds that he saw were darker, more mature, the sort of satins worn by spinsters, dowagers and chaperones, in mauves and browns and greys, the sort of satins favoured by the old.

IT WAS the third time that he'd knocked on Rosie Bowe's front door. The dogs recognized him now. They didn't bark. She let him in and put him in his usual place. There was an idling fire, and the smell of Sunday's beef stew, saved for the dogs and greening in the pot. Aymer leant across and put three sovereigns on the shelf above the hearth. He didn't want to justify the gift, or ornament it with a speech. He simply clicked each coin on the wood, so that she wouldn't have to guess how much there was. He understood her independent mind, he thought. He was the independent sort himself. And he was keen to avoid her independent tongue, as well. He couldn't forget her thrashing temper when he'd first offered her his help: the kelper's shilling and the soap. 'That in't no use,' she'd said, not guessing what a friend and benefactor he might be. 'It's a bad-luck shilling and we'll have none of it.' This time he wouldn't preach at her, but carry out his duties without a word. His promise would be kept and his debt settled. She could pick the money up, or leave it there for ornament, or throw the bad-luck coins out. That responsibility was hers.

Rosie dished a plate of stew. The dogs could go without. No matter how upset she was and wanting privacy, she could hardly let her visitor shiver in his chair and not provide the victuals for his journey back. The beef did not taste good, but Aymer forced himself to chew on it, and eat the horn of home-bake and drink the lukewarm minted water that she gave him. It seemed important that he should finish everything. These were her modest thanks to him, he thought. He occupied himself with food. Where should he look, but at his spoon and plate?

She stared at him, expressionless. If he looked up from eating, her mouth and eyes grew narrow in the half dark-ness. Her face became invisible. Her teeth and eye-whites disappeared. She gave no sign of breathing. If she had lungs, they must have been in her legs. She was ill at ease with Aymer Smith, but not as ill at ease as he was, alone with her. Despite the comforts of the fire, the chair, the smell of food, he felt displaced, a vagrant, over-feathered bird on a starling's nest. He was too big and cultured for that room. Nothing that he valued in himself had any value there. His modest wealth, his manners and his education – what did they count for? His charity? His Scepticism? His love of conversation and debate? His unexpected sympathy for dogs? His democratic spirit? His prodigious memory for Latin names? Which amongst these attributes should Rosie Bowe admire? Which of his parts and virtues could she burn for candle wax, and which would stew well with a turnip root? What use were manners for catching fish? Would Scepticism make a sauce? Would education batten down the roof against a lifting wind? Would love of dogs bring Miggy back? Aymer understood her narrowed eyes to mean, 'You in't no use to me!'

And he was right to some extent. For all his clumsy innocence, for all his clicking coins on the shelf, she didn't value him. He was no use to her. He'd disappear like all the other passing gentlemen on their pedestrian expeditions through Dry Manston. Rosie had met a hundred men like Aymer Smith. They weren't rare. Not in the summer anyway. They'd stop to sketch the cottage or ask the way. And then, what questions they would put! What was the folklore thereabouts? What were 'conditions' on the coast? What weather might be signified by easterlies? Which were the places where the seals came in? They'd make notes, persuade her to provide a plate of 'whatever's cooking on the fire', look Miggy up and down as if she were a horse, donate a penny, then make their farewells – their plates not empty and their eyes not looking into hers, yet claiming that their lives had been enhanced by this encounter and exchange.

But Rosie's life hadn't been changed. She wasn't enhanced by meeting gentlemen, and feeding them. No matter how they loved the 'emancipations' of sea and air, they didn't stay for long enough to make their mark on her.

They soon grew tired of pauper food, and Rosie's conversation. They'd come for landscape, beauty, history. They didn't want to taste her life. They disappeared without a trace. Like Aymer would. Except that he'd not grown tired as quickly as he might. He had at least stayed long enough to taste her life. And, by the looks of it, he would leave an empty plate.

Rosie watched him forcing down the stew, and tearing off small bites of home-bake as if he expected it to bite him back. He wasn't used to wooden spoons, or eating off his lap, or chewing outskirt cuts of beef, or sitting on uncushioned wood with nothing overhead but a thatch of turf. She ought, she knew, to take the plate away. But let him eat like dogs before he goes, she thought. Let him get the tough and joyless taste of it. Let him gag.

She was fascinated by the man's timidity. He was as nervous as a child. He didn't even dare to push his plate aside. He'd rather make a penance of the beef. If she let him finish every scrap and then put a second helping on his plate, would he eat that as well? She'd rap his knuckles if he didn't eat it up. She'd box his ears. She smiled her first smile of the day. At last she couldn't watch him any more. 'You've had enough,' she said.

'No, no.'

She took the plate away and put it outside for the dogs. 'They're glad of it.'

'A dog that dines on beef is king,' said Aymer.

Rosie laughed out loud at that. 'And what's a king that dines on beef?' she asked. 'Is he a dog?'

'That is not logical,' said Aymer, glad to have this gristle

for his intellect, and be free of gristle in his mouth. 'A king
that dines on bones might well be called a dog, I think you
will agree. But the vice versa is not true. A dog that dines
on bones is still a dog. You would not say he was a king . . .'

'If they was beef bones, though?'

'Then what?'

'Then dogs and kings might share a plate, and that
would be a day worth living for, in't that the truth?' Aymer
thought it was the wittiest of truths, and told her so.
Again she narrowed her mouth and eyes, and seemed both
unamused and unflattered by his laughter and approval.

He tried to find some common ground with her. He'd
see how sharp and witty she could be on other topics. But
she didn't want to talk about the beauty of the kelp, or the
bizarre case of blindfolded Lotty Kyte, or hear the great
debate between Wind and Steam. She hadn't any views to
share on Blind Superstition. Nor did the tumbling of the
Cradle Rock much interest her. The fishermen were idiots
if they thought one man had pushed it down. 'It must've
been those Americans,' she said eventually. 'I saw them on
the headland yesterday. There's nothing to be feared of
them. Not now. They've gone. And Miggy, too.' At this
her eyes were narrowed even more. She screwed them up.
She hid them with her hand.

'Your daughter, Mrs Bowe, will be well under way by
now. I am happy that the sea is placid for her,' said Aymer.
'She will be sorely missed, of course. But Ralph Parkiss is a
decent young man. I had the pleasure to be acquainted
with his character. And he with mine. He would regard me
as a friend. And – you will believe me, I am sure – he will

regard your daughter with affection. Do not alarm yourself on his account. There are few better sons-in-law, though he be only young and poor. It may be that there are men of better standing and more generously provisioned . . . ah, that is . . .' Aymer, too, put his hand across his face, to hide his embarrassment. 'I do not mean myself, of course. Though I am neither young nor poor. I would not make a son-in-law for anyone. I am not the husband kind. I was foolish to have ever entertained the thought of it . . .'

Again, Rosie Bowe was imitating seals. She tried to trap their calls inside her mouth. She tried to swallow them. Aymer thought, at first, that she was trying to suppress a sneeze. But he had wept enough himself to recognize a stifled sob. What had he said? Why should she care that he would not make a son-in-law for anyone? Was that so sad for her?

He almost asked her not to waste a tear for him. He wasn't worthy of her sympathy. But there was something in the way she cried that kept him quiet and gave him time to realize the shaming truth, that no one cried for Aymer Smith. Her tears were for her daughter and herself. They were unstoppable. She'd drawn her legs up to her chest and had her hands laced round her wrists. Her head was on her knees. She had halved in size. She was like a woman out of Bedlam, hot, white-knuckled, volatile. Why should she care if Aymer Smith was there and watching her? She didn't know the protocol of grief. Her cheeks were wet, and then her lips. Her chin was leaking on her dress. Her nose began to run, and she was sniffing back the tears and swallowing them. Her breathing next: her lungs were working overtime.

Her throat was wet and windy, and the noises that she made now belonged to gulls, not seals. Her shoulders shook. Her body lost its bones. Her hands were knotted wood. Her hair was weed. She said, 'This is bitter . . .'

Aymer Smith was too ashamed to move at first. 'Can I do anything?' he said. She didn't hear. She banged her fists against her head. She threw her head back on the wall. His three sovereigns rattled on the shelf.

'I beg you, Mrs Bowe . . .' He took one step across the room and put his right hand on her shoulder. 'Come, come, you will upset yourself . . .'

Her head came up from off the wall; her forehead rested for a second on his hip, and then her head went back again and bounced against the wall.

'I beg you, Mrs Bowe,' he said again. 'You are damaging yourself.' Perhaps he ought to throw some water over her. He couldn't see a bucket or a bowl. There was only beef stew in a pot. That wouldn't help. He put both hands behind her head and tried to steady it. She was surprisingly strong, and Aymer was too gentle. He should have held her by the ears or hair. Instead he clasped her head tightly to his body, and called for help. He didn't have a name to call. The nearest neighbour was a quarter-mile away. His sister-in-law, Fidia, would have quietened Rosie straight away, with a glass of water and a slap, both in the face. He'd seen her do it with their kitchen girl. But calling 'Fidia!' would be no use. And simply calling 'Help' seemed too theatrical. So he called out, 'Anybody! Anybody!' And it worked. Nobody came. But it had startled Rosie. She stopped trying to break away from Aymer. Had that been his intention? He wasn't sure of anything, except that dreams and nightmares were the same.

So the oddest thing had come about. Steam and Wind were reconciled. This pair of awkward, independent Contraries were pressed together like two pigeons in a storm – though they weren't as plump as pigeons. Rosie could feel his rib cage on her face and, now that she was quiet, she heard his stomach dealing comically with stew to the quickening percussion of his heart. She'd always liked a man's hands on her head, his fingers hard on her skull and hidden in her hair. Her tears had made Aymer's shirt-front damp. He smelled of good soap, and dog. She didn't want to pull her head away and face him. What could they say to save their blushes? Besides, his hands around her head were calming her. Miggy had not hugged her Ma for years. So any hugging at that time would help.

What did she want? She didn't know, except that she was in no hurry to begin the last part of her life alone, a piece of salted granite on the coast. She might as well . . . She might as well, she told herself, have someone hold her in his arms, even if that someone was this creaking, timid stick. When he had shouted, 'Anybody! Anybody!' he had expressed her feelings too. Will anybody ever hold me to their heart again? Will anybody try? He'd had his chance to take his hands away. But he'd left them in her hair. She put her own hands on his waist and then on to the lower part of his back. He could be anyone she chose. She only had to keep her eyes shut tight.

She chose to look at him. 'Come on,' she said. 'You can.' She pushed aside the sacking curtain that divided the room and tiptoed across the cold bare earth to the box-bed. He didn't follow her. She had to go back to the fire and pull him by his wrist. She ought to feel ashamed, she thought, pressing him like this. Any man she'd known before had pulled *her* wrist. This one was reluctant even to be pulled. Did she disgust him? Was he just shy? Was he one of those men, like Skimmer or George at the inn, who only liked to be with other men? She put her arms around his waist again. 'It in't important, Mr Smith,' she said. 'Just put your hand back where it was, so that I can get the crying out of me.' Aymer put one hand onto the nape of her neck and pushed her hair up on to her crown. He put the other hand behind her back and pulled her to him so that his lips were on her forehead. His lips were dry. She did cry for a minute or two, though Miggy was confused with Aymer in her mind. She couldn't prise the two apart. Who was she hugging? Why? That dry-lipped kiss drew out her final sobs. She took deep breaths. She wouldn't grieve any more for Miggy. She had to settle to her life.

Rosie had never known a man as slow as Aymer. His lips and hands had hardly moved. They were standing like two dancers at a ball, waiting for the music to begin. She *had* to settle to her life. She pushed her hands beneath his parlour coat and pressed her head against his chest. She could feel his body tensing. Was he excited by her now, or was he repelled? She held him tightly, one hand spread out across his back, the other underneath his arm. She couldn't kiss him though, not on the mouth. His cock was growing hard.

'I only need someone,' she said.

'I can't.'

'You can.' She dropped a hand on to his trouser front, and pressed him there. He doubled up. She thought his legs had given way, at first. His body sagged. He gasped so loudly that the dogs outside jumped up against the porch, and one began to bark. He reminded Rosie of the first boy that she'd ever touched, when she was seventeen. And Aymer, really, was just a boy, despite his age. He'd been slow with her, she realized, because he didn't know the way. This was a voyage frightening and new for him. Rosie was his first. And she would have to take command or wait forever.

She took him through the sacking, pushed him on the bed, tugged his boots off, and unbuttoned him: the jacket, the shirt, the cuffs. She pulled his trousers down, and joined him on the bed. She didn't take her own clothes off. She was embarrassed by her bones. She stroked him on his chest and legs, but wanted really to be stroked herself. At last he found the courage to explore her. His hands were shaking when he pushed her smock up to her throat and put his fingers, then his mouth, onto her tiny breasts. She had to take his other hand and press it in between her thighs. He pushed so hard she almost doubled up as well. It seemed so odd that she should be excited by this man and that he – hesitant and clumsy, at first – had become so urgent and engrossed.

When Aymer finally ran his fingers up her legs, her hands went dead on him. She fell over on her back, closed her eyes and simply held his body close. Again he didn't seem to know the way. His fingernails were too long. His shirt sleeves tickled her. He didn't know how delicate she was, or what to touch. She let him fumble for a while, and then she helped him, holding his fingers between hers until there was no dryness left. If he thought that he would be the centre of attention, he was wrong. She concentrated on herself – looking at him, talking to him only when his hands and fingers were too rough or slow. She didn't try to touch him any more. He was not there – except to be her serving gentleman. But she was more there all the time – getting bigger, narrowing; becoming stretched, tense, bloated . . . tremulous. She climaxed on his fingertips.

Aymer looked both startled and afraid, she thought. 'Are you quite well?' he asked, evidently alarmed by all her noise and agitation. He must have imagined that she was feverish, or suffering from fits.

'I'm well. I'm well,' she said. 'And what of you? Let's see.' She put her hand down on his cock. It wasn't hard, but it was stiff enough to rub. He rolled on top of her and butted at her legs. She put his cock inside. He wasn't slow. Ten thrusts and that was it. The bubble burst. Not sexually. His orgasm was nothing much. It had been better in the inn's dank alleyway. No, the bubble was the trance that had bewitched him the moment he had touched her hair. It was the same trance that he had felt, less fleetingly, with Katie Norris. To be alive and in such half-a-dream was rhapsody. But this was odd and unexpected for Aymer Smith. The instant his virginity was lost with his ejaculation, there was no longer any rhapsody. There was no trance. This was sober. He'd never felt so wide awake, and stripped. There – and it was not a dream – was the straw-packed bed, the threadbare blanket and the woman's flushed and bony face, eyes closed, her legs spreadeagled under him, and daylight making curving slats across her chest. What had he done? What would his brother say?

Aymer tried to be polite. He asked if he should bring a drink, or mend the fire, or throw the blanket over her. But all the time he spoke, he was gathering his clothes from off the earthy floor and dressing hastily. He muttered thanks. He almost put more money on the shelf, but had no coins left. He wished her all the good fortune in the world. 'I promise you, dear Mrs Bowe, that I am in your debt . . .' The truth is Aymer ran away from her, out of the door and past the dogs, along the six-mile coast to Wherrytown, where he would have plenty to repent, including Mrs Yapp's bill and his farewells to George. Get out of town, he told himself, with every stride. Get on the *Tar*. Get home.

Rosie wasn't sorry that he'd gone. Nor was her life enhanced by him. Though it was changed. Aymer had left her something more valuable than coins. She wasn't quite pregnant yet. Her egg hadn't voyaged down into her uterus and implanted. But the egg was fertilized and it was moving. By Sunday she would be with child. The guess in Wherrytown would be that Rosie's new baby would be black. Everything unusual on the coast would, from that day, be put on Otto's bill. When no one could remember Aymer Smith or put a name to any of the Americans, or their ship even, the African would still be talked about. In fact, he gave a lasting phrase to Wherrytown. If anything went wrong – the harvest failed, the yeast went flat, a coin or a button disappeared – they'd say 'Blame it on the African!'

or 'Otto's been at work again.' Otto fathered many babies on the coast, not only Rosie Bowe's.

But for the moment Rosie was still alone with no one but herself to love. And she wasn't the sort to love herself. She rested on her wooden bed and conjured up the *Belle*. She could think more calmly of her daughter now. She was an optimist again. She pictured Miggy on the ship. It was. her marriage day. The captain would anoint her with sea water beneath the canvas canopies, the rigging vaults and the mastwood spires. Blindfolded Lotty Kyte and the woman with the lovely, sandy hair would be the maids of honour. Miggy would lie down with Ralph that night, in their creaking cabin out at sea, a seashell ring on her finger, his arms about her waist, the blood-red ensign round her throat. And they would shortly be together in the Lands of Promise.

15. The Lands of Promise

THIS WAS Aymer's final night in Wherrytown. He had the whole inn to himself. George neglected him. Even Mrs Yapp had disappeared – she'd gone to Walter Howells's for some celebration of their own. There was no one for Aymer to talk to. When he heard Wherrytowners coming back from Evensong, he was almost tempted to stroll up to the chapel and the chapel house to see Mr Phipps. Just for the company. It might, he thought, be an amusement to conclude the conversation he had started that morning with the preacher on the quay – Blind Superstition, and the Bible as a Chart. But he guessed that Mr Phipps would hardly welcome a Sceptic interrupting his supper. So Aymer stayed at the inn and had to eat alone. Cold ham and pickles. Solitary pie.

Aymer, as the only guest, could choose to sleep in any of the inn's twenty empty beds. He hardly dared to sleep at all, in fact, in case he missed the Wednesday's dawn departure of the *Tar* and the liberating taste of salt-free city air which beckoned him. He'd already packed his bag and dressed for the voyage by ten that Tuesday night. He wouldn't go to bed. He took a blanket to the parlour. He put his chair next to the grate, facing the window that opened on to the lane.

The fire would keep him warm until the early hours. And, if he dozed, he would wake as soon as there was any daylight in the window. He tried to read at first, but he was tired of Mr Paine. He couldn't concentrate. Rosie Bowe had disconcerted him. He tried to put her out of mind. He shouldn't blame himself. The fault was hers. She'd misconstrued his charity.

Where was her daughter? How far out at sea? Aymer stared into the fire. Would she be happy in America? Too late to worry now. No *need* to worry now, in fact. Aymer could put right in his mind's eye things that might go wrong in life. That was his major skill. He couldn't quite remember Miggy's face. No matter – he'd improve on her. He imagined her in Wilmington. She wasn't gaping. She wasn't fidgeting her feet. Nor wearing breeches. She was breathing through her nostrils, not her mouth. He gave her better skin and hair. He ribboned her. He put her in a simple cotton dress. He imagined her heavily pregnant, too. That, surely, was the spirit of the emigrant. And she was more lively in her speech, more generous, more womanly. America was suiting her.

He put her in a rocking chair, and spread one hem of her cotton dress across the arm. He served her a slice of honey cake, and a jug of some new drink. He couldn't recognize its smell. He put her foot up on the balustrade of the veranda. Maize, tobacco, sweet potatoes, and snap beans were growing in the plot below. (Would there be snap beans in America? Aymer wasn't sure.) There were chickens. There was sun. Whip was rolling in the grass.

Aymer shut his eyes and put himself into the scene. He was standing in the garden, looking up at Miggy. 'In't you too hot?' she said. No, no, that wouldn't do. She had to speak again, and this time with the slight brogue of the Carolinas. 'Aren't you too hot? Put on your sun hat, Mr Smith.' Oh better, yes.

'I can't wear that foolish hat.'

'Then you will bake.'

Aymer baking in America! Just the thought of it made him smile. Again he imagined himself in Wilmington with Miggy, *Margaret*! This time he was sitting on a stool underneath a shag-bark tree. He put his back against the trunk and began a pencil sketch. The artist Aymer Smith! Another life, another dream. First he roughed in the framework of the rocking chair, and then he marked in Miggy's black hair against the curving headrest. Then the outline of the jug. Then her ankles and her black boots, a happy balance with her hair. He left the paper blank for her white dress.

'What will you do with it?' she said.

'The sketch?' She nodded slightly, hardly moved her lips. She didn't want to spoil the pose. 'I'll finish it and give it to Ralph. He can take it with him when he goes to sea. You'll always be with him.'

'What will you draw for Ralph and me, so that you'll be remembered too, for your generosity?' She forgot her pose, and waved her hands towards the house and garden. 'Your sovereigns have paid the rent on this.' Aymer shook his head, both in the parlour and in Wilmington. He didn't want their gratitude. Why could no one understand that simple fact? 'Perhaps you'll do a portrait of yourself,' she said.

Now Aymer almost had her face: undramatic, self-possessed, determined. She had one hand cupped underneath her belly, supporting her first child – two weeks from being born. Its head was tucked in above her bladder; its bottom pressed against her dress, and its heartbeat was racing on her fingertips. She stretched her legs. She was content – she'd heard that Ralph would be back in a day or two from his voyage on the *Belle* to Norfolk in Virginia. Her face was flushed and full. She wasn't the ouncy girl she'd been at Dry Manston, dressed in breeches, thin-lipped and mistrustful. Nor was she the shoreline pessimist, expecting nothing from her life but the repetitions of the seasons and the sea. Here was a woman pioneer, roots up, and free. Aymer looked at her, imagined her, and he was proud. He had been right to let her go.

'Shall I fetch the map?' he'd say, if he could only walk in on her now. He'd take it from the table drawer and hold it for her in the sunlight. 'Find Wilmington first.' That was easy for her. She had found it many times. She only had to spot the W, and Ws were easy. 'Now Norfolk, Margaret. Your finger must go north.' And there was Norfolk, spread across the coast. The *N* was on the reaches of the estuary; the *f* was on the beach; the *k* was knee-deep in the sea. 'Now read for me the places Ralph will pass before he comes back home.' She'd read: Cape Hatteras. Raleigh Bay (pronounced uncertainly, but Aymer smiled and didn't shake his head). Cape Lookout. Onslow Bay. Cape Fear.

'You see, it isn't difficult. You're reading well. Read for Ralph when he comes home. Read something for your baby when it's born. We can resume our lessons later on. I will teach you script.'

'I'll never learn. I in't . . . I'm not that clever.'

'You will. I'll not leave here till you do. Just think what they'll say in Wherrytown, Margaret, when you write home in your own hand.'

'I'll write down how it's all thanks to you.'

'You'll tell them how you're missing Wherrytown.'

'I don't miss anything.'

'Nor anyone?'

'Well, there's my ma. I think of her. I do. But I'm to be a ma myself, so there's the sense in it. I don't expect my baby . . .' (she'd drum her stomach with her fingers) '. . . to stick to me for ever more . . . I'll love it though while it's here. If it's a girl we'll give it mother's name. That's only right. We promised her. She'll be American. Miss Rosie Parkiss.'

'She'll be the belle of Wilmington, Margaret. And what if you have a son? The beau of Wilmington, I suppose.'

'We'll name him after you, to mark your generosity to us. Master Aymer Parkiss. Don't that sound high-falutin'? Oh, my! He'll be the mayor!'

'He'll be the captain of a ship.'

AYMER wasn't quite awake, nor quite asleep, when he invented Captain Aymer Parkiss. The parlour was too dark and quiet for sleep. And far too cold. The fire had not survived. He wrapped the blanket round his legs. He was tempted to ring the parlour handbell for George or Mrs Yapp. Would either of them come? He'd like some fuel for the fire, another blanket and a warming drink. But it was far too late – or far too early – to summon them. He guessed the time was two or three o'clock. The window-panes were black. There would be at least three hours more of Solitary Pie before the glass thickened with any light. He'd have to ruminate the time away, grazing on the minutes of the night with only chimeras for company.

He'd had enough of Miggy Bowe and her offspring in Wilmington. He'd settled them. They didn't trouble him. Now his thoughts had turned to Katie Norris and how, in this very parlour, he'd first set eyes on her. It wasn't hard to recall *her* face. She'd worn a shoulder cape. She'd had black ribbons in her hair. The parlour grate had been cold and empty then as well: 'We were hoping for a bit of fire,' they'd said. *A bit of fire in life*, Aymer thought to himself. What fire could he kindle in his own, cool life, in those dark hours in the parlour? What else but some device to bring him back to Katie Norris? They'd have to meet again. In Canada, of course. That was possible. If Aymer was to keep his resolution to travel more in future, to see the greater works of man in Florence, Paris and Edinburgh, then why not travel to Canada as well to see dear friends?

He could imagine her in Canada, and ready for his visit. Their landscape was quite clear to him. He'd seen the prints of immigrants by Mr Gay in his *Illustrations from the Colonies*: 'Glorious morning! What a fine country. Here at last is Canada!' He was acquainted with the trees, their Latin names, the timber huts, the never-ending lakes, the distant prospect from the migrant ships of Cap Tourmente and the Laurentians. What would he do if he arrived in Montreal, Aymer wondered. Canada was big. How would he find the Norrises? He saw himself on unpaved streets, with wooden boards for pavements, and buildings in grey limestone and timber. All the men were tall and bearded. All the women wore thick boots. He'd look at every face he passed. He'd check the colour of the women's hair. One day, surely, he'd meet Katie on the streets. 'Why, Mrs Norris,' he would say, 'the world is smaller than we think . . .' But, no, that wasn't right. He knew he wouldn't meet her on the streets, or in the market places, or coming out of church. She wouldn't be in Montreal. The Norrises hadn't gone to Canada for streets and marketplaces. Their dream had been a piece of land, a cabin in a clearing, privacy. They could be anywhere, from Sturgeon Falls to Lake St John, from mountaintop to shore.

But Aymer could meet Lotty Kyte instead. He'd see her by the river harbour, handing advertising bills out for her brother's firm to new arrivals. She'd not remember him. How could she? She'd been blindfolded when they met in Wherrytown. Aymer hadn't seen all of her face before. But no one could mistake the fleshless angles of her body, and that voice. 'My brother can supply . . .' He'd introduce himself, remind her about Wherrytown, and ask if she had any news of the Norrises. She had, she had! They'd cleared a piece of lakeside land a few miles north of St Jean-Luc. They'd built themselves a little hut. They'd even ordered furniture from Chesney Kyte, who else? Lotty, who helped her brother in the factory office, had sent a letter to the

JIM CRACE

Norrises only last week informing them that Chesney would deliver their beds and sideboard and their chairs by wagon in a few days' time. Could Aymer go with him? She'd ask.

What gift should Aymer take the Norrises? He'd buy a beaver hat for Robert. *Castor fiber.* And an ambered whalebone comb for Katie's hair. It seemed to him that Wherrytown was Montreal. He had to stay awake that night, not to catch the *Ha'porth of Tar* along the English coast but to be on time for the wagon journey north, in Canada. He'd report to the Kytes at dawn. Chesney and his eldest boy would drive their four horses out of Montreal with furniture for five families roped to their wagon. There'd not be space for Aymer on the driving bench. He'd sit on one of the Norrises' new chairs, watching the freshly printed ruts behind the wagon disappear into the flood plains to the south.

Aymer stared into the darkness of the parlour, and devised how the wagon ride would end with him and Katie . . . what? Arm in arm? Embracing? He guessed it took two days to reach the Norrises. Their cabin was a woodshed and a single room made out of pine logs, pine planks and maple frames. Their land was black from burning. Nothing grew between their cabin and the lake. Geese were picking through the ashes. The Kytes couldn't get their wagon within fifty yards of the house. Too many trees were felled. The way was blocked by uncleared trunks and branches. Robert Norris was standing with a saw, down at the water's edge, among the geese. He seemed more square, less clerkish, younger even. He had a beard. He pushed his spectacles up on his forehead when he heard the men

268

approaching. He couldn't believe his eyes. He hugged Aymer like a brother. 'I knew that we must meet again,' he said. They walked together, arm in arm, between the trunks of trees to where the wagon had been hitched. Together they lifted down the furniture. 'Now we have everything we need,' said Robert, and that 'everything' included Aymer too. 'We wouldn't wish to welcome you to Canada without the offer of a bed and chair.'

'And is your wife quite well, and happily disposed to her new life?'

'Oh, she is well! Why don't you leave the furniture to us? Go to the cabin and surprise her there. She'll be so happy to see an old friend such as you. She misses conversation.'

Aymer saw himself in Canada. He crossed the clearing like a young man, leaping over logs, not faltering, not caring if he fell. He couldn't wait to see her face, to push the comb into her hair. She was singing in the cabin. He pressed his nose against the knots and eyes of the window glass. At first he couldn't see the room. But then he found a square inch of the glass that wasn't puddled. He could see the aura of the candlelight, and then the naked body of a woman, standing in a bowl of water. Her back was turned against the window and her hair was up. Her thighs were strong and freckled, just as he remembered them, although their tones were split in curving arcs of flesh, orange-warm from the candle flame, pink-cold from the window light. She was the salmon and the thrush. Her hair was sand. She sang. She washed herself in Aymer's soap.

When she'd finished washing, Aymer fixed her in the

bowl, dripping dry and struggling to find the verses of her song. As she sang she told a rosary of love on the double loop of chink-shells at her throat, his, hers, his, hers, his. *Lacuna vincta.* Aymer fancied that she searched for him, his chink-shells, the beauties that he'd found for her in Wherrytown. 'I thank you, Mr Smith. A lovely one.' Was Aymer looped forever round her neck? She stepped out of the bowl onto a piece of wood. She wrapped herself in cloth. She turned and faced into the window light. Such health and happiness, she had, such hope. Canada. Canadee. Canadee-i-o.

He'd wait outside and listen to her voice. He'd listened to her singing once before, when they'd stood together at the chapel wall – 'For Death is but the Shaded Sea . . .' This time she'd sing a lighter tune, but with such care and with such girlish and unconscious gravity that Aymer wouldn't dare call out her name for fear of ending it.

WHAT HOPE for Otto, though? Could Aymer realize some health and happiness for him?

Aymer had fought Otto off, banned him from the parlour. He didn't want to spend the night with him, contemplating what he'd suffered since the tackle-room door had been thrown back. But there was no escaping it. Aymer had to try and find a happy ending for the African as well. He put his head into his hands and pressed the palms onto his eyes until all the nighttime was excluded. He could feel his pulse tapping on his forehead and in his fingertips. There was, at first, a flat and bruising darkness beneath his eyelids from the pressure of his hands. Then heavy patterns came: the pheasant wings, the bark and bracken, the tapestries, the blue-red fogs, and finally the deep-brewed tropic undergrowth that he was hoping for. Aymer tried to impose Otto's face onto the pulsing darkness, but Otto's face, like Miggy Bowe's, was hard to recollect. So Aymer concentrated on the tackle room. That was easy. He could remember it. The single window and the draughty winter light. The door, the bolt. The saddles and the saddle-cloth. The floor bricks and the straw. And in the straw a body sleeping.

Now Aymer could imagine Otto emancipated at Dry Manston, wrapped in his blanket and looking down from Cradle Rock at the *Belle*, idling on its sandbank. There'd be a rising dough of clouds coming in from Canada with snow. He'd bang his forehead with his fist. What kind of freedom had he found that tricked him into this? Was he supposed to wade out to the *Belle* and climb aboard? Should he descend the companion ladders to the orlop deck, put his ankles back in chains?

Aymer pictured Otto squatting on the frosty ground. The grass seemed petrified. He had encountered frost before, but on the *Belle*'s rigging, not on land. What would he do with frost? He'd test it with his feet. He'd flatten it. His footprints were *engrav'd in frost. But soon forgot.* His blanket hung across his head. He swung from side to side on the pivot of his feet. He was a Cradle Rock of cloth. This was far too punishing. Aymer had to make him move, to look for help inland from some soft Radical, from some Samaritan, from George, perhaps. He had to make him run. The track was pitiless at first. It thwarted him. No shelter yet. No inn to welcome him. Freedom's not the open sky, Aymer thought. It's sheets, and heat. It's Victuals, Viands and Potations.

The light was lifting as Otto ran, through the frost, the mud, across the unforgiving rocks. He seemed illuminated by some sharp and icy sun. He was like a boy, dodging through the heather and the gorse, leaping granite, skirting the low branches of wind-distorted trees. That wasn't hard. Not hard for boys. But it was hard for Aymer to make the landscape change, to find a route for Otto between the granite and the thorn into the distant, humid fields of Africa. Aymer pressed his palms more firmly on his eyes and tried to make the land and earth come vaulting at him in a thousand forms, and every tumbling form a little warmer than the last, and every fleeting smudge of earth more succulent and odorous and dark and tropical. He tried to speed the landscape from grey and white to deeper green and yellow so that he could imagine the miracle of Otto home again. But he failed. No matter what he improvised, the landscape wouldn't change.

Aymer looked towards the parlour window. It was slowly taking shape. His eyes were tired, but he could recognize the frosty truth – that Otto's home was not in reach and never would be now. If he lived and had survived the snow, he could only be a ten-day walk away at most. He had his feet to carry him, and nothing more. Yes, Otto might be met again. Huzzah for that! He might be glimpsed. But it would only be on some *English* street. That was both a chilling and a strangely hopeful thought. It left the shadow of a chance that Aymer still could make amends.

He concocted their encounter. He'd see Otto . . . where? In the market? Begging at the church door? Working in some warehouse by the marsh? Taking refuge in a stable room? He'd be transformed by his cold freedoms, that was a certainty. Much thinner, yes. His skin would be dry and dull and chapped. But there'd be something better than before. Something in his face, something in the angle of his eye, would be startling. Oh, what a meeting they would have, thought Aymer, his eyelids heavier than stone, the parlour window silver now with the first of Wednesday's light, and with the last of Wherrytown. What have your travels taught you? he'd ask Otto. What have you learned away from home? What have you seen? But Otto would not say a word. He'd be joyful to have found a friend, of course, but far too weary to describe such cold, such bafflement, such heavy seas, such dislocating winds, such ships.

16. Good Boots

CITY AIR makes free? Well, yes. It was a liberation to be home again amongst the soft civilities of city life, and free from the embarrassments of Wherrytown. But Aymer Smith affected not to like the taste of city air that much. He was a travelled man now, amphibious between the country and the town. His blood was spiced with salt. He wasn't an innocent any longer. He took to wearing his tarpaulin coat and his heavy boots at every opportunity, to the factory, to debating rooms, to the subscription libraries, in the streets. 'Your brother has begun to look just like the pudding man,' Fidia Smith complained to her husband, when she had spotted Aymer, hatless and 'dressed for the fields', window-shopping like a vagrant in King's Avenue. 'He'll have a basket on his shoulders next, and will be selling plum pudding by the quarter yard.'

Privately Matthias didn't agree with Fidia's opinion that his brother was 'affected, but not improved' by the trip to Wherrytown. 'His stay amongst the hobnails and the corduroys has been no benefit,' she said. 'If an ass goes travelling, he'll not come back a horse. More's the pity.' On the contrary, Aymer had matured, Matthias thought, in everything except his dress. Yet to have him safely back was not entirely a relief. There'd been so little tension in the works while Aymer was away. Orders could be given and not questioned. Changes which were 'not in the interests of Fraternity and Justice' could be made without a pious argument. And men could be sacked. Indeed, Matthias had dismissed three of the hands who had, at Aymer's instigation, set up a Works Committee, and one other man who had poor eyesight. There would be a fine commotion, Matthias had expected, when Aymer got back from his mischief-making along the coast. But unexpectedly his brother didn't mention their dismissal. Perhaps he didn't notice it. He made more fuss when consignments of almost pure sodium carbonate, *méthode Leblanc*, were delivered to the factory yard in jogging-carts. Though even then the fuss he made seemed dilettante and not, Matthias judged, without the spice of irony. Aymer claimed he missed the cumbrous wagonfuls of kelp ash: six horses and six thousand flies a load. He missed the smell. This, surely, was a tease.

'Where is the beauty in it?' Aymer asked, on his first encounter with the new soda. He fetched the ancient folio of seaweed specimens from what had been their father's roll-top desk, and thumbed through the heavy pages with their browning fans of kelp and their Latin names in browning ink. Matthias could see no beauty there, though Aymer was extravagant in his appreciation of the weeds. 'If only you could see these living kelps in water, Matthias. You would imagine you were at a royal ball amongst the finest ladies . . .'

'And why would I imagine that? I cannot understand how I must confuse fine ladies with seaweed.'

'You would understand if you could see the living kelp. It is quite beautiful, I promise it. But you will not persuade me that this new material has beauty in it.'

'Its beauty, Aymer, will not be seen until our ledgers are complete, and then you will be able to admire it in the profits column,' said Matthias. He felt quite well disposed towards his brother for a change. Aymer had lost his argumentative edge. He seemed less preacherly, and more resigned. He complained less of minor illnesses. And, best of all, he displayed a less dutiful interest in the factory. Some days he left at lunchtime, and didn't return. On Saturdays he didn't come at all. He seemed too preoccupied with private matters – the very thought of which made Fidia laugh – to bully for the shorter working day or profit-sharing schemes.

'What private life?' said Fidia.

'His books, perhaps?'

'Ah, yes, his dusty volumes. Pity them, Matthias. They have to tolerate the tedium of sitting open on his lap for hours long with only him for company and his bad breath for ventilation.' Fidia laughed politely into her glove. She was relieved that it was only books that kept her brother-in-law preoccupied. She didn't want a 'private life' that might secure a wife for him – or offspring, God forbid. She and Matthias had a son who would inherit the soap factory in its entirety if Aymer could only remain steadfast in his bachelorhood. The sooner he grew too old for parenting, or – better – contracted some ailment that was fatal rather than imagined, the happier Fidia would be.

*

IT WAS an afternoon in mid-January 1837 when Fidia had spotted Aymer in his tarpaulin and his boots outside the shops in King's Avenue. Her brother-in-law had been standing with his shoulders up against a wall watching the military band which exercised along the avenue on Fridays. They'd marched past him twice already – first playing a hornpipe and then a doleful coronach – and Aymer had been marching with them like some schoolboy when he saw Fidia, hurrying fatly across the street ahead of him. He took his refuge up against the wall until she disappeared into the haberdashery. Neither of them knew that they'd been seen.

When the band assembled round the King's Hall steps for the tattoo, Aymer went up to look more closely at the drummer's face. He was an African; that much was clear from fifty yards away. And he was large; though hardly large enough to topple the Cradle Rock. Even when he got close, however, Aymer was not certain that he'd found his man. The nose was right, small and depressed. But his face was pulled out of shape by its chin strap, and the hair was hidden by the regimental cap. His drumming was indifferent, Aymer thought, though he didn't count himself as musical. He stood through two more pieces and endured the posturings of their final marching display, which was unaccompanied except for Otto – was it Otto? – beating time.

The soldiers put down their instruments and drank from water flasks. The drummer was talking to the buglers. He was ten inches taller at the very least. Aymer circled them. He didn't want to call out, or even seem to stare. He wasn't even certain what to do if he recognized the man. As he got

closer he could hear the drummer talk. It was more compli-
cated than *Uwip, Uwip*, and pitched too high. Aymer grew
more certain that, if he called out Otto's name, the man
would not turn round. At last he pulled off his regimental
cap. His head was bald above the temples, and what hair
there was was slightly gingered. 'Otto,' Aymer said, at half-
power. One of the buglers looked at him and yawned.

The drummer wasn't the first – or the last – dark face
that Aymer would pursue. Since his return from Wherrytown he had been struck by how many there were in the
city. They haunted him. He let them. Otto's life and his
seemed pleached together, like the woven branches on a
hedge. Of course, there were other concerns that might
have bothered him. Should have bothered him, perhaps.
The plight of Rosie Bowe, for one. Whenever he walked in
the streets, Aymer couldn't avoid encountering rough twins
of Rosie: thin, tough women with no vanity, and with only
the same unpinned black hair and pauper clothes to soften
the knuckle and the sinew of their frames. But Aymer didn't
waste a glance on them. The women that he turned for
were fleshy and sandy-haired, or black.

Aymer was unsettled by what he called 'our Africans',
both the women and the men. Most – and that's not
more than forty, say, throughout the city – were the sons
and daughters of liberated British slaves; laundry maids and
cooks, footmen, valets and coachmen. There were a few
who'd broken away. There was a freeman carpenter who
called himself William King; because, he said, he would
have been a Hausa king, if he'd not been born in London's
Battersea. And there was Susan Sack (or Sew-and-Suck as

she was called), a mulatto seamstress working in the Mart-way tenements. She was a nursemaid, too, labouring both with the hems and with the infants of fashionable ladies. She had no nipples, it was said. She had brass thimbles on her breasts, and any child that she suckled had rusty lips. There was a black prostitute called Cleopatra, too, though no gentleman would admit to any acquaintance with her. Even when she greeted men by name in the street, her familiarity was passed off to their companions or their wives as sauce or lunacy. Who could she be? What could she want? Her nipples might be brass, for all they knew or cared. Their lips weren't brown with rust.

Whenever Aymer saw black citizens, no matter what their station, he would catch their eye, press a sixpence on them, and enquire, 'Are any of your brethren recently arrived?' He would describe Otto, down to the glassy scars around his ankles, but no one yet had seen or heard of such a large black man. They were used to unsolicited donations, and odd requests. They were used to being stared at, too, and being shooed away like cats. Aymer's sort was not a rarity – but even if they had seen Otto, huge and scarred, riding down King's Avenue on a camel they wouldn't have told a stranger.

Aymer though, through his persistence, had managed to befriend a local black coachman called Scipio Jones who worked for a wealthy estate-owner on the city fringes. Each Saturday morning, Scipio came with the family barouche to the city square, where he waited for his mistress below the salon rooms in the Royal Hotel while she played cards, drank tea and displayed her latest heavily flounced crinoline, decorated mantle or pagoda sleeves amongst the crapes, tarlatans and bombazines of her acquaintances. Scipio had to come down from the warmth and comfort of his hammer cloth and stand sentry by the horses, so that if any of her friends should leave the card tables and look out, they'd see him there in his show livery, his polished buttons and his braid, attending on her fine horses and her carriage. 'Don't fidget, Scipio,' she'd said. 'Horses fidget. Coachmen do not move.'

Aymer hadn't mistaken Scipio for Otto. He was too small and plump. But he had offered him the sixpence and asked his usual questions when he'd first spotted him on New Year's Eve outside the Royal. Scipio was cold, despite his jacket and his hat. He had to warm his hands at the horse's nose and hope that no one had left the card tables and was watching him. He was glad to engage in conversation with Aymer. To talk politely to a stranger was not fidgeting, surely – but it was warming. Aymer blocked off some of the wind. No, Scipio hadn't seen anyone as large as that, he said. Nor anyone with ankle scars. But he would keep his ears close to the wall and would be happy to oblige with information. Aymer could return each Saturday and Scipio would report what he had heard (and take another sixpence for his pains).

Scipio had nothing to report on the first Saturday of the new year, but on the second he had 'double news', of a large black drummer in the regimental band, and of an itinerant boxer – 'an American, by all accounts' – called Massa Hannibal. So it was thanks to Scipio that Aymer was outside the King's Hall on the following Friday. And thanks to him as well that on the Friday night, Aymer Smith put on his boots and tarpaulin and went to see the boxing contest in a district of the city that he'd never seen before. As it turned out, Massa Hannibal was not an African, nor American. At most he was an octoroon. His accent was Italian. His hair was straight and greased to slide the blows. The blackest things about him were the bruises on his cheekbone and his arms from the previous night's fight. He'd zinced his chest with horizontal stripes, he wore bead anklets and he babbled some invented African language when he came into the ring. His opponent – King Swing – was a bald man, bandy and unbruised. All the money went on him.

Aymer had only come to check on Massa Hannibal. He didn't wait to see the fight. He gave his ticket to a wheedler waiting at the door. He was in a hurry to be home. It had been easy to find the warehouse where the fight was held. All he'd had to do was to follow those carriages with only gentlemen inside, and then stay with the crowd. But getting back into the quarter of the city where he had rooms was not as simple. He couldn't find a chair to take him there. And none of the rattling four-wheelers, drays or raddle horses waiting outside seemed equipped for passengers. There were no drivers, anyway. They'd bought cheap seats at the fight and weren't for hire.

The warehouse was on marshy ground below the river, amongst workshops and surrounded by ditches which weren't successful in their main task of taking human dung away. The smell was stifling, but still the place was busy with people (and their pigs and dogs) who didn't mind the

smell of waste and poverty enough to build their slum courts
somewhere else. Aymer followed alleyways that went uphill.
That was his strategy. He was bound to find the upper town
that way, but as he walked and left the marshes behind, his
fears increased. The homes were scarcely lit. Each contained
dark figures hunched around low light.

Laughter and loud voices went from house to house,
through open doors and windows. Aymer didn't feel concealed by the darkness, but disclosed. Low light throws
long shadows, and Aymer's shadow corrugated down the
alleyways, dipping into homes, flattening on the walls of
beer houses and tommy shops, running up front steps,
and slatting across the faces of people watching from their
windows. The dogs were large and importuning, bounding
out and barking at him with their haunches in the air and
their tails on springs. Slab-faced women – making baskets
from the marshland reeds – whistled at him. Men didn't
step aside immediately when he asked for room to pass, but
offered him their bottles or their pipes, or asked what he
was looking for. Their friendliness was frightening. What
might it lead him to? Where might it end? He was glad
that he was dressed so democratically. They might mistake
him for a wagoner and not consider him a man worth
robbing or beating up.

He must have said good evening fifty times and forced a
hundred smiles before he reached the first paved street and
the reassuring sound of decent shoes on stone. Well, it had
been an adventure, he decided within a few minutes – not
one that had located Otto, perhaps, but one that was an
education. One ought to know the city of one's birth,

including those parts that were not well furbished. He doubted that Matthias could boast of such a visit, not at night at least. And Perfidious Fidia? Well, Fidia hadn't been anywhere. Aymer looked forward to telling them about the boxing contest and enlightening them about the common, marshy end of their city. 'It would be wrong to regard as low and mean in character those people whose homes are low and mean in build,' he might say, and (stealing one of Parlour George's saner comments) he could add, 'A man is not a horse because he happens to be born in a stable. The Romans did not crucify a horse, I think.' He was smiling broadly now.

WILLIAM BAGNALL and his brother Bagsy had followed Aymer to the boxing match. Bagsy had, in fact, put a half-crown on King Swing to beat the 'African'. He wasn't pleased when Aymer occupied his seat for only five minutes and then – inexplicably – left the warehouse before a single blow had been thrown. There would be an opportunity outside to throw some blows themselves, but Bagsy would have liked to see how Massa Hannibal would cope with Swing's right hand. Still, there were debts to clear and a sovereign to be made, from Walter Howells in Wherrytown. And all they had to do was give this man a beating, and send proof.

They'd thought, when Walter Howells's letter had arrived before Christmas, that it would be a simple matter. They would intercept this Aymer Smith outside the Soap Works after dusk. It wouldn't be hard to identify him. They merely had to ask one of the workers. And then there were a hundred alleyways and dark corners thereabouts where they might lay hold of him. They'd waited three evenings running at the works, but their quarry had already left, mid-afternoon. On the fourth day Bagsy Bagnall went alone early in the morning and, for a ha'penny, discovered from the works caretaker that Aymer Smith observed no time-table these days but could be recognized from his thin figure, his tarpaulin coat and his walking boots. He lived alone, Bagsy was informed, in rooms above the assay house in Whittock's Court.

'Don't sink into a conversation with Mr Smith, unless you must,' the caretaker warned. 'He has such words, your head'll spin.' Bagsy Bagnall was amused by this. He knew whose head would spin. It wouldn't be his.

Bagsy waited at the entrance to the court that afternoon. He was cold, but he was happy to be idle. He'd burned two pipes of best Virginia and helped himself to a purse from an unattended carriage before Aymer returned home, and no mistaking him. If ever there was a man deserved a beating, he was it. Look at the clothes he wore. Look at that bony, educated face, those soft and fussy hands, that self-esteem. Bagsy, hidden in the gateway, waited to see which door in Whittock's Court led to Aymer's rooms. When Aymer was about to step into the hallway, Bagsy shouted, 'Mr Smith!' Aymer turned around and peered into the empty court. No one. He had half expected to see Otto standing there.

The Bagnalls had left Aymer in peace over Christmas and the New Year. There was other work to do. Will Bagnall had obtained a list of which local gentlemen and wives would be attending the major balls and concerts of the season. 'They're out, we're in,' he told his brother, choosing to burgle the houses of the younger people who might be expected to stay late. They'd made a decent haul of jewellery, some silverware, some gold, a cavalry sword, and had only been discovered once, by a housekeeper who, at midnight, should have been asleep. Bagsy had to knock her down and gag her with a curtain sash. But by the middle of January Will Bagnall was keen to settle his accounts with Walter Howells. So on that Friday of the boxing bout, they'd followed Aymer from his rooms, and gone with him down to King's Avenue. They'd endured the marching band, and waited while he inspected the musicians on the steps of King's Hall. There'd been an opportunity, when Aymer was returning to his rooms, for Will and Bagsy to finish their business. Whittock's Court was both dark and deserted. They could give him a good dextering, leave him and his bruises on the steps of his front door and be away within two minutes. What could be more pleasing and efficient? But they'd been too slow with their decision and Aymer had been too speedy with his key.

They'd followed him that Friday evening too, though there was little opportunity to confront him, with so many people walking in the same direction for the fight, and so many carriages and conveyances about. If the streets had been full of ladies or children, then no matter. But to give Aymer a beating in the presence of men distinguished only by their shared regard for pugilism wouldn't be sensible. Nor was it sensible to set about him in the marshy alleyways around the warehouse. The people there would be quick to lend a hand to Aymer. Two men on one? They wouldn't tolerate it in their slums. So the Bagnalls waited for the quieter streets of the upper town before they went to work. They were certain that Aymer hadn't known that he was being followed. They'd walked quietly in the muddy lanes. But surely now, with their stolen leather shoes resounding on the paving stones, he would notice them a few yards to his rear and try to get away.

They didn't give him the chance. They ran at him and swept him off his feet into a stable yard. They banged him up against a wooden door. The horse inside backed away and snorted in the darkness. 'Your name? Your name?' they said to him. If he had answered Robert Norris, say, or Ralph Parkiss, would they have hesitated and held their punches, fearful of making a mistake? Will Bagnall might. He only had his brother's word that this tarpaulin was their man. His brother's word wasn't worth much. But nothing would stop Bagsy now. It didn't matter whom they'd got inside the stable yard, or what his name was. Bagsy wanted to express himself. He'd missed the boxing for this. He'd squandered half a crown.

'What do you want?' said Aymer. He was winded and could hardly speak.

'Shut up!' said Bagsy. He took a short length of solid, six-ply rope out of his pocket, gripped both ends and pressed the middle tightly across Aymer's throat. 'Just say your name. Say it. Say it.'

Aymer gave his name as best he could, but couldn't say it clearly.

'Give us something with your name on it,' said Will Bagnall.

'Hurry up.'

'Haven't anything.'

'Do what he says!' Bagsy, who wasn't the tallest of men, pressed his rope more firmly on Aymer's throat. He brought his head down sharply on Aymer's chest and at the same time brought a knee up into his groin. Aymer's legs gave way. He was as tall as Bagsy Bagnall for a moment. Then shorter. Then on the ground.

Will searched the pockets of Aymer's coat. All he found was a half-sovereign and some pennies. He knelt down on the cobbles and the straw, put his hand on Aymer's head and said, almost gently, 'Aymer Smith? Is that your name?' Aymer nodded. 'Have you been recently in Wherrytown?' A groaning Yes. 'It's him,' Will told his brother.

'I know it's him.'

'Go on, then. Get it done.'

Bagsy kicked Aymer once, on the shoulder. His ankle twisted with the force of it.

'We hear you're a thief and not a gentleman,' said Will Bagnall, while his brother shook his foot in pain. 'We hear you don't settle your accounts. So we're settling them for you. Speak one word of this and we'll visit you again. We know your rooms in Whittock's Court ... and we might call on you at any time. And you'll get a whipping.'

Bagsy was more careful with his second set of kicks. He aimed for Aymer's softer parts, his chest and stomach, then his buttocks, then his legs. He stopped and stepped back. 'That's it,' he said. Aymer wasn't badly hurt, just bruised and terrified. He groaned and stretched out on the ground.

'Good boots,' said Bagsy.

'Get 'em then.'

Bagsy pulled up Aymer's legs and tugged off his walking boots and his hose. He let the legs drop back onto the ground. Then, as a final flourish, he stamped on Aymer's ankles and his feet. The tarsi cracked. Walter Howells had asked for broken bones. The Bagnalls had obliged. He'd asked for broken teeth as well. Bagsy found a cobblestone and brought it down on Aymer's mouth. Aymer had never known pain so fierce and concentrated. His mouth was wet and red and stony. The Bagnalls collected two of his teeth as evidence for Walter Howells that they'd made a decent job of it. They covered Aymer in straw, then left the yard. If they hurried they might get back to the warehouse before the boxing finished. If King Swing had won, there'd be some winnings to pick up. Easy money, easy times.

Aymer Smith had wet himself. His bladder had been kicked and bruised. When he regained consciousness and found enough strength to limp, barefoot, for help, his trousers were soaked and icy cold. He didn't look the least like a gentleman who'd encountered some misfortune. He looked more like a beggar in a dirty wagoner's coat, lame and urinous, and with a black hole for a mouth. He leant against the outer wall of the stable yard. He couldn't stand without the wall. He tried to call for help, but couldn't make the words.

The first people to notice him crossed the road. The second – a group of high-collared bucks who'd been at the boxing match – pointed at him, stared for a few moments and stayed away, leaving Aymer in an empty street. At last a carriage stopped a few gates down but, even though

Aymer waved his hands, the coachman wouldn't look at him, and soon had driven off. What could Aymer do to save his life? A man who thinks he's at death's door when he's only got a cold, or who wears a sling when all the bruising on his arm has healed, is not the sort to shrug off such a beating. He must, he thought, have lost several pints of blood already. His liver and his heart had been damaged, he was sure, punctured maybe. His face would be beyond repair. He'd have to hide behind a scarf. He'd be an invalid.

Aymer had to save himself, and quickly, or (he imagined) he would bleed to death, or die of cold, or his organs would give out. There was a doctor who had rooms opposite his own in Whittock's Court. But Whittock's Court was far away, and uphill. Twenty minutes' walking even for a healthy man. Two minutes, though, at his wounded pace, would bring Aymer to his brother's city house. It was just a street away. He had no choice. He'd rather be with Fidia than die. He held on to the wall and, moving one limb at a time, as if he were scaling some treacherous rock face, he traversed along the pavings and the wall until he reached his brother's wrought-iron gates and pulled the night bell with both hands.

FIDIA WAS horrified. Her nightman, Samuel, had come into the house, wearing his boots and carrying his lantern. Two rules broken. He'd not observed any of his 'procedures'. If he had something urgent to communicate, he should – in the absence of Matthias and his valet – have summoned Emma, the housekeeper. She would have written a note for Fidia and called a maid to deliver it on a hand tray with a curtsey and a cough. Instead the nightman had knocked roughly on her drawing-room doors while she was entertaining friends and sharing the latest indiscretions over cards and Madeira, and had come into the room, even before she'd rung her bell. What must her friends, Mrs Bellamy and Mrs Whittaker, have made of it?

'I hope this matters, Samuel,' she said.

'So begging you, ma'am, it's Mr Aymer at the gate.'

'And selling pudding by the quarter yard?'

'No, ma'am. I've left him in the porter's room, and he is in no condition to walk a step but wants me to help him come inside.'

What, drunk? she thought. This was embarrassing. Mrs Whittaker could take the gold rosette for gossiping. This would be common knowledge throughout the city, and much embroidered, by breakfast-time.

'Then leave him there, if he will not come himself,' she said. She turned towards her cards again as if her brother-in-law was not worth the worry. Whatever his business, it could wait.

'I cannot leave him, ma'am.'

'Good heavens, Samuel! You should not bother us. I am entertaining for the moment. Tell him that Matthias is away at the estate this evening and that I will join my husband there tomorrow. So Monday is the earliest that we can spare any time for him. He knows our timetables. Tell him, yes, that we can see him Monday.'

'He might not last till Monday, ma'am, the state of him.'

Fidia raised her eyebrows for her guests — exasperated

and embarrassed, but trying to appear amused. Aymer was a trial for her. She had no patience left. She laughed. She said, 'The family cuckoo. Can't leave me in peace for five minutes.'

'Perhaps you ought to see he is quite well,' said Mrs Bellamy. Mrs Whittaker nodded in agreement.

'Oh, I suppose I must disturb myself if we are to enjoy our privacy at all. Excuse me, ladies, while I attend to this,' said Fidia. She would attend to Samuel, too. He needed reprimanding and reminding that his place was out of doors. 'Samuel is disposed to overcolouring the simplest things,' she told her friends. 'Where is my shawl? I should not want to take a chill . . .'

Samuel, for once, was not exaggerating. Aymer was a dreadful sight. He looked as if a horse had kicked him in the face. Fidia had to take him in, no question of avoiding it – he *was* related. What had her brother-in-law done to deserve such a bloody face? She was in little doubt that the beating was deserved. She would have liked to have rapped her little fists on Aymer's jaw herself, on many occasions, if only to keep him quiet. He wasn't talking now, though. His breathing was constricted, and he was moaning like a chimney pot. Was he sleeping, or unconscious?

'Why didn't you express his situation, Samuel?' she demanded. 'You have caused me to seem cruel. I don't believe that he is drunk at all. What made you speak of it? There is no smell of drink. He is not a drinking man besides, despite his oddities. You had better hurry straight away to Fowlers and fetch the physician, if there is one on a Friday night. Do hurry up. Haste is only vulgar within the house. You may run. And do not thrust your hat back on your head. It is rowdyish.'

A boy was sent to call sedans to take both of her visitors home. Emma made a bed up on the second floor. ('Not the good sheets, Emma. Mr Smith is bloody, and . . .' She would not say what else.) The servants carried Aymer up two flights of stairs, his bare feet covered with a napkin. They put him on the bed, still in his coat, and Emma sat with him until the physician arrived, a little after eleven and a little the worse for drink. Fidia sat in her drawing room, and waited. She couldn't concentrate to read. It would not do to practise her piano or go to bed. She played patience and finished the three half-glasses of Madeira while, two floors above, Emma and the doctor stripped her brother-in-law, washed him with warm water, applied poultices on his bruises, cauterized his wounds with candle wax and checked his ribs and limbs for breakages. They missed the fractured ankle bone, but that would mend without them anyway and provide him with an interesting limp.

Finally they turned Aymer on his side and laid his face on a surgical dish. The doctor swabbed his mouth out, cleaned the fragments from his tongue and lips, then left him to his dreams.

'This will be a year of dentistry for him,' he said to Fidia when he was ready to go. She shuddered at the thought. 'I think you might sit with Mr Smith for tonight. He will be feverish and certainly will be in pain. I will leave some Greenoughs Tincture for his mouth. And some powdered laudanum. I'll come again tomorrow. Don't be too con-

cerned for him, Mrs Smith. Your husband will be whole
again in time, other than the teeth, of course . . .'

'My husband, sir, is in the country,' said Fidia, horrified
for the second time that night. 'That gentleman is a relation,
that is all, and my concerns for him are only charitable.' She
looked down at her game of cards. She had a decent run of
hearts. Her spades had let her down. 'Will he be fit enough
to go back to his rooms tomorrow?'

'No, Mrs Smith. I beg you, let him rest. He should stay
in bed until this time next week. He will be feverish.' Fidia
went across to her piano and struck a single note. A black
one. Sharp. She must remember to warn her daughters and
her son when they woke that Uncle Aymer was about. They
should avoid his room.

When Aymer woke on Saturday the pain was hardly
bearable. His chest and thighs felt as heavy and inert as
iron. In this he didn't differ much from King Swing who,
contrary to all the bets, had been defeated in fourteen
rounds the night before by Massa Hannibal. But King
Swing's face wasn't much harmed. He was only bruised
around one eye. The upper part of Aymer's face was
colourless. It hardly showed on the pillowcase. Both eyes
were clear and moist. But everything below his nose was
blue and swollen. His lips were a pair of overripe damsons,
bloated, syrupy and sapped together by dry blood, with
stripy wasps of scab feeding at the juice. His cheek and chin
were stripped of skin. His jaw was bruised. He'd almost
bitten through his tongue. It looked as if a three-inch
worm was squashed across it. But his gums were worst
of all. What teeth remained were shaken in his head, like

gravestones in soft earth. The gravestones tilted and the earth was lifted up and split.

It was odd that he could think and see so clearly, yet hardly breathe or move, and that he should be so reassured and in such brutal pain at once. It was the bed that settled him and made him feel so like a child: its freshly laundered smell, its punched-up pillows, its quilted counterpane, its height and buoyancy. He looked around the room for clues to where he was. The windows were ten feet tall at least – an opulent house – and the room was full of calming winter light, yellow, penetrating, cool. Everything seemed sharp and mutely colourful. A silver candelabrum on a stand, which burned fine-smelling whale oil. A walnut dressing table and closet. Two brocaded chairs. A bedside table with a washing bowl and a pot pourri. A white marble fireplace. A watercolour of some ochre church in Italy or Spain. Hand-painted wallpaper, the latest fashion. This was no hospital. It smelled of furniture and cloth – and money.

At first he thought he was in Wherrytown. Inside some better inn. The footsteps in the corridor would belong to Mrs Yapp. Or George. How happy he would be to see the parlourman. But when Emma entered with fresh poultices and he saw his nephew and his nieces staring in and giggling, he knew exactly where he was.

Emma pressed cold flannels to his forehead and his face. She put him back onto the pillows. 'You mustn't move,' she said. She pushed his eyelids up. She felt the temperature of his hands and the nape of his neck. 'You're doing fine.'

'What day is it?' He sounded drunk. It hurt.

'It's Saturday. Excuse me, sir, but you're not allowed to

talk, not until your mouth is on the mend. Mrs Smith says I am to keep you quiet at all costs. You mustn't smile. You mustn't talk or smile. You must just rest. Shall I draw back the curtains, sir? Don't say.' A wedge of light spread out across his bed. Emma took the flannels off his face. She spooned some water in his mouth, and gave some Greenoughs Tincture and a draught of laudanum. He couldn't swallow it. It made a sticky pool between his lips and then seeped into the splintered cavern of his mouth. He had to fight a sneeze.

Then, while Emma changed the dressings on his wounds, he had sufficient time (before her draught of laudanum returned him to the night and to the sweetest dreams of all) to recall the details of the Friday evening, the endless crack and thud of it. And he remembered every word they said. Shut up. Your name? Your name? You're a thief and not a gentleman. Good boots. I know it's him. Say it, say it! Have you been recently in Wherrytown?

AYMER SMITH was at the end of tired. He was sleeping now, and truly dreaming: his landscape was a childish one. A beach, some dunes, some kelp, a granite headland, gulls, the numbing blanket of a sea-stunned sky, a dog. He put his shoulder up against the Cradle Rock. He had the strength. He rolled it back onto its pivot stone. He set the Rock in motion. He made amends. He put the world to rights again. Helped only by the muscle of the wind, and by the charity of dreams, the Cradle Rock ascended and declined.

A public announcement from
Oliver's Register of Ships and Shipping
Toronto, February 1837

A SAILING BARQUE, *The Belle of Wilmington*, with a burthen of 1,800 tons, and commanded by Capt. R. Comstock for Southern Maritime, is sunk in the Cabot Strait of Nova Scotia at 46.72°N and 59.85°W with a loss of 17 hands and in excess of 40 steerage passengers.

It was in transit from emigrant ports in Europe for the quarantine at Grosse Island in the St. Lawrence and getting up to windward in calm seas when, striking ice, was holed. No soul survived save one small dog and which was put ashore below New Waterford by the Glace Bay steamtug. 31 bodies are recovered and none identified but buried with the orders of the magistrate and at public expense in consecrated ground at Sydney. The wreck, at 80ft. in depth, is buoy marked and flagged in open passage.

All claims regarding Salvage Rights and Insurances to MSRS. HART & HICHISSON of Port aux Basques and Glace Bay. *No dealings with the next of kin, or other parties, except by Attorney or similar.*